Punishment by Fire

By

Mary Schaffer

ISBN-13: 978-1500877804

ISBN-10: 1500877808

Books by this author:

Jim Crawford mysteries:
Chance Encounter
Elements of Deception

Ed Flanders mysteries:
Death in The Home Place
Punishment by Fire

Dedication
To the many people whose words of encouragement have
kept me writing instead of giving up.

Forward

"Mr. Flanders, how do you feel about making your living from other people's misery and problems? Even their deaths!"

Ed Flanders removed his reading glasses and put them in his pocket. He looked down at the young woman poised to record his answer to her question and smiled slightly.

"For most of my life," Ed said, "I was in law enforcement, primarily in the F.B.I. In general, people in law enforcement view their job as *helping* people during difficult situations. The same applies to many other professions — firemen, doctors, nurses, etc." Ed paused then continued, "As a law enforcement officer, I also found personal satisfaction in catching what we call "bad actors," preventing them from more bad actions, and bringing some form of justice to their victims."

Ed paused. "Now, I find myself, as a writer of non-fiction, in a different position. People in mass media — and that includes *me* as a writer and *you* as an aspiring journalist — find their personal satisfaction in telling the story."

Motioning toward the three books stacked on the table beside him, Ed continued, "Whether I write about the catching of a serial killer or review a case involving a serial killer punished or long dead, I try to balance the two people that I am. Catching the chat room killer, of course, prevented further deaths. Revisiting the other cases is largely a matter of adding perspective and new techniques to old information; I have re-told the story."

With an expressive shrug, Ed finished, "Do I enjoy the money I receive?" He smiled. "Of course. But I try to never lose sight of the people — both living and dead — whose story I am telling."

When the young woman would have added a follow-up question, Joe Chambers, the moderator of the panel, interrupted. "Sorry, Folks," he said, "we are out of time for questions. In fact, we are completely out of time for this conference. Won't you join me in thanking our guests for this symposium on law enforcement and the media?"

Chapter 1

"Blood, and fire, and billows of smoke!" The old man's voice ruled the night. "The sun shall be turned into darkness and the moon into blood."

The clock boomed into the cold, dimly lit room. It startled the young boy in the rough, white linen robe where he sat on a wooden bench. The old woman also dressed in white continued murmuring songs under her breath.

The old man waited while the clock chimed the hours with a slow, discordant clamor. One. Two. Three o'clock.

The old man nodded at the time and beckoned his grandson to him. On feet numb with cold, Jesse Springfield approached his grandfather who stood beside the copper bowl filled with glowing charcoal, the only heat in the room.

The woman followed. They stood, the three of them, side by side. Without a word, the old man and old woman opened their robes to expose their left shoulder. The woman wore a white undergarment that almost covered the scars.

The old man held his grandson by the shoulder as he recited the words. "And there appeared unto them cloven tongues like as of fire and it sat upon each of them." As he finished the verse, the old man reached into the bowl to recover the intricately carved brass stamp that he ordinarily used to emboss leather. Before the boy could protest, the old man had moved the boy's robe aside and branded the cross into the boy's shoulder.

Even as the skin sizzled and nerve endings screamed pain messages to Jesse's brain, the smell of singed flesh spread in the small room.

Howling with anger and pain, the boy yanked, trying to free himself from his grandfather's hold. "God damn you! You son of a bitch!" he screamed.

"How dare you use the Lord's name in vain!" the grandfather screamed. He dragged the boy to the door of the room that served as a chapel. Just outside the room, he shoved the boy into the repentance box that stood in the corner. "Pray! Repent! Seek forgiveness!" the grandfather emphasized each word with a shove propelling the boy into the walnut hulls that filled the repentance box.

For seconds after his grandfather returned to the whitewashed room, Jesse trembled. His shoulder was on fire. His right leg, always weak, throbbed. When the sharp edges of the walnut shells were finally transmitted to his brain, Jesse managed to stand. He let the heavy robe drop to the floor. He stifled sobs and wiped away the tears that streamed down his face.

Dimly, he could hear his grandfather repeat the words about cloven tongues of fire. He heard guttural groans as his grandfather, Oather Springfield, re-branded his wife Esther and then himself.

Jesse gagged. What little was left in his stomach after a day of fasting was hurled into the repentance box.

With his eyes accustomed to the dim light and limping more heavily than usual, Jesse turned to the kitchen to find a kerosene lamp. The family had electricity, but it wasn't used on holy days.

Jesse heard his grandparents begin to chant verses about a wrathful God who destroyed evil.

"I'll show them evil," Jesse said. He left the lamp unlit but took the kerosene can and began to pour its contents on the floors and furniture. As he poured kerosene into the prayer box, he saw that the key to the chapel was in the door lock.

He turned the key. "Pray," he said, softly. "Pray."

He poured the last of the kerosene on the heavy robe. He returned to the kitchen for matches. He lit several and set them on the robe. He waited until the robe began to flame. Then he went outside and crossed the street. He sat on the steps of the neighbor's house and waited.

Jesse Springfield was still sitting there when the volunteer firemen arrived too late to extinguish the engulfed house. He was still sitting there when the sheriff came and took him, barefoot and dressed in only a pair of homemade trousers, to answer questions about the deaths of his grandparents.

Chapter 2

February, 2012

"I am very curious," Ed Flanders said, "about the reason for your invitation to dinner. For all this." Ed's words were directed at the beautiful woman sitting across from him, but his glance included the very exclusive Tallahassee, Florida restaurant and the pre-dinner martinis.

"Is it so odd that I would want to have dinner with you?" Nell Jones said with a smile.

"Yes," Ed said, bluntly. "Yes, it is." Ed Flanders was vain enough to keep his 65-year-old body in decent shape. His hair, once dark blonde, was almost completely gray and worn short. Accustomed to wearing suits on the job, Ed was at ease in whatever clothes the occasion merited. All things considered, Ed thought he was doing okay. Still, Ed knew there must be some reason, some real reason, that the attractive blonde about, Ed guessed, thirty years his junior had invited him to dinner.

Nell's smile deepened. She sipped her martini.

Ed tried a different tact. "You said you wanted my help," he said. "How may I help you?" His voice took on the tone of the professional investigator.

The two had met the previous day as presenters at the Criminal Justice and the Media symposium held at a small university in Tallahassee, Florida near Ed's home. Joe Chambers, the head of the Criminal Justice Department had gotten a variety of people connected with both law enforcement and journalism to present facets of their occupations to the combined students of the Journalism Department with his own.

An old friend of Chambers, Dr. Nell Jones had agreed to participate months before the symposium was scheduled. In the interim, she had been named Chief Medical Examiner for the state of Arkansas. Jones and her staff carry a heavy responsibility: they make the final determination for cause and circumstances of deaths sent to them from across the state. No matter what other officials said or thought, the final authority was Dr. Nell Jones. Her status made her the star attraction at the symposium.

At the reception for presenters and students the evening before the symposium began, Nell had approached Ed, saying, "Mr. Flanders, could I invite you to dinner Friday night after the symposium ends? " She hesitated and added, "I need your advice—maybe your help."

"Only if you call me 'Ed' and allow *me* to take *you*," Ed had said.

Nell Jones had frowned. "I've already made reservations," she had said.

"Okay," Ed had said, "but it's still my treat."

Now, Ed looked across the table. "Dr. Jones?" he said.

"I thought you agreed to call me 'Nell,'" she said with a broad smile. Then she sobered. "I'm sorry. I'm doing this all wrong," she added. "I have a question to ask you."

"Fire away," Ed said.

"Were you ever assigned to the Kansas City, Missouri, FBI office?"

Surprised at the question, Ed leaned back in his chair. "Yes," he said, "Yes, I was." He thought a second and added, "A *long* time ago."

"And do you remember Joanna Jones?"

"Joanna?" Ed said, frowning a bit. He searched his memory. *"Joanna Jones?"* he thought. *Jones? Jones?"* Finally, he remembered. "Do you mean Jo? Jo Jones?" He said then added. "Of course. Of course, I remember Jo."

"That's my mother," Nell Jones said.

"My word," Ed said. "Jo Jones." He looked intently at the woman across from him. "I see the resemblance now. Your hair is lighter and you wear it longer. You're a bit taller, I think. But, yes, you look a lot like your mother did all those years ago." He smiled again. "Jo Jones," he repeated. Before either of them could comment further, the waiter arrived with the appetizer.

As Nell took a first bite of the calamari, Ed asked, hesitantly, "How is your mother?"

Between bites, Nell explained that her mother was retired and lived in Arkansas, part of the time in Little Rock with Nell but mostly in a house on Greer's Ferry Lake, less than two hours north of Little Rock.

"She retired from the Bureau?" Ed asked.

"Oh, no," Nell told him. "She left the FBI soon after I was born. Went back to school. Got her Ph d. in Criminal Justice and taught for years at a university in Mississippi."

"And your father?"

"He's well. Still lives in Kansas City." She paused, added, "They divorced when I was four."

"Sorry to hear that," Ed said.

Nell shrugged and changed the subject. "And you?" she asked. "Are you married?"

"No," Ed said. "My wife died a number of years ago." Their conversation ceased when beautifully grilled sea bass was presented by the waiter.

When they had finished dinner, rejected dessert, and requested coffee, Nell re-opened the conversation. "So, you retired from the Bureau?" she asked.

Ed smiled. "Thirty years — more or less — on the job, and I retired."

"And became a writer," Nell said.

"And became a writer," Ed agreed.

"My mom has read your books," Nell said. "She recognized your name and photo on a display in a bookstore." Nell added, "She enjoyed them a lot."

"I'm flattered," Ed said and added, "especially when someone in the business finds my writing creditable."

"She told me about a case you worked together. One that looked like murder-suicide."

Ed thought a minute and then said, "I remember that case. Fort Leonard Wood, Missouri." He grinned. "Nickname: Fort Lost in the Woods, Missouri. The backside of the universe." He grinned again. "You think I'm kidding? It's — I don't know — 200 miles from Kansas City. On back roads. We had to stay on the base. Old Army base." He rubbed his hand across his face as he thought. "The base was still commissioned — may still be commissioned for all I know. Some kind of special training there even way back then."

He paused, trying to remember details. "We stayed in some sort of barracks made into guest quarters." He thought. "I remember the case. Young army guy and his girlfriend found dead on the base. Initially looked like a murder/suicide with the soldier killing his girl. We were able to determine that it was a double homicide. They caught the perp in Arizona or somewhere." He nodded as he remembered. "It's hard to remember details. Too many cases in a career."

He looked at Nell. "I do remember how thorough your mother was. She was remarkable. Excellent skills. She was the one who found the discrepancies. Many times in my career, I thought back to the way she thought and re-thought the crime scene. I learned a lot from her."

"You were partners on the case, then?" Nell asked.

"Yes," Ed said. "We worked together, but she was in charge."

"Really?"

"Really." Ed smiled across the table. "Jo was a rising star in the Bureau. Women, especially smart women with good skills, were getting a lot of attention. I'm a little surprised she left the Bureau."

Just then, the waiter arrived with coffee. When the coffee had been poured and the waiter gone, Ed said, "So tell me about you."

"By the time I can really remember, Mom and I were in Hattiesburg, so it was school in Mississippi. Summers with my dad and his family in Kansas City and my grandmother in Iowa. I knew, way back, that I wanted to be a pathologist. UNC. Assistant ME in Little Rock. Then, out of the blue, Chief ME job there is open and I get it." Nell Jones shrugged. "That's about it."

Ed took a drink of coffee as he considered the obviously well-rehearsed recital he had just heard. *"More to her story than these bare bones,"* he thought. He also realized that her credentials were impeccable. The University of North Carolina, or UNC, has a reputation as one of the top in the nation for training medical examiners. In addition, moving into a job as top medical examiner for a state usually took years of work.

"You're not married?" Ed asked, noting that her maiden name.

"Nope," Nell said. "Too busy. Too particular." She set her coffee the cup down and changed the subject. "When my mom saw the program for the symposium and realized you were a presenter, she told me I should talk to you."

"I'm glad you did," Ed said. "It's good to hear about Jo and to meet her daughter."

"There's a little more to it than that," Nell said.

"Uh-oh," Ed said.

"I think I may have stumbled across a serial killer" Nell said, speaking quickly. Then she sighed. "Actually, a case that came to my office and one that my mother found out about are so similar that I think they may be connected." She sighed again. "Or maybe not. Maybe it's just a coincidence."

"Young lady," Ed said, "in law enforcement, we do not believe in coincidence. However, let me warn you: two cases do not make a serial killer case." He smiled to soften the words.

Nell grinned. "That's exactly what my mom said."

"I have a suggestion," Ed said. "Let's go back to the lounge of the hotel, and you can tell me the whole story." As he spoke, he signaled for the bill.

Chapter 3

February 24, 1996

"Dr. Sales," the chairman of the committee said, "you really feel that Jesse Springfield is ready to be released from this facility?"

"Yes, yes, I do," Roberta Sales, resident psychiatrist and caseworker for Jesse Springfield said. "As you know," she continued, "I have worked with Jesse extensively during the past five years. During that time, I have become convinced that Jesse has overcome the tragedies that had impacted his early years and culminated in the deaths of his grandparents. Jesse has come to acknowledge and accept his past and is now ready, I am convinced, to move back into normal society."

She opened the folder on the table in front of her. "If I could," she continued, "I would like to review with you the history of Jesse Springfield and his commitment to our institution."

The committee was meeting to consider whether or not to release Jesse Springfield into a step-down program. A psychologist, a social worker, a policeman, and the head of the psychiatric hospital would listen to Dr. Sales and then interview Jesse himself.

"Jesse Springfield, Jr. was born on January 17, 1978 to Jesse Springfield, Sr. and his live-in girlfriend, Angel Harmon in Miami Beach, Florida. The father was 26; the mother, barely 17. By the time Jesse, Jr. was seven, his father had left the boy and his mother for good.

"At birth, the boy had a dislocated hip. Although surgeries were largely successful, the boy continued to walk with a limp that was more pronounced when he was emotionally distressed.

"By age 8, Jesse was, to all intents and purposes, the man of the family. His mother had given him control of the welfare check, the food stamps, and occasional money from his father. Jesse paid the rent and utilities and bought whatever food was cheap and fast. He gave his mother money for cigarettes and cheap beer or wine.

"According to his school records and a report from his third grade teacher, he was bright although his attendance was sporadic. The teacher noted that he was 'a sweet boy with a lovely smile.' She added that 'if he said or did anything wrong, he would apologize profusely and promise to do better.'

"Angel Harmon, Jesse's mother, had a succession of boyfriends and spent most of her time in an alcohol-induced state. In February 1988, Angel and her latest boyfriend were killed in a car wreck."

Dr. Sales looked at each member of the committee. "As much as we might deplore the haphazard way Jesse had been raised, the worst was yet to come." She cleared her throat. "After his mother's death, Jesse was sent to live with his father. Less than six months later, Jesse, Sr. took the boy to his parents' home and left him for them to raise. Oather and Esther Springfield lived in Stoneville, a village of less than a thousand people here in West Virginia."

Although the policeman nodded, the other committee members didn't recognize the small town.

"Oather and Esther Springfield were in their 70's when Jesse was left with them. Oather Springfield," Dr. Sales continued, "had been a master craftsman working in leather but, over the years, focused more and more on embossing leather covers for Bibles."

Sales consulted another page in her folder. "I interviewed Reverend James Wentworth, pastor of an independent fundamentalist church in Stoneville. Reverend Wentworth had known the couple for a number of years and had helped Springfield market his leather skills, enabling Springfield to make an adequate living."

Sales read from her notes: "Wentworth and his church consider themselves to be Pentecostals, a general branch of Protestantism, that focuses on—let me quote—the ability to defeat the enemies of Christianity through spiritual power. This power, they believe, is given now in the same way it was to the apostles as recorded in the Book of Acts in the Bible."

She looked at the group. "Wentworth admitted that he had been concerned about the intensity of Oather Springfield's religious fervor. The Springfields attended the church Wentworth pastored but also worshiped in what Oather Springfield called "the sanctified room" in the Springfield home, a room that was once the dining room. Painted white, the room contained only a rough wooden bench and a table."

She continued, "Wentworth said that during the three years Jesse lived with his grandparents, he had attended church with them. Wentworth added that Jesse had a difficult time adjusting to life with his grandfather's increasingly rigid demands."

Sales stopped her prepared presentation and looked at the committee members, focusing on the social worker. "Can you imagine how difficult it must have been for this child to come from Miami to Stoneville? The difference could not have been greater! In Miami, Jesse had been free to do as he wished— I'm not saying that was good, just that it was his life—but with his grandparents he had no freedom at all." She shook her head sadly. "Poor kid," she said.

She visibly drew herself together and continued with her report. "Reverend Wentworth also verified Jesse Springfield's account of the "repentance" box, a wooden box about 2 feet by 3 feet that was located just outside the sanctified room. The bucket of broken walnut shells that Wentworth saw gives truth to Jesse's story that he had been made to kneel in the shells and pray for forgiveness for various sins. In addition, the scar on his upper left chest matches the cross that Oather Springfield embossed on the leather Bible covers he made." Dr. Sales cleared her throat.

"The rest of the story is Jesse's. You have copies of his statement to the police in your folders. Jesse told approximately the same story to the psychiatrist who recommended that he be placed in our facility rather than being tried for the murder of his grandparents. Numerous times, Jesse said, 'I did a bad thing.' The sheriff joined the psychiatrist in the recommendation, stating that 'given the severe circumstances, it is no wonder the child lashed out at the adults.'"

Dr. Sales looked at each member of the committee. "Although the details have changed—as Jesse's perception of the events of those years has changed, the basic story of what happened in 1991 has remained the same."

She closed the folder. "Jesse became 18 in January. We must decide whether to further incarcerate him or to begin to return him to society."

"I think," the chairman of the committee said, "we are ready to talk with Jesse himself."

Roberta Sales left the chair situated in front of the committee and went to the door. "Come in," she said to the young man waiting outside.

Jesse Springfield entered the room and walked a little hesitantly to the chair.

At eighteen, he was just 5' 7" tall and slender. His short, dark blonde hair was slightly rumpled. He wore a white, long-sleeved shirt and dark slacks. He sat down on the chair and rested his hands on his knees.

He drew a deep breath and looked at the man in front of him, the head of the facility and chair of the committee. Jesse had spent five years preparing for this meeting.

Jesse Springfield had learned almost from birth how to manipulate adults. Doctors, nurses, teachers, social workers, and his mother had all succumbed to the sweet smile and the shy hesitation that Jesse perfected. He was able to convince most adults that catering to his wishes was their idea.

Two people were unaffected by his posturing: his father and his grandfather. "Conniving little piece of rat shit," his father said. "Always faking it. Faking being happy. Being sad. Being sorry. Fake. All of it." Oather Springfield, believing that the Holy Spirit had given him the power to bring sinners to repentance, was uninfluenced by anyone's actions, especially those of a young boy.

Sitting on the steps watching his grandparents' house burn, Jesse had reverted to the strategies perfected in his earlier life. Tears in his eyes, he had told the fireman, "I did a bad thing." He said the same thing to the sheriff and to the psychiatrist. Each time he made that statement, he touched the place where his grandfather had burned him, slumped his shoulders, and lowered his head. He was sitting in that forlorn-looking stance when the psychiatrist said, "We are going to take you to a hospital where we will help you get better."

Jesse trembled. "Oh, yes," Jesse had thought, "no trial, no prison. I'll just get better."

Now the time had come for Jesse to prove that he was "better." "Just enough sincerity. Just enough understanding of what I did. Just enough insecurity," Jesse thought. "Do this committee like you do that stupid bitch of a psych-doctor. Like you did Mommy."

"Jesse," the social worker said, "you understand that we are meeting today to discuss allowing you to move into a group home?"

"Yes, Ma'am," Jesse said. He met her eyes for just a second and then looked down again. *"How stupid do you think I am?"* Jesse thought. *"Do you think I'm as stupid as you are?"* He kept his head down.

"If you are allowed to move outside the facility, what are your plans for the future?"

With his head down, Jesse admitted, "I'm not sure."

The social worker frowned. "You have graduated from high school through our online computer program. Do you enjoy working with computers?"

"Not really," Jesse said. "I, uh, learned to use it for my school work but that's all."

The lie came easily. He had been told that the computers were carefully monitored, so Jesse had stolen the screen names and passwords of other inmates and used them for research into child abuse, into underage criminals and their rehabilitation. Over the years, he had read every paper written by Dr. Roberta Sales and those written by the head of the hospital.

"You don't like the games available on the computer here?" the social worker continued. They had, of course, accessed the records of Jesse's time on the computer.

"I'm not good at games," Jesse said softly, almost mumbling. *"Games?"* Jesse thought. *"What do you think we are doing now? Playing a game, Stupid. And guess who's winning?"*

"It's okay that you aren't good at games," the social worker said.

Jesse allowed a quick upward glance at her and a quick, sweet smile. She smiled back but approached the question of Jesse's future again. "Do you plan to continue your education?"

Jesse allowed his shoulders to slump again. Then he looked up, met the social worker's eyes. "I don't know. Maybe," he said. He looked down and then back at the social worker. "I haven't spent much time thinking about the future," he said, a look of sadness spread over his face. He looked down again.

The social worker's voice softened. "I understand," she said, "but we need to know what you would like to do."

"Oh, what I would *like* to do" Jesse said, looking at her once again, "I'd like to get a job where I could work with people." He allowed enthusiasm to brighten his voice and light his eyes. "I've been working in the kitchen here for two years. I really like that. Working with the cooks and, you know, serving food to people."

The social worker smiled. "You know, Jesse," she said. "I may have just the job for you. What do you think about working in a pizza place?"

"Oh," Jesse said, "pizza is my favorite food." Then he ducked his head. "I think I could do good in a place like that." Jesse sighed deeply. "If I had the chance."

The head of the institution reminded Jesse: "You know that moving to a group home means that someone would check on you and your room every day, don't you?"

"Yes, Sir."

"For two months, you would have to report to Dr. Sales twice a week."

"Yes, Sir," Jesse said. He looked from the man to Roberta Sales and smiled a tiny smile of acknowledgement.

"After that, if you are showing that you can handle life outside the institution, there would be weekly and then monthly appointments," the chairman said.

Jesse rigidly controlled his emotions. *"Yes!"* he thought. *"Yes! I've fooled all of you."* He said, "I know that. I promise I would do everything to be good." *"I'm winning the game,"* Jesse thought. *"I just have to keep pretending for a few more minutes. Have to keep fooling these idiots."*

"Young man," the police officer's voice broke into Jesse's thoughts. "Young man," he repeated, do you understand what you did and why you have been here for the past five years?"

Jesse had expected this question. "*Yes,*" he thought, "*that mean old son of a bitch burned me. His wicked, ugly wife did nothing to protect me. And I burned them. And I would burn you if I got the chance.*" Jesse's shoulders slumped, and then he looked directly at the policeman.

"Yes," he said, keeping his voice quiet and still, "I know that my grandfather hurt me." Jesse touched the place on his upper left chest where his grandfather had burned him but quickly dropped his hand back onto his leg.

"I know that I acted in anger." He drew a deep breath and looked down. "I was angry for a long time, but I'm not angry anymore." He met the policeman's eyes. "I forgave them for hurting me." He allowed his eyes to widen. "I hope they have forgiven me." He allowed his shoulders to slump, his hands to fall, his eyes to be downcast again.

The committee chairman looked at the two other members and then at Dr. Sales.

"I think that will be all," he said. "Thank you, Jesse."

Jesse sat bowed over until Dr. Sales touched his shoulder. Jesse kept his head down so they would not see the contempt in his eyes. "*Five years in this shit hole,*" he thought, "*with these stupid jerk-offs.*"

Jesse allowed Dr. Sales to lead him out of the room, her hand on his shoulder. She felt him tremble and said, "It went very well, I think." She added, "We can make plans for you to move into Wheeling to the group home."

"*Freedom,*" Jesse's thought had been so forceful that he had trembled. "*I made it work. I made it work.*"

Once he had been committed to the psychiatric hospital, Jesse had immediately begun to use his strategies. Staff members were treated to his wide-eyed sweet expression. In return, he received special treatment.

Other inmates—especially those with a criminal background—were befriended for their knowledge. It was all a game. A contest between Jesse and the rule makers. If he won the game, he got freedom. If they won, he stayed in the psychiatric hospital for good.

He carefully studied actions of his own and of other inmates. His best chance at winning, he decided, was to fool Dr. Roberta Sales, the psychiatrist. Pleasing her became his primary goal, but he never over-played the role he had chosen: shy, dependent, insecure, not too smart, immature.

He had forced himself to acknowledge the killings of his grandparents and to act as if he had put it in the past.

He even met with Reverend Wentworth, and pretended to pray for forgiveness.

Today, Jesse knew that he was the winner.

Jesse allowed himself a moment of celebration: *"That was easy!"*

Chapter 4

"Nell looks a lot like her mother," Ed thought a half hour later as she entered the hotel lounge. At the hotel, Nell Jones had gone up to her room while Ed found a table at the quiet end of the lounge and ordered coffee.

Now, Ed watched as she, having caught his eye, crossed the room, passing the men sitting at the bar without a glance. Ed grinned. *"Same walk as if she owns the world. Same way of getting every man's attention and never noticing it."*

"I ordered coffee," Ed said.

Nell Jones nodded her approval and sat across from Ed. She placed two manila folders on the small table between them.

"First," Ed said, "let me remind you that I am not a criminal investigator. I'm a writer. Like the young lady said this afternoon, I make my living from writing about other people's misery."

"I thought you handled that question very well," Nell said.

"Thank you," Ed said. "She may have just wanted to impress her professor with her gutsy question." He shrugged. "However, I tried to give her a straight answer. I really do have a foot in two camps."

He cleared his throat. "It is hard to give up being the investigator. In fact, I came awfully close to getting a policewoman killed because I thought I could be both investigator and writer. Now, I focus on bringing truth into my writing. If I find a crime to investigate, I call for help *immediately.*"

Realizing that his voice had taken a sharp note, Ed added, "But, of course, I have more leisure time for looking at cases now than I did when I was an actual investigator. Computers are better too." He smiled again.

He looked at the folder but didn't touch it. "Tell me about your case," he said quietly.

"Why do some cases just stick with you?" Nell asked. She obviously didn't expect a reply. She continued. "I can rationalize it," she said. "Not the case," she added, "but my reaction to it."

Ed waited.

Nell Jones took a deep breath. She switched into her professional mode, the one that enabled her to be objective and to give accurate reports.

"I have a case I've worked on that involves the murder and arson of two elderly people. At first, I thought it might have been a murder/suicide, and it might well have been." Nell's hands raised, palms up in a "Who knows?" gesture. She continued. "But the positioning of the bodies and the trauma to the victims makes me think it may have been a double homicide with a fire to cover up the crime."

"What kind of positioning do you mean?"

"The bodies were found in the kitchen with the male victim lying face-down on the floor and the female forward in a kneeling position at the sink."

Ed looked both thoughtful and puzzled. "And the trauma?" he asked.

"Of course, there was extensive damage from the fire to both bodies," Nell Jones said. Ed nodded his understanding. "The male was near the door into the living room and was discovered with the dining table across the middle of his back. However, his death was the result of a blow to the back of the head. He was dead before the fire started. No carbon residue in mouth, throat, or lungs."

"Perhaps he fell and pulled the table down on him?" Ed asked.

"That doesn't explain the blow to the back of the head," Nell countered. "The edge of the table top was at his waist. There was nothing near him that could have caused the trauma to his head."

Ed rubbed his chin as he thought through the information he had just received. Finally, he asked, "What about the other victim?"

Nell continued, "The female was in a kneeling position facing the sink adjacent to the stove where the fire started."

"Kneeling?" Ed questioned.

"Yes," Nell said. "Kneeling or semi-crouched facing the cabinet below the sink." She looked at Ed and said, "She died of smoke inhalation as a result of the fire, but she also had blunt trauma to the head. Blunt force trauma to the front of the cranium."

"The front of the head?" Ed asked.

"Yes," Nell Jones said.

"Tell me about the fire," he said.

"A skillet of oil on the cook stove caught fire. A nearby tea towel carried the flames to the curtains. Both the ceiling above the stove and the wall near the curtains caught. The house was a wooden structure. The flames quickly accelerated. A neighbor returning home saw the smoke and called 911. The neighbor started toward the house, but it exploded into flames before he got there."

Ed waited.

"I've tried various theories," Nell said. "First, was it an accident? She is cooking; he comes into the kitchen and falls. She goes to his aid. The oil catches fire. She tries to get back to the stove but slips, hits her head on the sink and falls to her knees unconscious. The house burns. An accident."

"But there's the blow to the back of his head," Ed said thoughtfully.

Nell nodded then said, "Next theory: murder/accidental death." Ed's raised eyebrows asked the question. Nell continued. "She is cooking; he comes into the kitchen. She hits him on the back of the head and shoves the table over him to make it look like an accident. Then she realizes the cooking oil is on fire. She tries to get back to the stove and so on. She murders him; her death is an accident."

"I guess that's possible," Ed said.

"Alternatively," Nell added, "she killed him and then started cooking. And you know the rest of the story."

Ed frowned. As he thought about the entire situation, his frown deepened.

"That's what is giving me fits," Nell Jones said. "It just doesn't make sense."

To lighten her mood, Nell grinned. "Do you suppose she killed her husband of sixty years and then started cooking lunch? Was she planning on cooking him?" Her laugh was forced.

The two of them sat silently for several minutes, each lost in thought.

Finally, Nell broke the silence: "I don't have enough hard evidence to call it a double homicide, so I have left the cause of their deaths as undetermined." She frowned. "I hate leaving it like that."

Ed nodded. "I can see that this is really bothering you." Ed leaned forward. "What I don't see is what you want me to do. If anything."

"Let me tell you the other part, the coincidence," Nell said. "Then maybe you can help me make sense of everything."

"Okay," Ed said.

"I worked the case I just told you about," Nell said, "back in May of last year." She paused then quickly spoke. "The female victim, the elderly woman, was the same age as my Gran. Gran, my mother's mother, died less than a year ago."

She let out a deep breath. "I think that's why the case stayed in my mind. I think that's why I didn't talk to Mom about the case."

Ed nodded. People in fields that deal with human tragedy cannot become emotionally involved in every case they work. Occasionally, however, a case becomes personal. Ed had never mentioned those cases that had touched him to anyone either.

"Fast forward to this January," Nell said. "I´m at Mom's, and she's not really depressed, but a little bit down. She had gotten a letter from a guy asking for her help. A guy serving a life-time sentence in prison."

Ed's eyebrows rose in question.

"Here's the story," Nell said. "About ten years ago, to help out a probation program, Mom hired a guy in his late 20's to work as a handyman."

Ed frowned.

"Drugs, drinking and driving, fights, some petty theft," Nell answered Ed's unspoken question.

Ed rolled his eyes.

"Anyway," Nell said, her grin agreeing with Ed's unspoken disapproval of the situation, "Dean March was a wizard with Mom's garden. So much that she helped him get a job with a landscaping firm."

Ed still looked skeptical.

"Just as you are thinking," Nell said, "by 2008, this Dean March was back to drinking and drugs. He argued with his grandparents over money one Saturday afternoon. That evening, they were bludgeoned to death and their house burned. The next day he was charged with their murder. He was convicted and sentenced to life in prison."

Ed waited.

"In the letter he wrote Mom, he said she was his last hope. No one will believe that he is innocent or will fight the evidence against him."

Now, it was Nell Jones who waited while Ed considered the two stories.

"I see similarities," Ed said, finally. "Tell me why you, um-m-m-m, concluded that there might be a serial killer." He avoided voicing his exact thought: *"why you jumped to the conclusion,"* and kept his voice neutral instead of allowing his extreme skepticism to show.

Nell Jones enumerated: "Two elderly couples, killed in their homes with blunt force trauma to the head, and their houses burned." She paused, added: *"If* I call it a double homicide, and *if* you believe Dean March, both crimes by person or persons unknown who presumably burned the houses to cover the crimes."

"The evidence against this March fellow?"

"Circumstantial," Jones answered. "Substantial. Very damning. But still all circumstantial."

Ed sat back and steepled his fingers. He wanted to rub his hands over his face in frustration. In the time since he had apprehended a serial killer whose victims were chosen from people involved in an online chat room, a number of people had approached him with "cases" they thought he should solve. Some were actual cases that still plagued law enforcement officials. Some were cases presented by family members of murder victims or missing people who hoped Ed would tie things together and then solve the murder or disappearance of their loved one. Others, like Nell Jones, had noticed similarities in two or more murders and imagined that they were on the track of a serial killer.

Because Ed had started this writing career looking for little known serial killers, he paid a bit of attention to all the cases that were presented to him. *"Even the crazy cases,"* Ed thought, *"the crazy cases like this."*

Nell Jones interrupted his thought.

"When I read the letter Dean March wrote to Mom," Nell said, "I kept thinking that the two cases were too much alike to be coincidence." She spread her hands in a what-am-I-to-do gesture. "Then we had a third coincidence: you."

"Me?"

"You," Nell repeated. "The same time Mom got the letter from Dean March, I got the program for the symposium with your name listed as a presenter." The smile that hinted at dimples deepened.

"Ah-h-h-h," was all Ed said.

"I brought a copy of the ME report on the couple from Little Rock," Nell said. She touched the folder. "And a copy of the letter from Dean March." She shrugged. "I did a couple of other things: I got the copies of the police reports from Mississippi. I also copied newspaper reports of the case, especially the trial." She indicated the folder. "Then I checked with Mississippi crime statistics for similar cases. I also checked our files in Arkansas for the same thing." Her look and shrug told Ed that her search for other cases had been unsuccessful. "I brought the reports with me," she said quietly, "just on the off chance. Just in case you were interested."

"What does your mother think about the connection?" Ed asked. "She has damned good instincts."

"That's exactly what she said about you," Nell said with a smile. "She credited you with finding the murderer in that case you worked together."

"Your mother found the discrepancy that changed the case from possible murder/ suicide to double homicide," Ed said. "After that was determined, it was easy to find the killer."

Ed looked at Nell. "Now," he said, "tell me what your mother thinks about the two cases you have brought to me."

Nell Jones frowned. "She sees the coincidences between the two cases. Like you, she says that in law enforcement, no one believes in coincidence."

"But?"

"But she's much more concerned with the Mississippi case than the two cases together."

Ed waited.

"Mom really wants to believe that Dean March is innocent," Nell explained. "She was on vacation in London and then teaching there for a semester the year of that fire. By the time she got back to Mississippi, Dean had been found guilty and sentenced to life in prison. If there *were* a connection between the two cases, Dean's innocence might be proved." Nell Jones drew a deep breath. "She said if anyone could connect the dots, it would be you."

Ed frowned. "Although I think it's a long, long shot," Ed finally said, "I'll take your information and see what I can find."

"Really?"

"Really," Ed said. "It may take several weeks, but I'll get back to you with whatever I find."

Chapter 5

May 1997

"Oh! Oh! Oh, Shit," Jesse's voice was nearly a shout. It was accompanied by the sound of breaking glass. "Oh! Oh!" Jesse stood in the pizzeria kitchen, looking helpless. A broken coffee carafe, a broken cup, and spilled coffee at his feet.

"Oh, my God," Tony Valenti said. He grabbed Jesse and turned him to the sink where he began running cold water. He held the young man's left arm under the running water.

"I'm, uh, I'm so sorry," Jesse said over and over.

Tony Valenti looked at the reddened hand and arm of his young employee. "It's okay," he said. "It's gonna be okay," he continued.

Jesse had been working at Lenny's Italian Restaurant and Pizzeria since his release over a year earlier. A program sponsored by the West Virginia government and the federal government paid most of Jesse's salary and paid the management to employ Jesse. It was part of a rehabilitation program.

Lenny's had been a Wheeling landmark since the 1960's when Leonardo and Graziella Valenti had opened the pizzeria and then added other Italian dishes to their menu. By 1997, their son, Tony, had taken over the ownership and management of the business.

Now, Tony had his mother, who had come into the kitchen at the sound of the noise, take Jesse to a near-by walk-in medical clinic.

Less than an hour later, the two were back at the restaurant. Jesse's left hand was red and a bandage covered a part of his arm just above the wrist.

"Second degree," Graziella said. "That doctor, he said second degree burns. Said Jesse would be okay in a couple of days."

"He gave me some medicine to put on it," Jesse added.

"Do you want to take off work today?" Tony asked.

"Oh, no, Mr. Tony," Jesse said. "The doctor made it feel a lot better. He said it's not real bad. Just second degree. Like Miss Gracie said."

Jesse looked earnestly at Tony. "I think it will be nearly well by Monday when Dr. Roberta is here." He lowered his head. "We will tell her about it when she gets here," He added softly, "but she worries about me. All the time."

Tony and Jesse had the same thought: *Do we have to report this to Dr. Sales?* Tony didn't want trouble. Jesse had proved to be an excellent worker. The money from the rehab program was good. Jesse didn't want Dr. Roberta to ask questions—about anything, especially about burns.

"I don't think we have to tell her," Tony said, "especially if your arm is much better by then." He added, "And if you promise to be very careful."

"I promise," Jesse said. He made himself look sincere. "I will pay you for the coffee pot and the cup I broke," he said. "It was my fault. I just picked it up wrong, and it slipped."

"Don't worry about it," Tony said. "It was an accident. You don't owe me for the coffee pot. We got more. We got more cups too." He put an arm around the young man's shoulders. "So long as you is okay, everything is good," he said.

Jesse kept his head lowered. *"It's working fine,"* he thought. He looked at the bandage on his arm. *"Safe,"* he thought, *"I am safe. Safe from the bastard who yelled at me and grabbed me. Safe from the fire. Safe from anyone wanting to send me back."*

It had all started two days earlier, on Wednesday, Jesse's normal day off. Jesse had come in for a couple of hours to fold and assemble pizza boxes; the next weekend was the Memorial Day holiday, and Tony expected take-away business to be better than normal.

As Jesse approached the restaurant, his arm was grabbed by Lloyd Davis, an itinerate preacher, who often stood on the street corner outside Lenny's. "You," Davis said in a booming voice, "have you found salvation through our Lord, Jesus Christ? Are you ready for Judgment Day?"

When Jesse tried to pull away, Davis gripped Jess's forearm tighter. "For Judgment Day is upon us. We must all kneel. Kneel and repent. Repent of our sins." His grip pushed Jesse downward. "Fall on your knees and repent. Lest the fires of hell consume you."

As Jesse pulled away, Davis put a card in Jesse's shirt pocked. "The road to salvation is narrow," he said. "Many will not repent in good time. Beware the fires of hell."

Jesse ran into the restaurant. Looking over his shoulder, Jesse thought, *"You Bastard, I'll give you the fires of hell. You just wait."*

Jesse went into the back of the restaurant and, while he folded the cardboard boxes, thought about the man who had yelled at him. When he finished folding and stacking the boxes, he reached in his pocket for the card, the man had placed there. On one side were scripture verses; on the other side, the name and address for the preacher.

When Jesse left the restaurant by the back door, the bastard was still yelling at people on the street.

Jesse, having checked the address on the pizza delivery map, walked the four blocks to the store-front church where Lloyd Davis held services.

From the shadow of a building across the street, Jesse looked at the five stores that shared a single roof. First was a flower store, then one selling women's clothing. Third was a greeting card and gift store. The fourth store was fairly dark, with no inside lighting, but Jesse could read several words: Davis, Church, and Holy. *"Ah-h-h-h,"* Jesse thought, *"that's his so-called church."*

The fifth store — the one on the end was also fairly dark. The door was open and, by looking carefully, Jesse could see stepladders inside.

As Jesse watched, three men came around the side of the building. They were wearing paint-stained clothes: one man wearing white coveralls, the other two in old jeans and t-shirts. *"Break time for the renovation crew,"* Jesse thought.

He had planned to go behind the building to see if there was a back door to the church.

"I can do this," Jesse thought. He walked down the sidewalk and crossed the street in front of the greeting card store. Then he walked to the end of the building, to the place where the men were squatted next to the building, smoking and drinking sodas.

Approaching them timidly, Jesse said, "Um-m-m-m, any chance of me getting a job here?"

"Sorry, Kid," the oldest of the three said, "the boss isn't here. Besides, I don't think we need anyone else."

Jesse made his shoulders droop.

"If you come back tomorrow about ten," the man said, "the boss will be here. You can talk to him."

"Okay," Jesse said, allowing his face to brighten. "Thank you."

"You a painter?" one of the other two asked.

"That's what I been doing," Jesse lied, "but the job finished." He shrugged and tilted his head in a way he had practiced. "We was renovating a old store out east of town," he said, talking softly.

"Smoke?" the man said, offering Jesse a cigarette.

"No thanks," Jesse said. "You gonna be working here long?"

"Probably another week or so," the man said.

"We'd be through quicker if that damned preacher would leave us alone," one of the other two said.

"Preacher?" Jesse asked, looking confused.

"Next door to where we're working is some kind of church," the man explained. "That preacher is always complaining. He doesn't like the paint fumes. The stripper we used on the wood counter is too strong." The man shook his head.

The third man spoke. "If he complains one more time, I'm turning him in." He looked at Jesse. "He sleeps in the back."

Jesse looked confused again.

"He's not supposed to," the man explained. "It's a business not a residence."

The second man explained further. "When we quit, we lock everything in the back room—the ladders, the drop cloths, the paint, everything." He looked at Jesse who nodded his understanding. "Trouble is," the man continued, "The heating and air guys haven't finished back there and both backrooms is using the same vent system."

The oldest man said, "Wouldn't be any trouble if that preacher wasn't sleeping back there." He looked disgusted. He looked at his watch and stubbed out his cigarette. The other two stood also. Jesse walked with them toward the back of the building, thanking them again for their information.

As they went inside, Jesse took a quick look down the alley behind all five stores. Each store appeared to have a wide, solid door to the outside. There were no windows.

With a farewell wave, Jesse walked back to the front as the men went back to work. He walked slowly past the storefront church. Quick glances showed him the door to the back room where the workers said the preacher slept.

That evening, Jesse stood across the street in the shadows and watched the stores. By seven, the workmen were gone; the other stores shut and dark. Wednesday night church service in the store front began at 7:30 with about fifteen people in attendance.

Jesse watched for a while, but the preacher's voice irritated him. "Bastard," Jesse said softly. Then he went home.

The next night, when Jesse got off work at ten, he went back to his place across the street from the strip mall of five stores.

Lights were only shining in the store front church. Jesse could see the man who had grabbed him. Jesse watched as the man — the bastard — closed the book he was reading and shut off the lights. A light from the back room shone briefly.

When Jesse had been in the mental hospital, he had befriended an old man who had related his criminal past to Jesse. "Crazy like a fox," the old man said. "Couldn't take no more prison, so I got crazy. Crazy like a fox."

He taught Jesse all he knew about breaking and entering, about opening locks, about defending yourself.

Jesse had learned well. He had added a black jacket to the black pants he wore for work. He had on a plain black baseball cap pulled low. For reassurance, Jesse put his right hand into his jacket pocket where he could feel the padlock inside the sock.

"I don't hold with no guns," the old man had said. "Guns will get you hurt. Get you sent away." He had showed Jesse how to put something solid — he preferred a padlock or a pool ball — into a sock. "Get a good grip on the sock and hit the bastard," he had said. "If it don't kill him, it'll for sure give you a chance to get away."

Jesse carefully crossed the street. A slender thread of light from under the storeroom door showed that the preacher was still awake.

Jesse quickly opened the back door to the storeroom used by the renovation crew. He picked up a two-liter bottle of paint thinner, sloshing some of it on the drop cloths near the vent. He also took a small shop towel — one of the red ones about a foot square, sticking it into the left side pocket of his jacket.

Then he went outside and set the paint thinner down beside the back door to the storeroom of the so-called church. He knocked on the door. When there was no answer, he knocked louder.

Lloyd Davis knew he should not open the door. According to his contract, he could not sleep in the building. If it were the police or a fire inspector, he would be in trouble. He hastily put shirt and pants on over the pajamas he wore and went to the door.

When he saw Jesse standing there, he recognized him. "You're the boy from the pizza place, aren't you?" he asked. "I talked to you yesterday."

"Yes," Jesse said. "I came here to talk to you about sin and hell and fires. About fires and billows of smoke and repenting."

"Come in, Son," Lloyd Davis said. Since he was standing in the doorway, he turned and stepped back into the room. Jesse followed him.

Jesse pulled the sock from his jacket pocket and swung it, striking the older man on the head. Lloyd Davis fell to the floor unconscious.

Jesse stepped back to retrieve the paint thinner.

As Lloyd Davis began to moan, Jesse poured the paint thinner over him, making sure that some of the liquid was near the door. Davis began to move, trying to pull himself up. Jesse threw the paint thinner can toward the vent.

Jesse pulled the shop cloth from his jacket and reached in the other pocket for the cigarette lighter he had bought earlier that day. It wasn't there.

"Where's the lighter?" he thought, beginning to panic. Then he remembered. He had put the lighter in his pants pocket. *"So I wouldn't lose it,"* he thought as he took it from his pocket.

Jesse stepped outside the building and lit the shop cloth. He bent and reached out to start the fire. The paint thinner ignited with a whoosh that sent flames into the building and up Jesse's hand and arm.

Jesse pulled his burned hand and arm to his chest, holding it with the other hand.

He watched with satisfaction as the flames ignited Lloyd Davis's clothes. Davis, now fully conscious, tried to roll, to put out the flames.

Jesse listened to Davis scream. One long scream. The next intake of breath drew the flames into Davis's body, searing his mouth and wind pipe, destroying his lungs.

Jesse took a deep breath inhaling the smell of the fire — the oily smell of the paint thinner mixing with the heavy smoke from clothing and the overwhelming smell of burning flesh.

Then Jesse calmly walked away.

In his apartment, he looked at the burn on his hand and arm. *"They will see it tomorrow at work,"* he thought. *"Jesse,"* he told himself, *"you have to think about what to do."*

His plan had worked. A splash of hot coffee on the already burned hand, the dropped pot, the broken cup, the trip to the doctor had all been according to Jesse's plan. Even letting Mr. Tony suggest that they not tell Dr. Sales had worked in Jesse's favor.

By the next Monday, when Dr. Roberta Sales entered the restaurant, Jesse's hand and arm were healed. Jesse waved a hand in greeting when Dr. Sales entered the restaurant but continued working in the kitchen.

During the first three months after Jesse had been released from the psychiatric hospital, the two had met a number of times. At first, they had used the office at the group home on Mondays and Thursdays.

One day, wanting to see Jesse in more ordinary surroundings, Dr. Sales suggested that she come to Lenny's. Her meeting Jesse there had quickly become a ritual. Dr. Sales would arrive on Monday afternoon about 5:30 and order dinner. When Jesse took his dinner break at 6, he would bring his pizza and join her.

Their dinners together, continuing over the next year, had helped Jesse change their relationship. One night, he had called her "Mom" and immediately apologized, saying, "What I meant was you are the mother I always wanted." He reinforced that bond from time to time.

"She is my cover," Jesse often thought. *"If I ever get in trouble, I can turn to her. She will protect me."*

With no husband or children of her own, Roberta Sales was an easy mark for Jesse. She bought him nicer clothes and better shoes than the ones provided by the state. Her task, as she saw it, was to make Jesse feel better about himself.

Jesse's task, as he saw it, was to take whatever he could without her realizing he was taking. He made it look as if he were reluctant to receive gifts or money but sincerely grateful for any little courtesy.

Roberta Sales had found in Jesse Springfield the perfect son: quiet, dependent, grateful, caring.

Jesse Springfield had found in Roberta Sales the perfect stepping stone: she held his past and his future, but she was gullible. She mistook Jesse's deliberate actions for true kindness and sweetness.

At their dinners together, Roberta Sales drank wine; Jesse drank root beer, partly because he was still underage and partly because it emphasized his pretended immaturity.

Today, Dr. Sales moved quickly to a serious matter.

"Did you hear about the fire the other night?" she asked.

"Yes," Jesse said. He didn't look up but took a bite of pizza.

"A man died," she said. She looked at Jesse, but he didn't react. "Very sad," she added.

"Mr. Tony wasn't sad," Jesse said. He looked at her with widened eyes. "Mr. Tony didn't like him."

Dr. Sales fought to control her shock.

At the same time, Jesse fought and controlled his laughter. *"Got you, didn't I?"* Jesse thought. He had wondered if she would mention the fire. *"Ask me about him,"* Jesse thought. *"Better yet, tell me about him and the fire."*

"Tony—uh, Mr. Tony—knew Lloyd Davis?" she asked.

"Lloyd Davis?" Jesse made himself look confused.

"The man who died in the fire," Roberta Sales said. "Lloyd Davis."

"Oh," Jesse said, "the yelling man."

"The yelling man?" Sales was confused.

"Yes," Jesse said. "He stood on the corner out there. Mostly on Wednesdays. But other times too. Yelling at people." Jesse took a drink of root beer. "Mr. Tony told him to go away. Said he was driving off business."

Jesse took another bite of pizza and sat with his head down, chewing.

"What was that preacher yelling?"

Jesse swallowed the pizza carefully, said, "Things about go to church or God."

"Did he yell at you?" Sales asked. *"His answer will show me how he feels about religion,"* she thought. *"What he remembers about his grandparents. How he feels about the way they treated him."*

"Me?" Jesse said. He looked at her in surprise. "No," he said. "That man was not welcome in the restaurant. He was out there mainly on Wednesdays when I don't work. I hear Mr. Tony yelling and his mama yelling, but not at me. They just yell. All the time."

Jesse suddenly looked uncomfortable. "Oh," he said, "Dr. Berta, I like it here. I didn't mean nothing bad about Mr. Tony. I like my job here. Very much."

"I understand," Roberta Sales said. Then she said, "They arrested the man who owns the building where the fire was. Did you know that?"

"I saw that on the television," Jesse said. "The man on the television said that owner set the fire to get money from the insurance. He said that preacher wasn't supposed to sleep there. But he did."

"How did all of that make you feel?" Dr. Sales said.

Jesse appeared to consider the question thoughtfully. *"What do I say?"* he thought. *"How do I show just the right amount of concern but not too much?"* Finally, he sighed. "I think that man, that preacher, was unhappy and angry. I think he is in a better place now."

When Jesse went to the kitchen to get a dessert for each of them, Dr. Roberta Sales smiled to herself. *"He's doing fine,"* she thought. That he didn't shy away from discussing the fire and the preacher's death reassured her.

"Jesse has moved on," she thought. *"Such a sweet boy,"* she told herself. *"I'm glad I convinced him to get his own apartment. I'm glad he really likes working here. Yes, he is doing well."*

In the kitchen, Jesse scooped ice cream into two dessert dishes. *"Stupid people!"* Jesse thought. *"Grabbed me, didn't he? Told me I was going to burn in hell, didn't he?"* Jesse carefully added whipped cream to the ice cream. *"Who was it that burned?"* Jesse snickered.

He had avidly watched the story unfold on the television. First, there were pictures of the strip of five stores, the two on one end in ruins. Then the fire chief, looking somber, told about finding the body of the itinerant preacher in the ruins of the back room, dead of smoke inhalation.

Jesse laughed out loud when the reporter announced that the owner of the building had been arrested for arson. The reporter had told the shocking story: the only thing the owner said about the fire was that the preacher wasn't supposed to be sleeping in the building. *"Stupid, stupid people!"* Jesse thought again.

Jesse carefully carried the tray with the two sundaes back to the table where Dr. Sales sat. *"Here you go, you stupid cow,"* Jesse thought. He smiled and said, "A special treat for a special friend."

Roberta Sales considered refusing the ice cream but couldn't hurt Jesse's feelings. She smiled broadly and began to eat.

Jesse began to eat too. *"I have to stay ahead of them,"* he thought. He smiled. *"It gets easier and easier,"* he thought. *"I am the smart one. Not them."*

Chapter 6

March, 2012

"What was I thinking?" Ed said. His words echoed in the empty house. A week had passed since the night Nell Jones had handed him the two manila folders, the same manila folders that were unopened in the To-Do file basket on his desk.

"You weren't thinking," a voice in Ed's brain spoke, *"you were flattered. Flattered that a young woman wanted your help. Pleased that an old colleague remembered you and thinks you have 'damned good instincts.'"*

Ed nodded agreement to his thought then sighed. Whatever the reason, the folders were on his desk reminding him of his promise to give the two cases a look.

Having discussed the case he mentally dubbed the "Arkansas Case" with Nell Jones, Ed opened the folder with the letter from Dean March and the reports on the "Mississippi Case."

Ed began with the letter Dean March had written to Joanna Jones. Ed skimmed the first page where March proclaimed his innocence and begged Joanna to help him.

The second page was, March explained, his recollection of the events of Friday, May 9, 2008.

First, March explained that he had been living in a shabby trailer park in Hattiesburg. He stated that he drove the 24 miles south to the area where both his grandparents and his mother lived. He admitted that he had been drinking and, also, that he hoped to get money from his grandmother and his mother. He wrote that he had argued with his grandfather over his drinking and drug use.

March did not know the exact time he left his grandparents home but thought it was about 4 o´clock in the afternoon. He drove on to his mother's house where he drank a couple of beers with his stepfather. His mother gave him $20.

Taking the back roads toward Hattiesburg, March ran out of gas about half way home. He walked to a nearby gas station where he bought a 2-gallon gas can and filled it with gas. He stated that he poured most of the gasoline into the tank but saved some to prime the carburetor. When he flooded the carburetor and the truck wouldn't start, he passed out.

Early the next morning, he woke up, started the truck and drove home. The deputy who had been watching his house arrested him. Still smelling of gasoline and still hung over, he was taken to jail and charged with the deaths of his grandparents.

He ended his story with a statement: "I was in no way responsible for the deaths of my grandparents. I was not angry with them. I had been drinking, but I had not done any cocaine in over 10 days. I am innocent."

When Ed looked at the police reports, he realized that Nell Jones had gotten only the reports made available to the public. They held little information: the initial responder from the sheriff's department listed the date and time of the call from the 911 dispatcher. It gave the address of the incident and information about the victims. Then, as Ed expected, the report read, "See investigative report." Everything else that the deputy did or saw was kept from the public. Standard Operating Procedure.

The other police report was the same. Titled "Murder/Arson/Arrest," it listed the name of the deputy who had arrested Dean March at March's home and the date. Ed sighed. "See investigative report," Ed said. "No help here," he added. The reports were the bare-bones information available to reporters and others who would not be allowed access to the rest of the information gathered.

"Okay," Ed said, "maybe the newspaper will be more helpful." He read the clippings that told about the fire. A neighbor had seen and smelled smoke and had made the 911 call.

Ed noted that the neighbor believed that the Marches were not at home. "Regular as clockwork," the neighbor Linda Mayo was quoted as saying, "Mr. Leo and Mrs. Peggy go to that gospel singing over by Lucedale. Ever Friday night."

The chief of the volunteer fire department for that rural part of the county added that the fire was "fully involved" when the fire truck arrived some 10 minutes after the 911 call. She added that the job of the fire department was to ventilate and then to extinguish the fire.

Based on the information from both Linda Mayo and her husband Seldon, the chief had been unprepared for finding the two charred bodies. She had called for the sheriff and for the fire investigator.

Ed scanned the clippings that told of Dean March's arrest and indictment.

The trial was brief. Among the various law enforcement officers who testified, the only one of note was the testimony of the state medical examiner: the skulls of both Leo and Peggy March had been crushed with what appeared to be a single blow from a hammer-like weapon. Neither had carbon residue in mouth or throat. Leo and Peggy March were dead before the fire started.

Linda Mayo, the Marches' neighbor, testified to hearing an argument between Leo March and his grandson on the afternoon of the fire.

The gas station attendant testified that Dean March had purchased the gas can and gasoline. A still photograph taken from the CCTV film showed Dean March filling the gas can.

Dean March's mother, treated as a hostile witness, had testified that Dean had been at her home on the day of the fire and had been angry at Leo and Peggy March, her ex-in-laws. She testified that Dean and her boyfriend had drunk several beers before Dean left for Hattiesburg.

The final witness for the prosecution was the deputy who had arrested Dean. He testified that he had been sent to inform Dean of his grandparent's deaths, but Dean was not at home. He had been advised by the sheriff to keep checking the house for Dean's arrival. The deputy had told, in detail, of Dean's arrival, his drunken state, of the smell of gasoline on Dean, of the empty gas can in the back of the pickup truck.

When questioned by the defense attorney, he admitted that Dean seemed surprised — even shocked — that his grandparents had been killed.

The jury was out twenty minutes before they returned with the guilty verdict for each death. The judge sentenced Dean March to two consecutive life sentences.

"Where the hell was the defense?" Ed said. "Didn't that poor sucker even have a lawyer?"

The answer was easily found by reading between the lines: a public defender assigned by the judge. *"Probably little, or no, criminal experience,"* Ed thought.

Besides, Dean March admitted to all of it — the argument in the yard, storming off in his truck, his attitude at his mother's, buying the gas can and gasoline. All of it. Except the killing of his grandparents. He continued to scream his innocence of that crime.

Ed re-opened the manila folder. On the inside cover, Nell had written her mother's name, address, and phone number.

Before he had time to change his mind, Ed picked up the phone and dialed the number.

"Hello?" the voice was a curious blend of upper-Mid-West quickness and softer, slower Southern speech.

"Jo? Jo Jones?" Ed asked. "This is Ed Flanders."

"Ed," the voice sounded richer, deeper. "Ed Flanders." She laughed. "I'm not surprised to hear from you. Nell can be very persuasive. But, oh, it's good to hear your voice. How are you?"

"Fine," Ed said, "but confused."

"Confused?"

"I just read the reports on the death of the couple in Mississippi—the Marches—and I wonder why you are interested in the case. Seems pretty straight forward to me."

"Maybe I just want to believe in his innocence," Joanna Jones admitted. "Dean came to work for me when he was, I don't know, maybe late 20's. Fondness for beer? Oh, yes. And cocaine too," Joanna sighed. "But, Ed, I just don't think he killed them. He called them crazy. Said they were holy-roller religious. But he also said his Granny made the best biscuits and fried chicken in the world. He carried a pocket knife his Grandfather had given him when he was ten."

"Lots of people murder people they profess to love," Ed reminded Joanna. "I will say, however, that I was struck by the pitiful job his lawyer did."

"I know," Joanna said. "I keep thinking that if I'd been in the States at the time of the trial—you did know I was in London then?—I might have gotten someone better to do some *pro bono* work on Dean's case."

"*Well, shit,*" Ed thought. He said, "Better late than never." He drew a deep breath. "Make you a deal. You take a fresh look at the case, and I'll look at it again. Then let's meet with Dean March at the prison in Mississippi. He may not be innocent, but he at least deserves a chance at a new trial. He was shafted by his original attorney."

"Are you serious?" Joanna Jones said, surprise filling her question.

"Yep," Ed said. "I haven't made the run to New Awlins in the better part of a year." Thinking about the six-hour drive to New Orleans, Ed said, "Hattiesburg is a bit closer. I'll drive there. We'll see what we can find. Make a run to Parchman. Then you owe me dinner at Willie Mae's Scotch House."

"You're on," Joanna said.

"This is Friday," Ed said. "When and where in Hattiesburg?"

"How about Wednesday afternoon? As to where, give me your email address, and I'll find a good place," Joanna said.

After they exchanged email information, Joanna said, her voice hesitant, "This may be a waste of time."

"Dinner with an old friend at my favorite restaurant in the South?" Ed said. "Never a waste."

Joanna promised to send details to Ed and said good-bye.

Is there anyway I can charge this to my publisher?" Ed thought as he opened the folder to begin reading again. "Not a chance," he answered his own question and began to read again.

Chapter 7

May, 2003

Jesse Springfield whistled softly as he began to reassemble his special briefcase. He examined each item as he put it into its proper place.

First, he inspected the leather box originally designed to hold four to five cigars. On the outside of the box, the carefully-lettered label read "Adjustment tools." Satisfied that the box had suffered no heat damage earlier in the day, Jesse picked up the small box of matches and inspected that box too. *"As usual,"* Jesse thought. The matches were for absolute emergency use only. In fact, they had never been used. Still, Jesse always carried them. Just in case. He carefully wiped the wand-like lighter, the kind used to start charcoal, and slid it carefully into the leather cigar holder. He closed the leather box and strapped it in place in the briefcase.

Next, he wiped the chrome-plated rod and placed it in the briefcase. It was an exact fit, specifically cut to the length of the briefcase interior. The rod was marked in inches and half-inches. If asked, Jesse said it was an easy measuring tool. He had found it in a Nashville pawn shop and immediately realized its potential. A tool shop had cut and smoothed the ends.

A plastic package of hand wipes and a package of surgical gloves were also strapped into place. Another plastic package containing cable or zip ties, the ones long enough to be used as handcuffs was refilled and replaced.

Then Jesse checked the lid to the heavy plastic bottle clearly marked "Rubbing Alcohol." He wiped and re-wiped the bottle which held a liter of liquid — just a little bit more than a quart. He fitted the bottle into the briefcase, strapping it in as well.

He had explained to the seamstress making the insert that customized his briefcase, "The liquid in there is necessary in my work. I use it to sanitize things. But it is very flammable. I have to be very careful." He had showed her the warning label carefully glued onto the bottle. Today, as usual, the bottle did not contain rubbing alcohol. It had been filled from the can of kerosene Jesse kept in the garage attached to his apartment.

Finally, Jesse picked up the black leather wallet. It contained $30 in cash, a credit card and a Tennessee driver's license in the name Josh Faraday. Jesse put it into a box clearly labeled "Bandages and Compresses" and fitted it into the briefcase. "There you go, Josh," he said softly. "Stay there until I need you again."

Jesse looked at the interior of the briefcase, mentally checking to be sure that all supplies were in place, and closed the case. He wiped it once more.

After taking the gas can filled with kerosene back to the garage, Jesse took the special briefcase into the bedroom-turned-office and placed it beside the filing cabinet. If anyone asked why Jesse had two very similar — almost identical — briefcases, Jesse would say, "Christmas gifts. One from my boss. One from my adopted mother." Then he would grin shyly and say, "How could I get rid of either one of them?"

By 9 p.m., Jesse had finished a late dinner delivered from a nearby Chinese restaurant. The television was tuned to one of the Nashville stations, one that often added "Breaking News" to its programs. Not that Jesse expected the fire to be on the news yet. It might not be on until morning. Even then, there might not be much. The fire was in western Tennessee, near Memphis.

After the 11 o'clock news program was over with no report of the fire, Jesse went to bed. He didn't fall asleep immediately. Instead he reviewed the day.

"What do *you* want?" Mrs. Melinda Clifford had said when she answered the doorbell. She looked at Jesse in disgust. Recovering from knee replacement had made her move slower. It had intensified her already bad attitude toward people.

"I was in the neighborhood," Jesse said quietly, "and thought I should check to be sure that your walking canes had been adjusted properly."

"Of course, they are," Mrs. Clifford said. "If they weren't working right, I would have called your office and told them." She had puffed air through her lips in a dismissing gesture.

"Well," she said, "since you're here." She awkwardly turned, leaning heavily on the walking canes. "Come on," she said.

Without turning back to Jesse, she reminded, "Take off your shoes."

Jesse left his shoes on the doorstep as he had in three previous times he had been to the Clifford residence.

Mrs. Clifford led the way into the kitchen where Jesse could put his briefcase on the kitchen counter. "I can't have you scaring my good furniture," she said each time.

"Where is Mr. Clifford?" Jesse asked although he had watched James Clifford leave two hours earlier for the weekly prayer breakfast he hosted at a nearby restaurant.

"Prayer breakfast," Mrs. Clifford said in an abrupt voice. "He should be home in the next ten minutes." She frowned. "Waste of time if you ask me. Let 'em go their sinful, hellish ways." She looked closely at Jesse. "Didn't he tell you to come and pray with him?"

"Yes, Ma'am," Jesse said, "but I had to work."

"Not taking time to pray will bring down the fires of hell on you," Mrs. Clifford said. "You will be repenting and praying for forgiveness, young man. Be warned."

"Yes, Ma'am," Jesse repeated.

"I'm sure Mr. Clifford warned you about hell fire coming to cleanse the sickness of this world," Mrs. Clifford said.

"Yes, he did, Ma'am," Jesse said as he lifted the chrome rod from the briefcase. "If I could just have your canes," he said quietly.

Mrs. Clifford turned to sit heavily on a chair at the kitchen table. She handed Jesse both canes.

As Mrs. Clifford began to warn Jesse about scratching the counter, Jesse stepped behind the woman and hit her hard across the back of the skull with the chrome rod. Without a word, the woman fell to the floor of the kitchen.

Jesse tore a paper towel from a nearby roller and wiped the chrome tool. He put on surgical gloves and walked through the house checking the windows. He turned the air conditioner off. *"Slow the flow of oxygen,"* Jesse thought. *"Make the fire hotter."*

Back in the kitchen, Jesse bent and grabbed Melinda Clifford by her heels. He dragged her across the kitchen and through the hall.

The task became more difficult when he reached the carpeted living room, but Jesse yanked and tugged until Melinda Clifford's body was wedged between the sofa and the coffee table. An open Bible was on the sofa where Mrs. Clifford had apparently been reading before Jesse's arrival.

Jesse carefully picked up the open book and placed it over Melinda Clifford's face. "Read your way to hell," he said and smashed the book downward.

Back in the kitchen, Jesse removed the bottle of kerosene from the briefcase, carrying it into the living room where he splashed the sofa and upholstered chairs. He poured kerosene onto the big, open Bible and religious material on the coffee table.

Saving only enough kerosene to make a trail from the living room to the front door, Jesse doused the still body of Mrs. Melinda Clifford. "Body fat to make the fire burn hotter," he said.

Returning to the kitchen counter, Jesse transferred the cigar holder to his suit coat pocket and repacked the briefcase. Carrying his briefcase and Melinda Clifford's canes, Jesse walked back into the living room.

Contrary to portrayals on television and in movies, the wound on Melinda Clifford's head had left no trail of blood. Her instant death had stopped her heart from pumping. Only a smudge on the kitchen floor gave evidence of the trauma that had occurred there.

Jesse sat down in one of the wing chairs and waited quietly, watching the driveway from a safe distance. The kerosene fumes were strong. With the air conditioner off, the house was warm and stuffy.

Jesse breathed carefully, allowing himself to go back in time to that other place, that first smell of kerosene. The memory of that first burning, that first act of retribution, was interrupted by the sound of a car turning in the drive. The angle was good enough to assure Jesse that James Clifford was alone. Jesse heard the garage door opening. James Clifford was home.

Jesse moved to a spot behind the door from the hallway into the living room.

"Melinda?" James Clifford called. "Where are you?"

"We're in here. In the living room," Jesse answered.

Mrs. Clifford's body would be in sight when Mr. Clifford entered the room.

As Jesse expected, Mr. Clifford saw his wife's body on the floor and bent over her. As he did, Jesse hit him from behind. The blow to James Clifford's head was restrained: hard enough to stun the elderly man but not hard enough to kill him.

Working quickly, Jesse bound the wounded man's wrists and ankles with cable ties.

As he worked, he spoke softly. "Fire and repentance. Repentance and fire." Jesse's voice changed taking on a deeper, harsher tone. "Here, Jesse! Kneel in the repentant box and pray. Pray to have your sins forgiven."

Jesse's voice changed again, became childlike. "Please, please...." His voice strengthened. "Day after day kneeling in the box. The cuts never healing."

Jesse blinked. He looked at the two people on the floor beside him. "You didn't care. You just wanted God to send fire to cleanse me and all the other sinners. You asked for fire and smoke. You *demanded* fire and smoke."

James Clifford tried to struggle against the ties, tried to move away from the pervasive smell of kerosene surrounding his wife's body. He moaned and tried to speak.

"Time to go," Jesse said. He calmly turned from the man who began to cry.

"Help, help," James Clifford's voice grew stronger and louder. "Help me. Oh God, help us," he cried.

Jesse stepped carefully around the two bodies on the living room floor and picked up his briefcase. As he walked down the hallway, James Clifford's cries for help became louder, stronger.

Jesse stopped at the place where the trail of kerosene was closest to the front door.

"And God shall come to you in fire and billows of smoke," Jesse said. He took the butane lighter from the cigar case and clicked it. He bent and lit the trail of kerosene.

As Jesse watched the flame catch and begin to move along the hall floor, he put the lighter back into the case and into his pocket. He also removed the surgical gloves and put them in his jacket pocket.

He cocked his head, listening to the old man's frantic pleas, and then let himself out the front door. With the door securely closed, he slipped on his shoes and walked back to the car.

Jesse did not stay in the neighborhood to watch the fire. He would see the results on television. He would enjoy it in safety.

As he drove toward the entrance to I-40, Jesse kept an eye on the clock, counting off the minutes.

1 minute: the fire was still in the hallway. Kerosene burns slowly especially with limited oxygen to feed it. Jesse pictured it—the low blue flame running toward the carpeted living room. Now the flame reached the kerosene-soaked sofa and the body of Melinda Clifford.

In his mind, Jesse could hear the screams of James Clifford as his pant legs began to catch fire.

2 minutes: the fire is climbing up the sofa and wall. Heavy, smoke begins to fill the room. In his car, Jesse inhaled deeply as if he could smell the oily, acrid stench as the clothes and then the bodies of the Cliffords began to burn. *"Burning like candles,"* Jesse thought. Jesse inhaled deeply through his nose as if he could smell the burning flesh, the singed hair. Beside his wife, James Clifford chokes on the smoke that slowly smothers him. His growing unconsciousness eases the pain of his burning legs.

The smoke alarm above the cook stove in the kitchen sounds its shrill alarm. Jesse chuckled at the thought that there was no one alive to hear it.

3 minutes: the entire house is filled with smoke, consuming the available oxygen. Jesse imagined the sound of the fire trying to breathe through the small gaps around the windows, in the attic. The fire gasps for air. It is an audible sound. The heat is intense--distorting plastics, bubbling the paint on the walls and cabinets.

The Cliffords are now charred lumps on the living room floor. The area around them is charred as well.

Jesse grips the wheel as an intense wave of delight sweeps over him.

4 minutes: the house is near flashover. Combustible gases and hot smoke have nearly reached the point of ignition.

5 minutes: the house explodes. Flames shoot into the air. The crackle and roar of the fire is heard several blocks away. Smoke plumes into the blue sky.

"Fully involved," Jesse said, his voice rich with satisfaction. "Fully involved," he repeated the words from the fire department manuals he had studied over the years.

Jesse was still smiling an hour later as he pulled into a fast-food drive-through in Jackson, Tennessee and ordered a burger, fries, and large Coke.

Hours later, lying in bed, Jesse smiled again, picturing the charred remains of Mr. and Mrs. James Clifford one more time. Then he drifted off into peaceful sleep and did not awaken until 7:30 the next morning, his usual rising time.

Although it was Saturday and Jesse did not have to work, he followed his normal routine.

By 9:00, Jesse had done thirty minutes on the treadmill and eaten a nutritious breakfast. He had also watched with pleasure the news report of the fire in one of the communities that lie just east of Memphis.

Jesse knew that by Monday, when he called on clients in Memphis, newspapers there would carry all the details. He would add the story of the Cliffords to the others in his scrapbook.

Still thinking about the work he had done on Friday, Jesse went into his home office and sat at his computer.

First, he transferred money from an account in the name of a bogus company he had created to the account of Josh Faraday. Then he went into the account of Josh Faraday and paid the credit card bill for the car rental. There was, Jesse knew, a thin trail from Josh Faraday to Jesse Springfield, but that could not be helped.

Josh Faraday, his dream of becoming a singing sensation dissolved, had been pawning his guitar when Jesse saw him. They looked quite similar — Jesse and Josh — with the same height, weight, hair- and eye-color.

It had been a simple matter for Jesse to get rid of Josh but keep Josh's identity. Simple enough. Jesse had offered Josh dinner, had hinted at his spare room as a place to stay. Then while Josh sat at the dining table, Jesse had hit him with the chrome rod.

Jesse had wrapped the body in a blanket, loaded it into the trunk of his car and had driven to an abandoned farm near the Kentucky border. Dumping the body into an old well had been the most difficult part of the entire operation.

"Just another wanna-be country/western singer that didn't make it," Jesse said, as he drove back home.

Jesse as Josh had rented a room for long enough to get an updated driver's license, a credit card, and a bank account.

If any nosey neighbor had seen a car in front of the Clifton residence and noticed the license number, it would be traced to the rental company and then to Josh. Then the trail would go cold.

Jesse's main determination in life was to never again be sent to the psychiatric hospital. Never. Josh was simply a convenient part of that determination.

"Time to check in," Jesse said. He reached for his phone and keyed in the number. Dr. Roberta Sales answered on the second ring.

Chapter 8

March, 2012

"I suggest we walk through this as if it were a cold case that we had been assigned and knew nothing about," Joanna Jones said.

"That will be easy for me," Ed said and chuckled. "I know nothing—or next to nothing—about it."

They were seated at a portable table in the largest suite the hotel in Hattiesburg, Mississippi had to offer. Joanna had arrived on the previous day and, among other things, had commandeered the room and a table and chairs for their use. Ed had arrived just after noon, having broken speed limit laws in Florida, Alabama and Mississippi.

Over lunch, the two had caught up on the past—their own and that of several colleagues—and had laughed at the audacity of Joanna's daughter Nell.

Joanna had several folders on the table as well as pencils and yellow writing pads.

"I got copies of the total case file from the defense attorney," Joanna said. "Make that, 'I *bought* copies," she corrected, shaking her head.

"Good," Ed said. "Let's start with the first responder's investigative report. Ed read page one of the two pages and handed it to Joanna to read while he read the second page.

Virtually all of the information contained in the deputy's report had been in the newspaper: the 911 call, the arrival of the deputy followed immediately by the arrival of the fire department vehicles, the containment of the fire, the discovery of the bodies, the call for the sheriff, the identity of the bodies.

"Here's the report from Sally Jane Young, the volunteer fire chief," Joanna said. Ed's eyebrows rose. "The rural fire department was in danger of being closed because of incompetency in bookkeeping and administration," Joanna explained. "That was about ten years ago. Sally Jane took over and got everything, and everyone, in line." Ed nodded his understanding.

The report verified Joanna's defense of the chief. The 911 call had come into the fire station and to Sally Jane Young's home at 6:42 p.m. Mrs. Linda Mayo, in her backyard had smelled smoke and then had seen smoke above the house of her neighbors, Leo and Peggy March. Mayo and her husband had crossed the hundred yards between the houses but had not attempted to enter the house, believing that the Marches were not at home.

Fire Chief Young noted that the fire was fully involved, meaning that the house was in flames when the fire trucks arrived. Having been told by the deputy that the house was empty of occupants, Young had focused on the fire. Warning her fire fighters of the chance of back draft or flash fire, they had ventilated the building carefully. Firefighters managed to douse the flames, and Chief Young entered the building. The body of Leo March was found in the remains of the recliner he favored. Peggy March's charred remains were on the floor just inside the living room door.

Fire Chief Young had requested that the deputy call for the sheriff and the fire investigator. She had her firefighters guard the building until the sheriff arrived. She had also waited an extra hour and a half until the fire inspector arrived.

"Upon finding the bodies," Chief Young had written, "I observed damage that did not look like fire damage. In fact, both victims had extensive damage to their skulls. I was sure that this was no accident, but I did not want to make that call. That is the fire investigator's job."

"Good report," Ed said as he finished reading. "Interesting that the fire department had to ventilate the house." Ed frowned. "Was this an old house or a fairly new one? Would the Marches have had central heat and air conditioning?"

"I don't know about either," Joanna said. "However, if the Marches were preparing to go out, they might have closed the windows and doors."

"Right," Ed admitted. "Still, it's something to ask the fire chief."

He wrote "Q's for Chief Young" at the top of a page of yellow note paper and jotted down his question. *"Later,"* he thought, *"we'll deal with this later."*

Joanna opened the manila envelope that contained the fire investigator's report and 8x10 glossy, black and white photos of the fire scene.

Ed looked suitably impressed.

"I taught criminal justice courses for twenty-five years," Joanna explained. "I know a lot of people. People who know other people."

Ed grinned. The law enforcement network is strong from the local to the international level.

The report from the fire investigator was simple. He had been called by the rural fire chief and had gone to the scene. He had agreed with the volunteer fire chief that the bodies had been damaged by other than the fire. He had determined that the extensive burning had been caused by the use of an accelerant. He had called the case one of Murder/Arson and had sent the bodies to the state medical examiner.

The first photo showed the house exterior. Most of the roof on the left side in the photo was gone, exposing charred beams. At the center of the house, where there was a second-story, the structure was intact although the white paint was scorched. A blackened area above each of the remaining windows and door was either smoke or fire damage.

Photos from inside the structure showed that the intensity of the fire was confined to the living room. The wooden floor was burned through in places. In others, the wood was deeply charred.

Photos of the victims showed extensive fire damage. Leo March, sitting in his recliner, was a black skeletal mass. The floor beneath Peggy March and the wall behind her were heavily burned.

Close-up photos of each of the victims showed the crushed skulls that had caused both the fire chief and the investigator to determine the cause of each death to be murder rather than fire.

Having worked with crime scenes and crime scene photos for their respective careers, neither Ed nor Joanna reacted strongly to the ghastly appearance of the bodies and their surroundings. Joanna spread the photos out on the table, and they both continued to study them.

"I have an idea," Ed said. He turned to his laptop computer and typed a code accessing phone numbers not available to the general public. "Ah-hah," he said and keyed the number for David Martin, an arson expert with the FBI.

After Ed identified himself to Martin, he said, "I would like your opinion—strictly off the record, of course—on a fire. I have photos of a house fire that may was apparently used to cover a double homicide. I need more understanding of the fire than I have. The fire investigator determined that an accelerant was used."

"Fax me the photos," Martin said. "It may take a week or so for me to get back to you, but I'll give you my thoughts. Off the record, of course."

"Okay," Ed said although he was a bit disappointed.

"You want something faster," Martin said, his voice making the question into a statement. "Describe the photos to me. I'll give you an off-the-cuff analysis to get you started."

Ed described the photos one by one. Martin asked few questions.

Finally, Martin said, "Here are a few things that strike me. First, the investigator was right. An accelerant was used. Probably a slow burner. Something like kerosene or lamp oil."

"Not gasoline?" Ed asked. He was using the speaker phone so that Joanna could hear the conversation too.

"I doubt it," Martin said. "Gasoline goes 'Woosh' and is out unless it happens to catch something really flammable like curtains. The depth of the charring you describe doesn't fit a gasoline fire. At least, as a general rule." Martin was silent a moment then asked, "Do you have the fire department report?"

"Yes," Ed said.

"Check these things: what stage had the fire reached when the responders arrived; was the structure closed or ventilated; and did the responders mention a lingering smell of fuel," Martin said. "Either gasoline or diesel will most often leave a vague scent," he added.

"The fire was fully involved, and the firefighters had to ventilate the structure," Ed said. "There was no mention of odor," he added.

"If I were a betting man," Martin concluded, "I'd bet that the victims were murdered first. Then some form of slow-burning accelerant — not gasoline — was poured on their bodies and also around the house, especially in the room with the bodies. The house was either deliberately closed or was already closed. This intensified the heat and the damage once the gases in the enclosed space ignited."

"Very interesting," Ed said.

"Send me your photos and the reports," Martin said. "I'll get back to you with a full report. But I think it will verify what I just told you."

Ed thanked David Martin and ended the call.

"Well," Ed said. "That was interesting."

"Yes," Joanna agreed. "Very interesting."

Ed added a second question about the smell of gasoline to the questions for the fire chief.

Joanna opened the folder which held both the report of the arrest of Dean March and the investigative report that accompanied it.

The first page was identical to the one Nell Jones had given Ed. It was titled Murder/Arson/Arrest and contained, as Ed had noted, no details.

The other page was the investigative report that the deputy had completed.

"Not exactly a scholarly report," Joanna said as she read. "I hope he was not one of my students!"

Ed took the report when she finished. In the space provided, the deputy had typed, "On Saturday, May 10 at 12:48 a.m., I was assigned by the sheriff to make a death notification to Dean March at Number 213 in the Homestead Trailer Park on Highway 16 West. Upon arrival, I was unable to get a response from the house. I was instructed to resume patrol but to periodically check the address of the residence to see if anyone returned before my shift ended at 7. Upon approaching the residence at approximately 3:45 a.m. observed a vehicle entering the driveway. I approached the vehicle as the driver exited. As I approached the vehicle, I noticed a gas can in the bed of the pickup truck. The suspect smelled highly of gasoline and alcohol and appeared to be somewhat intoxicated. I placed the suspect under arrest and conveyed him to the jail where he was booked in connection with the crime."

"A non-scholar," Ed said, "who doesn't follow procedure or orders either."

"He had no real reason to arrest Dean," Joanna agreed. "But why did it snowball from there?"

"Path of least resistance," Ed said. "Dean March was an easy way to wrap up the case. No one had to investigate. March himself admitted to most of the evidence against him."

Joanna sighed. "Poor Dean," she said, "always his own worst enemy."

"I would say his attorney was in the running for 'worst enemy,'" Ed said. "He certainly didn't help." He shook his head. "Really lousy job of defending March."

"We need to talk to Dean," Joanna said. She turned to her laptop and clicked into the site for Parchman Farm, the Mississippi state penitentiary where Dean March was incarcerated.

As Ed had done, she set her cell phone to speaker and called the prison. Once again, knowing the right people worked for Joanna Jones. In less than ten minutes, she was speaking to the prison superintendent. Another couple of minutes and she had convinced the superintendent to let both Joanna and Ed interview Dean March on Friday afternoon.

The call ended, Joanna grinned at Ed. "All in who you know," she said.

"Now," Ed said, "get us an appointment with Fire Chief Young."

A quick directory search, a quick call, and Sally Jane Young promised to meet Ed and Joanna on Saturday morning.

"Okay, Miss Wise Guy," Ed said when Joanna finished the call. "Now, we need reservations at somewhere good for dinner. I need a martini and food. In that order."

"Reservations already made," Joanna said, grinning. "At a place with a bartender who makes a mean martini. Good food. Live music. 8 p.m."

"I'm going to go take a shower," Ed said as Joanna began re-assembling the packets of information. "Meet you in the lounge at 7:30. Be timely."

She grinned as he left her suite for his.

Chapter 9

"Jesse!" Warmth and delighted infused her voice as Roberta Sales answered the phone. "How lovely to hear from you!" Without waiting for him to respond, Roberta began a series of enthusiastic questions: "How are you? Still enjoying your job? Still liking life in Nashville?"

Jesse laughed. "Good morning, Mama Bert," he said. "I am fine. The medicine you suggested cleared my sinuses right up. I still love Nashville. I still love my job. I have to thank you again for making my life so good."

"Oh, Jesse," Berta answered, "you are the one who has made your life good. *You.*"

Five years earlier, when Roberta Sales, in her capacity as Jesse's psychiatrist, had begun to encourage him to do more than work in a pizzeria, Jesse had resisted. He felt safe and secure in his job and his life.

Then Roberta's nephew began to expand his medical equipment and supply business and needed a salesman and customer representative. Roberta practically forced Jesse to apply for the job. She coerced her nephew into giving Jesse the interview.

As she had hoped, the two hit it off immediately. Jesse had become a salesman. More importantly, he had become an excellent representative for the company. His specialty was in doing follow-up meetings with businesses and, especially, individual customers. His percentage of additional sales to repeat customers was exceptionally high.

For Roberta, the down-side to Jesse's success was his move to a new company territory. Working in Kentucky and Tennessee, Jesse's base was in Nashville. This meant that Berta rarely saw him.

She contained her impatience at the distance between them and waited for his more-or-less regular phone calls. *"Like most mothers waiting patiently for calls from their sons,"* Roberta often thought.

She had worried about the mother/son relationship that had developed between them. Jesse reassured her. "I know the difference," he had said. "Of course, you are not my mother. You *are* the mother I wish I had."

He had first shortened her name, calling her "Dr. Bert." When she was at ease with that familiarity, he had called her "Mama Bert" but immediately apologized.

Finally, she had said, "Since it means so much to you, you may call me 'Mama Bert' but only when we are alone." Jesse had ducked his head to hide his grin.

In the years since Dr. Roberta Sales had begun working with the young Jesse Springfield, she had gained a highly favorable reputation and renown. Her book on the rehabilitation of abused teenagers, particularly those who had committed violent acts, was acclaimed by many in social work and psychiatry.

"The youthful offender must confront the facts of the abuse," Sales said. "Confront the abuse, accept the abuse as a part of the past. Then, each youth must confront and accept the violent response made to that abuse. Combining that with positive re-enforcement and a caring relationship with a trained health-care provider offers the youth a better-than-even chance to lead a normal, life."

Jesse and Dr. Sales had made a video. Jesse, his face in darkness, had talked with Sales about his childhood, his mother's death, his grandparents' brutality, and their deaths.

He had related, in answer to Dr. Sales' questions, his role in their deaths. He had spoken about his realization and acceptance of his responsibility. As always, Jesse said he hoped they were in a better place and had forgiven him. In their video, the camera focus switched to Roberta Sales who, speaking directly into the camera, outlined the methodology she had used in treating Jesse.

The video was also successful. To Roberta Sales and those who followed her teaching, Jesse was the picture of rehabilitation.

Although Sales made a great deal of money from books, lectures, symposiums and the video, it was the acclaim of her peers and, most especially, the continued mother/son relationship with Jesse that were the most fulfilling.

On this Saturday morning, Mama Bert continued to ask Jesse questions and he, laughingly, answered them. With each response, Jesse added words of thanks to Mama Bert: for co-signing for the larger apartment and the new car, for sending him a beautiful cashmere sweater that just matched his blue eyes.

"And Susan?" Roberta asked. "What does Susan think of the sweater?"

"Susan loves it," Jesse said, "but Susan loves everything: sweaters, kittens, chocolate, anything purple, etc., etc., etc." The sarcasm was evident in his tone.

"You're not still dating her?" Berta asked.

"No," Jesse said. "She was just. . . . Well, she was just silly." Jesse didn't tell Berta that he had only dated Susan, the secretary at work, to quell any questions among the other salesmen about Jesse's sexuality — or rather the idea that he might be homosexual.

After several dates with Susan, Jesse, discretely using sniffs of black pepper, had sneezed his way out of Susan's dating life with an apparent allergy to her cats.

"As I have told you many times," Jesse added, his voice infused with warmth, "if I ever find a girl like you, I'll be happy. Until then...." Jesse allowed his voice to drift off to nothing.

They spoke for several more minutes with Berta asking questions and Jesse answering them. It never occurred to Jesse to ask about Roberta Sales' life.

After the phone call ended, Roberta sat for nearly half an hour reviewing the call, a smile on her face. Jesse, his home chores finished, took his car to the car wash and then stopped for lunch, the phone call forgotten.

Chapter 10

March, 2012

"Oh, Miz Joanna, I shore am proud to see you." Dean March's delight with seeing Joanna Jones was obvious. "I just couldn't hardly believe you was really here," he continued.

Drew was seated at a table when Joanna and Ed entered the lawyer/client room of Parchman Farm prison.

To Ed, Dean March looked like one of those extras in an old Western, scrawny and rather ferret-faced — the kind who was part of the gang of bad guys that rode into town and got shot.

"Dean," Joanna Jones said, "it's good to see you." Joanna and Ed took seats across from Dean.

Under the watchful eye of the guard, Ed laid a portable recorder on the table. Both he and Joanna had yellow note pads and stubby pencils for taking notes.

Ed was surprised when they were accorded such liberty with the prisoner. He had expected the normal visitor's room with other inmates and their visitors in a loud cacophony of sound. Either that or a room with a glass partition where inmate and visitor talked through a telephone receiver. However, they had been granted access to the prisoner although they were to be carefully watched.

Earlier that morning, Joanna and Ed had driven north and west from Hattiesburg about 3 hours to Parchman Farm, the main penitentiary for the state of Mississippi.

Actually, Joanna had driven while Ed made notes and outlined the main points of their coming interview with Dean March.

Joanna hoped that they could eventually prove Dean innocent of his grandparents' death; Ed was skeptical but thought they might get the man a new trial with a competent lawyer.

Joanna quickly introduced Ed to Dean, telling Dean that Ed was a retired FBI agent. Dean nodded in Ed's direction.

Joanna began the interview, saying, "Dean, we are going to try to help you, *but* we have to have the absolute truth from you. Do you understand that?"

"Yes, Ma'am," Dean said, "I didn't kill my grandparents. That's the absolute truth."

"What I want you to do," Joanna said, ignoring Dean's protestation of innocence, "is tell me about that Friday. I want to know what you did every minute." She looked at him.

"What time did you get up?" Joanna listened while Ed took careful notes.

"Well," Dean said, thinking back, "it was about noon. Maybe near one o'clock." He thought. "Must 'a been about one. Sun was beating down on that trailer roof." Joanna nodded. Early May in Mississippi is warm, often hot.

"Then?" Joanna prompted.

"I just set around a while," March said. "They was a couple beers left over from the night before and I drank them. Then I got to thinking about where I could get some money and I thought, 'What day is this?' and I figured out it was a Friday."

Dean March turned his hands palm-upward in a gesture that echoed his next thought. "Time to go south," he said, with a grin.

Joanna looked her question but didn't interrupt.

"See," March explained, "Mama and Roy — that's her live-in — get paid on Friday. I figured I could sweet talk her out of some money and ol' Roy out of some beer."

Dean leaned forward to confide. "Friday's a good day to go by Grandma and Grandpa's house too. I figured I could get a twenty out of her before she went to Singing."

For the moment, Dean March was lost in the past. Joanna interrupted his reflections. "So you decided to go south?" she asked. "What time was that?"

"Well, it was about two o'clock," Dean said, "but first I had to clean up." He shook his head slightly. "No use showing up at Grandma's dirty and wanting money. 'Cleanliness is next to godliness,' Grandma always said."

Joanna nodded her understanding. March rubbed his hand across his face as he might have after shaving that day.

"I must 'a' left Hattiesburg about three. Maybe a bit after. It's right near twenty-five miles from the trailer in Hattiesburg to Grandma and Grandpa's house," he explained to Ed.

"I got this 1980 Ford pickup—ol' Big Red, you remember it, Miz Joanna?—that gets maybe 13 mile to the gallon. So when I got to Grandpa's, I pulled up beside his garage."

He leaned over once again to confide to them. "On Fridays, when Grandpa filled up his car for the drive to the Singing, he filled the jerry can so he could mow the lawn on Saturday. I always parked where I could borrow a little gas." March grinned at his cleverness. "If I'd get to the house at just the right time, the gas can would be full. Grandpa would be getting cleaned up to go to Singing. Grandma would have her pocketbook handy for her sweet baby's baby boy. That would be *me*."

"Tell me what time you got to their house," Joanna interrupted to say.

"It must 'a' been about 4," March said. He went over his actions and the trip mentally. "Yep," he said. "About four."

"And when you got there?" Joanna urged him to continue.

March sighed and leaned back in the chair. "That day, Grandpa was standing on the porch when I drove in. I couldn't get no gas. He was watching too close."

March folded his arms across his chest. "I didn't even get in the house. Grandpa, he was standing there on the porch, leaning on them walking sticks and watching me. When I got up to the steps, he started preaching at me. Quoting them Bible verses at me. Telling me Judgment Day was a coming."

March's voice became a husky, sarcastic imitation of the old man's voice: "The wrath and revelation of the righteous judgment of God."

March grinned. "Ain't no telling how many times I heard that from him. Shoot, I don't even know what it means."

Joanna waited, trying to look patient. March leaned toward her and continued.

"Bout that time," March said, "Grandma, she come out on the porch. I started up the steps to give her a hug, but Grandpa stopped me. 'You'll not be getting money from us to spend on drunkenness,' he said."

Dean March looked angry at the memory. "I start telling him I just wanted to hug my Grandma, but he swung one of them crutch things he used to walk and shook it at me. Called me a 'bomination like he always did and said Satan had taken me. Then he put the end of that crutch against my chest and pushed just a little bit. 'Get away from here, Son of Satan,' he said. So I left. Got in my truck and drove the hell out of there."

March leaned back in his chair. "Don't that tell you I wouldn't harm them?" He looked from Joanna to Ed and back to Joanna. "Don't you think I could have pulled that old man right off that porch if I wanted to?"

He leaned forward again. "But I didn't, did I?"

March answered his own question. "No, I didn't. I left. And when I left, they was both standing on that porch. And that's the truth."

Joanna drew a deep breath. "Where did you go then?"

"My mama's house," March said. "She lives on down toward Popularville. 'Bout a mile—mile and a half—on down the road."

"What time did you get to your mother's house?" Joanna asked.

"Must 'a' been about 4:30, maybe a little bit later," March said.

"And?" Joanna asked.

"And me and Roy had a couple of beers," March said. "Mama asked had I had anything to eat and she said I should stay for dinner which she was just fixing to cook."

"Did you eat dinner with them?" Joanna asked.

"Nah," March said. "I had them beers and was ready to roll. Back to big Hattiesburg."

March looked at Ed. "I gotta explain something to you," he said. "Southern wimmen, maybe all wimmen, I don't know. Southern wimmen, they got a soft place for they men folks. My grandma and my mama both knowed I was no good. They both knowed I'd buy booze or drugs with money they give me. They knowed it. But wimmen just love they baby boys. They give them money and loves them even when they is 'going to hell' rascals." He nodded his head at Ed. He grinned a one-sided, mainly toothless, grin. "Mama give me a twenty-dollar bill. I got a fiver in my pocket. Twenty-five dollars and I'm ready to roll." He grinned and nodded at the memory.

"Then I'm half way back to Hattiesburg and run outta fuckin' gas. Pardon my French," he said. "Have to walk, shit, forever to get to that little backwoods gas station." March shook his head. "Lady Luck for sure wasn't with me that day."

"What time did you get to the station?" Joanna asked, trying to keep Drew March on track.

"Little bit after five, I reckon," March said, straining to remember. "Maybe closer to 5:30."

"You bought gas. Then what happened?" Joanna asked.

"I walked back to the truck," Dean said. Poured the gas in. Kept a little for the carburetor. Then it went to shit again." Dean's look of disgust returned.

"Damned if I didn't flood the damned carburetor," March said. "I was hot and sweaty and just set down in the shade of the truck and, well, I guess I passed out." He looked as surprised as he had then. "Next thing I knew it was middle of the damned night and pretty damned cold and damp. I been sitting there so long, the dew done settled on me." He laughed a bit at the memory.

"What time was this?" Joanna urged.

"Now, I can tell you that," March said. "When I was working for you, I bought a CD player and put it in the dashboard of my truck. It's got one helluva clock. I said, 'Well, son of a bitch, it's twenty-eight minutes after three!'"

"And then?"

"Then I drove on home," March said. "Took me 'bout fifteen minutes to get there." A look of sadness crossed his face. "I was just getting out of my truck when that deputy told me about Grandma and Grandpa and arrested me."

March made solid eye contact with Joanna. "I swear to you, I didn't kill them. I didn't even know they was dead. I thought he was taking me in for drinking and driving."

"Okay," Joanna said. "Now, just to be sure we got all the information right, we're going through this time frame again. Okay?"

March looked a bit confused but agreed. This time through, Joanna asked questions rather than allowing March to ramble along. Basically, his story remained the same; however, there were details that he remembered as she questioned him. He remembered looking at the clock in the pickup when he pulled into his grandparents' driveway.

"Shit," he said, "I was early. It was only 4:04. I always try to get there closer to six. They leave for the Singing at 6:15 on the dot. Every Friday. If I get there just about six, I get Grandma's lecture about sin and drinking, but I get money too."

"But you were early that day?" Joanna asked.

"Sure 'nuff," March said, shaking his head. "Got the old man's preaching. Got no gas. Got no money." His look reflected his disgust.

"How long were you at your grandparents' house?" Joanna asked.

"Hell," March said, "I wasn't there ten minutes. Like I told you, I didn't even get up on the porch."

"And then you went straight to your mother's?"

"Yeah," March said. "See. You go down highway 11 and turn to the right and down that little road just a little ways to Grandpa's house. But to get to my mama's, you go on down highway 11 one more mile and turn left onto that dirt road. They just live a little more than a mile apart."

"What time do you think you got to your mother's?"

"I was thinking it was later, but I guess it was more like a quarter past four. Mama and Roy just got home."

"Tell me about being at their house that day."

"Well, Mama was putting away groceries and fixing to cook dinner. Me and Roy sat out on the porch and drank a couple beers. Then Roy wanted to watch the television so he went in the living room and I went in the kitchen to talk to Mama."

"What did Roy want to watch on the television?"

"You know that man that comes on the TV ever afternoon and yells about the government gonna take our guns and mark us with the 666 and stuff like that? Well, Roy watches that ever damned day at 5 o'clock."

"So you were at their house at five?" Joanna asked.

"Yes, I was there," March said, "but soon as that yelling started, I was ready to head out. Kissed my Mama and took the twenty she snuck into my hand and left."

"Did you go back by your grandparents' house?" Joanna asked.

"Well," March answered, "I drove *by the road* to their house, but I didn't even turn off the highway. One dose of religion a day is plenty for me."

Joanna walked Dean March through the rest of the story without focusing on the gas station incident. She and Ed had agreed beforehand that he would question March about that particular time frame. It had seemed odd to both of them that during the trial, the prosecution had used a still photograph of Dean March pumping gas rather than showing the CCTV video.

When March had once again protested his innocence, Joanna nodded her agreement.

"Mr. March," Ed began.

"Call me Dean," March said.

"Now, Dean," Ed said, "I'm just a bit confused about your trip to the gas station. I'm just a city boy, myself, and just call for help." Ed grinned. "Could you just tell me about that again? Start with running out of gas."

"Well," March began, "I was on highway 11. Ol' Red just run out of gas. I pulled into a kind of driveway where they used to be a house, but it's been gone for years. I knew the station was just — oh — half a mile on up the road. I walked up to the station. Got the gas. Flooded the carburetor. Passed out. Woke up."

Ed knew instantly that March was lying. March had memorized this part of the story. A person telling the truth remembers details or tells the story in a slightly different but consistent way. A liar memorizes the story and repeats it exactly the same way. Ed would have to break through the lies to find the truth.

"The way I understand it, the gas station is about half way between your mother's house and Hattiesburg," Ed said. "Is that right?"

At March's emphatic nod, Ed continued, "So it was probably about 5:30 when you ran out of gas? Does that sound right to you?"

Dean March mentally walked back through his actions and nodded his agreement.

"So then you walked to the station to buy the gas?" Ed asked. March nodded. "What did you put the gas in?"

"Wouldn't you know?" March said. "I had to buy one of them gas cans. Used to be able to get a milk carton or a water jug or anything and buy gas, but now you have to buy a *legal* gas can. Cost me ten damn dollars. Then two-gallon of gas was damned over $7.00."

"You spent about $17.00 at the station?"

"Hell, no," March said. "Add $7.50 for a six-pack, and I had fifty cents left to my name."

"You bought beer?" Ed asked.

"I guess it don't make no difference now," March said.

"What doesn't make a difference?" Ed asked.

"My lawyer said to not mention the beer. He said the jury would know for sure that I was drunk and mad and bought the gas to burn up the house."

"Let me get this straight in my mind—I'm an old man and get confused," Ed said. "You went to the station, bought a gas can, pumped gas, and then bought beer?"

"No, no, no," March corrected. He spoke slowly and exactly to Ed using downward chops of the air with his hand to emphasize the items. "I walked to the station. Got the gas can. Got the beer. Paid for the gas can. Paid for two gallons of gas. And for the beer. Then I went outside and pumped the gas into the can and walked back to my truck. You understand?"

Thinking about the photograph or still taken from the CCTV video, Ed said, "What did you do with the beer while you pumped the gas?"

March looked at Ed as if Ed were some kind of idiot.

"I set the bag with the beer on the top of the gas pump," he said.

"Oh, okay," Ed said. "Now I understand." He nodded his head. "Now, explain to me about the carburetor."

"When I run out of gas," March explained carefully, "all the gas was gone from the carburetor. If I just put gas in the gas tank, I might run the battery down before I got enough gas pumped up to start the truck."

He looked at Ed to see if Ed understood. Ed slowly nodded to show his understanding.

"I poured most of the gas into the tank, but stopped with a little bit left to pour into the carburetor. That way, I could start the truck."

Once again, Ed nodded.

"But, I poured too much into the carburetor and flooded it." Dean looked at Ed. "That means I would have to wait about twenty minutes or so for everything to be ready to start. You understand?"

"Oh-h-h," Ed said, drawing out the word. "Okay, now I understand. Thank you." He scratched his head. "So, while you waited. . .?"

"I drank a couple of the beers."

"And passed out?" Ed asked.

"Yeah," March said. Suddenly, March seemed puzzled. "Yeah, I passed out. 'Course I hadn't had nothing to eat, but, hell, that don't make no sense."

Ed and Joanna watched silently as Dean March re-thought his day.

"I bet it was that damned 'shine," he said finally. "I forgot all about that." Suddenly aware of Ed and Joanna, March said, "That damned Roy had a bottle of moonshine, you know, home brew. I took a couple—maybe three or four—slugs of that." He scratched his head. "No wonder I was out like a light."

Ed broke into March's astonished remembrance to review the time from running out of gas until the moment when he awoke and started the truck.

March remembered drinking a beer as he walked back to the truck, remembered sloshing the gasoline onto the side of the truck, and remembered sitting down beside the truck in disgust when he poured too much gasoline in the carburetor.

With the lie about buying beer out of the way, Dean March's story made more sense, and the added details made it more complete.

Finally, Joanna said, "Dean, we are going to take the information you have given us and the other information we have been gathering to a lawyer I know. She works on cases such as yours. I can not promise you anything, you know that. You will hear from me as soon as I know anything."

As Joanna and Ed gathered notes and the recorder, Dean March thanked them repeatedly for taking time to visit him and to help him. Joanna promised again to keep him informed.

In Joanna's car on the way back to Hattiesburg, Ed said, "Boy, Joanna, you sure can pick 'em." He shook his head. "No wonder the jury found him guilty. He could have been the prosecution's star witness. Against himself."

"I know," Joanna admitted. "I know."

"I'm not sure I think he's innocent," Ed said, "but I do think we can gather enough information together for a competent lawyer to petition for a new trial."

For the rest of the way to Hattiesburg, they discussed the enquiries they would each make over the coming days.

Chapter 11

On Saturday morning, Ed and Joanna drove south from Hattiesburg to meet Sally Jane Young, the rural fire chief. They took Highway 11 which runs parallel to Interstate 59 using the same road that Dean March had used that day in May four years earlier, driving past the turns that March would have made first to his grandparent's house and then to his mother's.

Sally Jane Young, short, slender, grey-haired and dressed in jeans and a t-shirt, was inspecting the daffodils that were beginning to bloom in flower beds at the fire station. The main building, a combination of sheet metal and brick, was attractive and clean. Ed noted that there were large doors indicating three fire trucks, two smaller doors for average-sized vehicles and an office door. Water tanks and a fuel supply were secured behind fencing.

"Very impressive," Ed said. Joanna agreed. In years long past, there had been little or no help with rural fires. Now, throughout the country, volunteer rural fire departments were well equipped and operated efficiently.

After introducing themselves and complimenting Chief Young on her facility, Joanna took over the interview.

"As I told you on the phone," Joanna said, "we are taking a fresh look at the fire at the home of Leo and Peggy March."

Young stepped inside the open office door to retrieve a folder.

"Here are my notes from that incident," she said. "The call came in at 6:42 p.m. on Friday, May 9, 2008. The 911 operator with the Mississippi State Police called here. Immediately, the pagers of every volunteer fire fighter went off. Mine, even then, had more information. Within four minutes, I was here and so were four other fire fighters. We rolled out with the big truck at 6:51 and were on the scene at 6:54. A second truck with eight fighters arrived at 6:59. A deputy sheriff was already at the scene when we arrived."

She looked from her notes to Joanna. "When we arrived on the scene, the house was fully involved. The fire was throughout the house and flames had already broken out. The roof was already involved as well. My first concern was for possible occupants in the building. The deputy informed me that the house was empty. The neighbors had told him that Mr. and Mrs. March were gone for the evening."

She looked thoughtful. "Of course, they were inside."

She sighed. "Had we known they were inside, we would have tried to get to them." She dismissed the thought. "Not that we would have been successful. They were already dead."

"Yes," Joanna said. They stood silent for a moment.

Young continued her report, "Believing the house to be unoccupied, our concern was to contain the fire. We ventilated the building and put water on it. It took approximately 45 minutes to extinguish the flames."

She looked at Joanna. "Having been assured that no one was in the house, I waited nearly three hours to make my walk-through. Lot less danger of injuries to me or my people if we wait. When it cooled down enough, I did a walk-through, checking for hot spots to be sure the fire did not re-kindle itself. That's when I found the bodies."

She blinked and continued, "That's when it all stopped." She raised her arms at the elbows and spread her hands, palms open, toward Joanna. "I stayed in the living room area while others made a last check for hot spots. Then we vacated the building. I told the deputy to get the sheriff. I called for the fire inspector. As far as the house and the bodies went, my job was finished."

"Right," Joanna agreed. "One more question: did you notice an odor associated with a petroleum product when you finally entered the house?"

"I've thought about that," Young said. "No," she added, "No, I didn't."

She looked from Joanna to Ed and back to Joanna. "To tell the truth, I was pretty shocked to find the bodies. Really shocked. I stopped my people and called for the sheriff and the fire investigator right then and there. It was more than a house fire. I knew that for sure. I remember thinking—just before I found the bodies—now, what caused this fire? Then I found the bodies and, honestly, quit thinking about the fire, which was out."

She explained, "We deal with car fires some. The police always warn us about destroying evidence, so we're careful if we can be." Then she added, "Later, I thought about smell and I'm pretty sure there was no smell."

She looked at Joanna. "Not that I could be sure enough to testify to that in court. I mean, I just don't remember it. And I think I would."

"Could you give us directions to the place where the house stood? And also to the home of Sheila March?" Joanna asked.

"I'm ahead of you," Young said, with a laugh. "I thought you would want to go to the scene, so I copied that part of the map." She handed Joanna a sheet of paper with highlighted directions to the place where the March house had stood. She also pointed out the house where Dean March's mother Sheila lived and, finally, the house of Seldon and Linda Mayo who had called 911.

Joanna looked at Ed to see if he had other questions, but he had none. Both of them thanked Sally Jane Young for her time and her assistance.

They drove back to the place where Leo and Peggy March had lived and died. The ruin of the house had been cleared away. Only the vague outline of the foundation remained. The garage still stood some 40 feet from where the house had been. It was open and empty. A sort of lean-to made of two poles with a sheet metal roof was still attached to the side of the garage but had fallen into disrepair.

Ed and Joanna sat in the car in the driveway for several minutes, matching the scene before them with Dean March's story and the report from the fire chief. Then Ed maneuvered the car out of the driveway, down the road, and into the next driveway.

Linda Mayo had been watching through the curtains and came to the door as Ed and Joanna got out of the car.

"Can I help you folks?" she asked. In blue jeans and a flowered sweat shirt, Linda Mayo was finishing her weekly vacuuming and dusting. Later, she would go into town for a manicure and pedicure at the same salon where her hair would be re-bleached, washed, and dried by the same woman who had been doing it each week for over 25 years.

Joanna introduced herself and Ed. "We're taking a fresh look at the deaths of your neighbors, Leo and Peggy March.

"Come on in," Linda Mayo said. She seated them and herself at the table in the kitchen/dining room. They declined her offer of iced tea and cake.

"Could you tell us about the Marches?" Joanna asked.

That was enough of an opening for Linda Mayo. She gave them a detailed report of that day nearly four years past including everything she had done for the entire day. She had no doubt about the time that, in driving past the Marches' house, she had seen the confrontation between Dean March and his grandfather. "I always come home after I get my mani-pedi and my hair done," she said. "It was just after 4."

"Could you tell us a little bit about Dean March and his relationship with his grandparents?" Ed asked.

"It's a tragic thing," she said, "what drugs does to a family." She shook her head, a heavy frown on her face. "That Dean was a sweet little boy. Used to spend quite a lot of time with Mr. Leo and Miz Peggy. He didn't have what you would call a *normal* home life. What with his daddy — that would be Mr. Leo and Miz Peggy's son William — off in New Orleans. Supposed to be working."

Linda Mayo looked over the top rim of her glasses to indicate her disbelief. "And that mother of Drew's!" She puffed air between her lips. "Well, I'm telling no tales." Her look indicated that she had plenty of tales to tell. "Poor Miz Peggy, bless her heart, tried to teach that boy right from wrong. Of course, Mr. Leo did too. But he was a little harsh with the boy. I will say that."

Ed and Joanna waited.

"Then, as you probably know, Dean got into drugs and it was just off and on. Sometimes he wouldn't be around for a long time and Miz Peggy would just worry. And pray. Then, he'd take a spell and be all cleaned up and helping out and mowing the lawn. Things like that. Miz Peggy would be so happy. Mr. Leo would be too, but he didn't show it much. Just grumbled. Preached at Dean. Just like on that day."

She shook her head at the memory. "We already heard Dean was back on drugs. Glenda Jean at the beauty shop said he was. I didn't say such to Miz Peggy. It would just break her heart."

She sighed. "Anyways, there they are: Mr. Leo on the porch telling Dean he's been taken by the Devil; Dean standing on the steps to the porch cussing Mr. Leo something awful."

"Did you stop?" Ed asked.

"Good land, no," Linda Mayo said. "We knew not to get involved. It always worked itself out. Mr. Leo would yell; Dean would cuss. A couple weeks later, Dean would just show up. Get the riding lawn mower—they kept it right there by the garage—and mow the whole yard. Things would be good again."

"Do you and your husband go to the Singing?" Ed asked. "I don't quite understand all I've heard about that."

"Me and Seldon? Law, no," she answered. "Honey, that's way over by Lucedale."

She looked at Ed's frown of confusion.

"Let me explain," she said. "Mr. Leo and Miz Peggy grew up over there. Somewhere by Lucedale. But they went up North to work years ago. Somewhere like Detroit or Indiana or maybe Michigan. Anyway, when they moved back, their son William was living over here and that place next door was for sale. But they still had friends and such over by Lucedale. One of their friends was that woman preacher, Sister Murphy."

Linda Mayo paused then continued, "For, oh, I don't know how many years, she has a old timey singing on Friday night. Sister Murphy says, 'Don't let the Devil get a start on the weekend.' They have a one-room church. People come from all over. Sing lots of old hymns. Maybe a little testifying. But mainly, just singing. Most times, people bring guitars. Sister Murphy's grandson plays the keyboard or the piano."

She smiled at the memory. "I went a couple of times with Mr. Leo and Miz Peggy. But they stayed until near midnight. I'm telling you, this ol' gal has to get a good night's sleep. I'm just too old for that 'staying out late' nonsense." She laughed at herself.

"You called 911 that day?" Joanna asked.

"Ye-es," Linda Mayo made the word have two syllables. "Me and Seldon was sitting out on our patio. It's over here," she explained, "on the east side of the house. We was just having a glass of iced tea. Just sitting in the cool of the evening. Then Seldon said he thought he smelled smoke. And I got up and went to look. And it was black smoke."

She looked at both of them. "White smoke is wood or grass. Black smoke is worse. It's a house or a car or something like that. Anyway, I walked to where I could see and it was smoke all right. It was black smoke. Coming out like under the roof of Mr. Leo and Miz Peggy's house. Well, I just run back and called 911. Then me and Sheldon went over toward the house. I said to Sheldon—this is exactly what I said—I said, 'I bet Miz Peggy left something on the stove and went off to Singing.' That's what I said. 'Cause I was just sure in my heart that they was gone."

She sighed deeply. "Every Friday, sure as the world, at 6:15 they pulled out of the driveway. Sure as the world."

"How did you know it was after 6:15? That they should have been gone?" Ed asked.

Linda Mayo looked confused then thoughtful. "That is a *good* question," she said. "Let me think."

She began to reconstruct her movements. "When I got home, just after 4—you know, after I saw Dean and Mr. Leo—Seldon was using the weed-eater to clean up out by the patio. He come in and took a shower. Then we ate supper. The news was on the television, but when the news was over, he said we should take our iced tea out and sit on his clean patio."

She looked at Ed. "Seldon loves sports. Football—college or NFL—is his favorite. But he follows baseball. Hates tennis. Doesn't like golf much either. But he watches the sports ever night. Looks to see who's winning and losing. Things like that."

Content with her memory of the evening, she added, "So it must have been about 6:30 when we went outside. That's about when sports is over on the news."

"Would you have heard the Marches—or someone—leave their driveway?" Ed asked.

"No," she answered. "It's too far away and on the other side of the house."

She thought. "No, I wouldn't have heard. I was just sure. In my heart." She looked sad. "They were good people. A little bit strict. But good."

She sighed. "Well, me and Seldon told that deputy we were sure the Marches was gone to Singing. But, of course, they weren't. But there wasn't nothing we could have done. I comfort myself with that. They were already dead."

Ed and Joanna nodded and looked somber.

"You know, we stayed outside that evening, making sure no sparks or whatever got over by us," she added. "It must 'a' been near to ten o'clock when we saw Sally Jane and two other people got into what was left of the house. Well," she continued, "me and Seldon just stood there watching. That's dangerous. Going into a burnt-out building like that. Anyway, they just started gathering up their hoses and stuff so me and Seldon come on home."

She paused in her recitation. "It was late and we was fixing to go to bed when I looked out the bedroom window and saw the sheriff's car pull up. Seldon got his binoculars that he uses for bird watching. He says Sally Jane and the sheriff is talking and they go back inside that burned-up house. Well, we knew something was wrong so we went back over there."

She put her hands on her hips. "When we got there, the sheriff was opening the garage door, and there was Mr. Leo's car. Still in the garage. My heart just literally stopped. Just literally stopped. I said, 'Oh, my God, Seldon' 'cause I knew. I knew why the sheriff was there."

She shook her head in remembered sadness. "Poor old Mr. Leo and Miz Peggy. Poor old souls."

She sat a moment with her head bowed in silence. Then she looked up and began to speak again.

"Before we knew that it was Dean that killed them, I told the sheriff that Dean was their next-of-kin."

She looked at Joanna. "It was true. They hadn't heard from that William in years. He borrowed money from them and just disappeared. And that Sheila? She *used* to be their daughter-in-law. But even then, she didn't like them and they didn't like her."

She shook her head again. "It was a bad business all the way around," she said.

With no other questions for Linda Mayo, Ed and Joanna thanked her for talking to them and left her house.

"Are we ready for Sheila March or whatever her name is now?" Joanna asked as they drove.

"I am ready for a strong drink," Ed said.

"Maybe what's-his-name will share his moonshine with you," Joanna said with a grin.

Ed cut his eyes toward Joanna but didn't answer.

A dented mailbox, the word "March" barely discernible, marked the entrance to the driveway that led to Sheila March's house trailer.

The trailer that had been blue and white when it was new in the 1970's was still vaguely white. Pieces of rusted sheet iron had been haphazardly used as skirting to cover the underpinning, but there were pieces missing and others hanging by one edge.

A roofless porch of rough-sawn lumber had been added at some time in the distant past. An old green fake-leather sofa and matching chair sagged against the trailer wall.

Sheds of varying sizes, ages, and states of disrepair stood in the area that was more-or-less fenced. Paths from one building to another had been cleared; Johnson grass and weeds grew randomly elsewhere.

A rose bush had outgrown the trellis that was intended to support it. Daffodil blossoms showed through the grass beside the porch steps.

Seated on the sofa was a large, bare-footed man. He did not get up when Ed and Joanna approached. They stopped at the bottom of the steps.

"We're looking for Sheila March," Ed said. "Is she here?"

"Sheila," the man yelled. "Someone here looking for you."

At his yell, a yellow dog of indiscriminate breed came out from under the trailer and looked curiously at Ed and Joanna. It walked to where a cooking pot served as a water bowl, took a long drink, and returned to the shade of the house. A little black and white dog, some sort of mixed breed, barked from the doorway.

Sheila March, cigarette in mouth, picked up the little dog as she walked out of the trailer. She wore cut-off shorts and a tank top. Her hair was pulled back into a ponytail. The pulled-back part dark brown with grey streaks; the ponytail dull red.

"What?" she said, looking at Ed and then Joanna.

"Sheila," Joanna said, "I am Joanna Jones. Your son Dean worked for me several years ago when I lived in Hattiesburg."

This time it was Sheila and the man who waited.

"This is Ed Flanders," Joanna indicated Ed. "We are taking a fresh look at the deaths of Leo and Peggy March."

When neither of them spoke, Joanna continued, "I am hoping that we can obtain enough information to petition for a new trial for Dean."

Sheila looked at the man who raised his eyebrows slightly. "We don't know nothing that would help," he said, looking at Joanna.

"Dean told me that he was here the day his grandparents were killed," Joanna said.

"Yeah," his mother said. "He was here. And that judge said I was hostile. And I had to say that Dean was here and mad at that old bastard. Then I had to say that Dean and Roy was drinking. And that I gave Dean money." She threw the cigarette stub into a bucket beside the porch. "Lot of good that did Dean, didn't it?" She snorted.

"Get me a beer," Roy said to Sheila. "You want one?" he asked in the general direction of Joanna and Ed.

"No, thanks," Joanna said.

"Think I will," Ed said.

Sheila went back inside and came out immediately with two bottles of beer. She handed them one to Roy who turned the ring on his finger around and popped the top off of the bottle. She took the open bottle and handed him the other one. Then she handed the bottle to Ed.

"Now, that is cool," Ed said, watching the man open the other beer.

"Ain't it though?" the man said. "Come on up and have a seat," he added. He turned the ring, worn on his middle finger, to show Ed how it worked.

Ed stepped up onto the porch and sat down in the chair. Sheila shrugged her shoulders, went into the kitchen and returned with a plastic chair.

"Have a seat," she said to Joanna. As Joanna sat down in the plastic chair, Sheila sat down on the sofa.

"I didn't get your name," Ed said.

"Didn't give it," the man said. Then he grinned. "My name's Roy. Roy Goodson." He held out a fairly clean hand which Ed shook. "I was waiting to see if you was a bill collector or not," Roy said.

Ed grinned his appreciation of Roy's wisdom and raised his beer toward his host. He took a long drink. So did Roy.

"What business you in?" Roy asked. "You a lawyer?"

"A lawyer? Good lord, no," Ed said. "I'm retired." Then he added the line he had used many times when he didn't want to talk about his job. "I used to pick up garbage. Just working at keeping the streets clean."

Roy grunted his understanding.

"Joanna's an old friend," Ed told Roy. "She thinks Dean got a raw deal. I think maybe he did too."

Ed took another drink. "We're just trying to look at everything from that time to see what we can find. Then Joanna's going to talk to a lawyer friend of hers. Try to get Dean a new trial."

"Well, we'll tell you all we know," Roy said, "although it ain't much."

"You know, I don't know Dean," Ed said. He turned to Sheila. "Could you just tell me a little bit about him. Just to help me understand."

"Dean was a good little boy," Sheila said. "He was smart too. He was four when me and William split the first time. Them days, Peggy would come over and take Dean home with her. He liked going there. Peggy was a good cook. Sometimes William was there. Sometimes he was off working. Then, when Dean was ten, William decided me and him ought to get back together. Thought we ought to raise pigs. Borrowed $2000 from Leo to get started. That same day he got the money from Leo, he got a telephone call from the oil rig in Louisiana. They wanted him back. He was going to work a couple months. Then we'd have enough money to buy pigs and fence and everything. He left the next day. And never came back. I got a call from a bail bondsman in Biloxi saying William was in jail and did I have $500 to get him out. I said 'Here's his daddy's phone number,' and give him Leo's number."

She picked up the little dog and spent several minutes playing with it.

"Old Leo was a hard man before that. After that, he turned mean. Especially towards Dean. Said Dean was like William. Sons of Satan." She sighed. "I guess he was right. Dean got into trouble in high school. Got to doing coke. Drinking. Got sent away for stealing."

She sighed again. "Then he come back and was doing good. Living in Hattiesburg. Working for a gardening company. But it all went to shit." She shrugged her shoulders. "Same ol' Dean. Coming around begging money from Peggy or me."

"And that day?" Joanna asked.

"He got here not long after we got home from the store. Must 'a' been about four. Not much after. I was putting away groceries. Hadn't even started supper."

Roy agreed, "Yeah, it was pretty early. Me and Dean set out here and drank beer."

Sheila looked disgusted. "Drank beer?" she repeated, making it into a question. "*Beer?*" she repeated.

Roy gave her a silencing look.

"What the hell difference does it make now?" she asked.

She looked at Ed. "They was drinking home brew and chasing it with beer," she said, her voice slightly defiant. Ed allowed his eyebrows to rise in surprise.

"See," Roy explained, "me and Tony, my cousin, we makes home brew—you know—moonshine." He added, "We don't sell it. Just make it once in a while for ourselves."

"And you and Dean drank some that day?"

"Yep," Roy said, "we each had three—maybe four—slugs of it."

"Did you tell Dean's lawyer about the home brew?" Joanna asked.

Sheila sighed. "We did," she said, "but he said all that drinking made Dean look worse." She sighed again. "And he *was* talking crazy that day."

Joanna and Ed waited.

"Said he hated that old man. Said he should have pulled him off that porch and used that walking stick on him. See how he'd like that." She looked at both of them. "That lawyer said I shouldn't say nothing they didn't ask me. He said I should just say Dean was mad and drank some beer. And that I give him $20."

"Did you worry when Dean left that he might go back to the Marches' house? Might fight with his grandfather?" Joanna asked.

"Good lord, no," Sheila said. "Dean was all talk. He wouldn't hurt nobody. 'Specially not his Grandma and Grandpa. He was just blowing off steam."

"You tried to get him to stay?" Joanna asked.

"I was fixing supper," Sheila said. "I figured he didn't have nothing to eat at home."

"He was ready to get back to town," Roy added. "Get on with the weekend."

"Was he drunk when he left here?" Ed asked Sheila.

"Well, he was a little unsteady on his feet," Sheila admitted. "Took him two tries to get into that truck of his."

Roy grinned at the memory. "Hell, Ed," he said, "the boy had to drive. He was too drunk to walk." Roy laughed at the old joke.

"I have a question about the truck," Ed said. "What happened to it?"

"Nothin' happened to it," Roy answered. "It's right out there in that shed yonder." He waved an arm to indicate an area behind the trailer.

"Really?" Ed said. "How did it get here?"

"We went and got it," Roy said.

Sheila interrupted to explain. "Dean was in jail. The rent on the trailer was due. We went up to Hattiesburg and loaded what stuff Dean had into the truck and brought it here. Dean didn't want his truck sold. We just put it out there." She also motioned in the direction of various sheds behind the trailer.

"Yep," Roy said, "we just went and got his stuff. I knew where Dean kept the extra key. Damned good thing Sheila was following me coming home," he added. "I hadn't got out of Hattiesburg and damned if I didn't run plumb outta gas." He nodded his head vigorously. "Coasted into that station on fumes."

"Where was that station?" Ed asked. "Do you remember?"

"It was the one right there by the interstate," Roy said. "Maybe half a mile from Dean's house." He shook his head, remembering. "Took damned near $10.00 in gas to get a fourth of a tank and then barely got it here and backed into the shed. Gas guzzling piece of shit!"

Ten minutes later, Ed repeated Roy's assessment: "Gas guzzling piece of shit." He and Joanna had made a hasty retreat from the home of Roy and Sheila and, with Joanna driving, were on their way toward Hattiesburg.

He and Joanna both laughed.

"I'm just happy that he and his cousin hadn't made any home brew lately," Ed said. "Drinking a beer with a man to get him in the mood to talk is one thing. Drinking home brew that may or may not be anywhere near safe is another."

"We should be near the place where Drew ran out of gas," Joanna said. She had checked the odometer from time to time. "Not that there will be much to see now," she added. "It's been four years since the Marches were murdered."

As Ed nodded his agreement, the gas station came into sight. Joanna pulled up to one of the two pumps. Ed filled the car with gas and went inside to pay.

A short, round man with a full beard was behind the counter. Ed looked at the monitor of the CCTV mounted on the wall behind the counter. He could plainly see the pump area and the entrance to the station as well.

Ed paid for the gas and then introduced himself. "I'm taking another look at the deaths of Leo and Peggy March. They died in a fire about four years ago," he said.

"I remember that," the man said. "Bad business."

Ed nodded agreement. "I understand that their grandson Dean got gas here that day." Ed looked at the man whose expression didn't change. "Were you, by any chance, working here then?"

"I owned it then," the man said, "but I wasn't working that day."

"I don't suppose…," Ed began.

"He don't work here no more," the man said. "Don't even live around here."

Ed looked at the layout of the store and also at the CCTV monitor. The camera was well positioned to film the counter area, the front door and the gas pump area. There was — or had been — a video that would either support or disprove Dean's story of buying beer at the time he bought the gas and gas can. It could also show just how much the beer and home brew had affected Dean.

"The video tape of that day?" Ed asked.

"Sheriff come and got it the next day," the man said. He crossed his arms over his chest.

"Okay," Ed said. *"I need to talk to the sheriff,"* Ed thought. He thanked the man and left the store.

Chapter 12

"The sheriff will see you now," the secretary said. It was just past eleven o'clock on Monday morning. Ed and Joanna had spent Sunday compiling and typing reports. The lawyer in Jackson had promised to look at whatever information Joanna had compiled, but it had to be in good order.

Now, the secretary led Ed down the hall to an office where the door stood open.

"Come in," Sheriff Jim Ed Kelly said. He stood to shake hands with Ed, a big smile on his face. "Good to meet ya," he said. As tall as Ed at just over six foot, skinnier than Ed by maybe forty pounds, younger than Ed by at least a dozen years, Jim Ed Kelly had peppery grey hair and a broad grin.

"Have a seat," he said. "How can I help you?"
Ed introduced himself, not mentioning his FBI career. "I'm here to talk about the homicide that Dean March was convicted of."

"Are you a private investigator?" the sheriff asked.

"No," Ed answered. "I'm an old friend of Dr. Joanna Jones who used to teach at the university here and really believes in Dean March's innocence. She asked me to help."

"Why did she ask you?" the sheriff asked.

"I retired from law enforcement so she thought I might be able to give the case a fresh look," Ed answered.

"Oh," the sheriff said. "What city did you work for?"

"I was with the FBI," Ed answered. "I retired six years ago."

"How can I possibly help you?" the sheriff asked.

"Joanna took me to meet Dean March," Ed said. "Based on what I got from him, the investigation seemed pretty straight forward."

"Yeah," the sheriff said, "we did everything but catch him with the match in his hand."

"True," Ed agreed. "There's just a few things I'm confused about. Mind if I ask you a few questions. Just to clear things up in my own mind."

The sheriff grinned. "Tell you what," he said, "I'm starving. What do you say we go down the street to the diner and get some lunch?"

The two men left the office together, the sheriff telling the secretary where they were going. They walked a half block to the Dailey Diner.

"Howdy, Sheriff," the hostess greeted Kelly. As she led them to a table, she said, "Monday special is roast beef with all the trimmings."

"I'll have that and tea," the sheriff said.

"Make that two," Ed said. The hostess passed the information on to the waitress.

While they waited for their food, the two men talked their respective backgrounds and indulged in what Ed's wife had always called "police talk."

By the time the food arrived, both men were comfortable with each other. As Ed suspected, the tea was super sweet; the roast beef and trimmings, excellent.

As they finished eating, Sheriff Kelly scratched the side of his face. "Let me tell you a little bit about that murder," he said. "We don't get many murders here in Forrest County. Not more than two or three, maybe four, in a year. Makes Dean March killing his grandparents stand out in your mind, you know?"

Ed nodded.

"Of course, I already knew Dean March," the sheriff said. "Drugs. Petty theft. Sent up for stealing from a video store. Not a serious bad actor. Just low life."

He sighed. "Then we get two dead people burned up in their house. Fire chief calls it foul play. Or at least suspicious. Next of kin: Dean March."

He shrugged again. "Deputy goes to notify Dean about the death. Dean drives up. Drunk. Smelling of gas." The sheriff raised his eyebrows. "That's about it."

"Dean told us he ran out of gas near a station south of here," Ed said.

"Well, he bought a gas can and put gas in it, at any rate," the sheriff said. "We got him on the video tape."

"You have a tape?" Ed asked.

"Oh, sure," the sheriff said. "I went down to the gas station and got it."

"But the prosecutor used a still photograph taken from the video instead of the whole video?" Ed questioned.

"I'll tell you about that," the sheriff said, leaning forward. "Ol' Lee Gates—the man that owns that station—is a friend of mine from way back. High school football. Anyway. Lee's liquor license was up for renewal. Then that dumbass working for him sells Dean a six-pack when Dean's way over the limit already."

Ed looked a little confused.

"The prosecutor just wants to show Dean buying the gas. We pull that one frame from the video. It's righteous. Shows the date, time, and Dean pumping gas into the can. *Not*. Let me repeat. *Not* into a vehicle."

Ed nodded his understanding: The prosecutor got the evidence he needed; the sheriff's friend got his liquor license renewed. "Do you still have the evidence?" he asked.

"Yep," the sheriff said. "The video is in lock-up at the jail; the gas can and Dean's shirt and jeans with gas spilled on them is locked up at the storage locker at the county garage."

"Could I get a dupe on the tape?" Ed asked.
"I don't see why not," the sheriff said. "I promise you all it's gonna show is Dean, drunk and obnoxious."

The sheriff pulled a cell phone from his shirt pocket. "Let me take care of that right now," the sheriff said, "while it's fresh on my mind."

He quickly and made arrangements for a technician to copy the video. "Be ready for you by five this afternoon," he said. "If you want to look at the gas can and clothes, go out to the garage. I'll tell them to let you see what's there." He put the phone back in his pocket. "Anything else?" he asked.

"One more thing," Ed said. "When Dean was arrested, what did he have on him? Besides, clothes, that is. Do you remember?"

"Now *that*, I don't remember," the sheriff said. "Let me check on it," he added. He used the cell phone again, talking to his secretary and then saying, "She's checking." Another quick conversation with the secretary, and the sheriff shut the phone.

"We put his clothes and shoes in evidence because of the gasoline," he said. "According to Sadie, the list is short: a wallet with a driver's license and two quarters — you know: 50 cents."

The sheriff shrugged. "We gave the wallet and money to his mother. The clothes and shoes are still in evidence." He grinned.

"Anything else?" he asked again.

"I think that takes care of it," Ed said. He signaled for the bill and paid it. The two men walked back to the county building together. As they shook hands, Ed thanked the sheriff for his help.

"Ya got any more questions," Jim Ed Kelly said, grinning from ear to ear, "holler at me. We'll have lunch again." Ed laughed and raised an arm in farewell.

"You've already had lunch?" Joanna asked twenty minutes later. While Ed had been with Sheriff Jim Ed Kelly, Joanna had been meeting with the county fire inspector.

Ed shrugged. "What could I do?" he said. "He wanted to talk, but he wanted to eat, too." He smiled. "I'll drink tea — unsweetened, please — while you eat."

They sat on the terrace of a restored 1920's house-turned-restaurant. While Joanna ate, Ed recounted his meeting with the sheriff. "Once again," he finished, "Dean's attorney tried to keep Dean from looking like an angry drunk."

He shook his head. "If the tape shows what I think it will, it will show Dean as too drunk to do much of anything

While they waited for dessert—they had both ordered the house specialty, pecan pie, served with coffee—Joanna told Ed about her meeting with the county fire inspector.

"Nice guy," Joanna said. "Very good at his job. He had a number of photos and a video of the floor exam."

Ed nodded. The fire inspector would have taken a section of the floor, maybe 3 feet square, to the lab to check the burn pattern and the depth of the burn. Rather than keeping the actual sample after the case was settled, the inspector had used video cameras to show his examination of the section.

"Anything interesting?" Ed asked.

"Yes," Joanna said, a frown furrowing her forehead.

"Although he determined early that an accelerant had been used, he was never questioned by *anybody* as to what type of accelerant it was."

"The prosecutor didn't care," Ed said, "and the defense attorney didn't know to ask or didn't bother."

"Did I tell you what Dean's attorney said when he gave me the files?" Joanna asked then answered her own question. "He said, 'I kept him off death row. That was all I could do. They wanted to lynch him right then and there.'"

Both of them looked solemn for a minute. "So what did the fire inspector tell you about the burn?"

"The burn was slow and deep," Joanna said. "Because the house was closed completely—remember they were leaving for the evening—and the air conditioning units turned off, the fire would have burned slowly. He said maybe as long as twenty minutes from initial ignition to the time when the neighbors smelled smoke."

"And the burn pattern?" Ed asked.

"The accelerant had been poured on and around both bodies and down the hallway to the kitchen and door."

"Could it have been gasoline?"

"I asked that same question," Joanna said. "The inspector said it was highly unlikely. Almost impossible. Even if the gasoline had been poured there and left several hours, it would still flash rather than the slow burn the inspector found. He said kerosene or lamp oil seemed much more likely."

Both were silent as they considered this information.

"One more interesting thing," Joanna said, "the fire inspector took a photo of the riding lawn mower and the gas can. They were in that sort of lean-to beside the garage."

Ed nodded. He remembered the addition to the garage.

"One of those old Army-style jerry cans that hold about five gallons of gas," Joanna explained. "And it was full."

"Really?" Ed asked.

"Really," Joanna verified. "He specifically noted that the can was full."

The waitress interrupted them, bringing wedges of pecan pie and coffee. When they had finished dessert, Joanna said, "Let's go back to the conference table and put all our information in order."

Back at the motel, they took time to type reports on their meetings. When they had added those reports to the growing stack of material for the lawyer in Jackson, Joanna said, "Ed, do you believe Dean is innocent?"

Ed sat back in the chair and thought for several minutes.

"You know," he finally said, "I do." He leaned forward, rested his arms on the table between them and said, "I've thought—almost from the beginning—that he deserved a new trial. That his lawyer was incompetent. I still think that, but here's the question I can't answer: 'Why?'" He leaned forward.

Joanna waited, realizing that Ed was working his way through his thoughts as he spoke.

"Why did Dean go 'south' that day?" Ed asked. "To get gasoline and money." He looked at Joanna who nodded. "When he left his mother's house, why didn't he go back to his grandparents' house?" Ed asked. "Better yet," he continued, "why not wait until after 6:15 when they were gone and, at least, get gasoline? Maybe break in and get money or something of value."

"You're right," Joanna said, "but maybe he didn't think about all of that. He was drunk."

"Right," Ed said. "So he gets up the road twelve miles and either runs out of gas—his story—or buys a gas can and gas so that he can go back and burn the old folks up—the prosecution's view."

Ed looked at Joanna. "Why take gas back to burn their house when Dean *knew* they had a big can of gas there already? And *if* he went back, why didn't he put the gas from the jerry can into his truck? Or use it to set the fire?"

"The prosecution said he was drunk and not thinking clearly, just angry."

"Last question: why didn't he go home?" Ed said. "Why didn't he go home, take a shower, watch television, wait for someone to come tell him about the fire?" Ed frowned. "If he went back, killed them, and set the house on fire, what did he do then? Where was he between 6:30 or so in the evening and 3:30 in the morning?"

"Good question," Joanna said.

"In my experience," Ed said, "if a guy like March does a deed like this, he confesses. To someone. Goes home to Mama and tells her about the bad thing he did. Goes to a preacher or priest or drinking buddy. Or turns himself in. Dean March isn't a stone-cold killer. He's a weak, whiney, unlikeable drunk."

When Joanna would have protested, Ed stopped her with a raised hand. "We are not ever going to be able to prove that Dean didn't do this. Here's what I think we can do. When we get the dupe of the gas station video, I am betting it shows a barely conscious Drew. Otherwise the sheriff and his good buddy wouldn't have been worried about it. Add to that the information from the fire inspector on the accelerant and — unless I miss my guess — the confirming report from my buddy in the Bureau. We can cast real, concrete doubt on Dean's conviction."

Joanna agreed. All along, she had *wanted* Dean to be innocent. Because she was afraid her prejudice would color the results of their investigation, she had allowed Ed to lead and to follow his thinking.

She was pleased that he had affirmed her conviction that Dean had been judged unfairly.

"I agree," she said. "I'm going to add our reports and summaries to the other documents and present it to my friend, Myra Ingram, in Jackson. At the very least, I think she will agree to petition for a new trial." She looked at Ed. "I don't know how to thank you."

"Seems to me you agreed to buy me dinner at Willie Mae's Scotch House in New Orleans," Ed said with a grin.

Joanna grinned too. "You are right," she said. "That was our agreement."

"I say we get everything in order here," Ed said. "I'll pick up the video from the sheriff's office. We can box it all up and put it in the trunk of your car. Leave your car in the parking lot here and, tomorrow morning, be off for a trip to New Awlins," he said, using the drawled Southern pronunciation.

They spent the rest of the afternoon organizing and labeling the information for the Jackson attorney who would be back in the office in a week. Ed took time to add the video to their collection.

On his way back from the sheriff's office, he picked up sandwiches and a bottle of red wine for a quick dinner for the two of them.

By nine o'clock, the files were in three boxes on the conference table.

"Whew," Joanna said. "That takes care of that."

"I have one more detail," Ed said. He took his cell phone from his shirt pocket, looked through his contacts and pushed a number.

"Good evening, Nell," he said when Nell Jones answered the phone. "Nell," he said, "this is Ed."

Without waiting for her standard greeting, he continued, "No doubt your mother has kept you up to date with our progress in regards to Dean March. I will tell you that I agree with your mother that Dean is innocent. What that means is that someone else is guilty."

Once again, he spoke quickly, "The similarities that you and your mother found between your case in Arkansas and the one here still remain. However, let me remind you again: two murders do not a serial killer make."

Before she could protest, he began again, "The choice now is up to you. You can either accept that there are similarities and get on with life or you can pursuit the serial killer idea."

"I can't just accept that," Nell interrupted.

"Okay," Ed said, "then here's what I suggest. You have the resources. Take the states within an eight-hour drive of Little Rock, Arkansas and Hattiesburg, Mississippi. Contact all the medical examiners. See if they have cases that are couples — probably older couples — murdered or made to look like murder or undetermined with their house burned. That's three indicators to consider."

Ed continued, "I'd say you're looking from Texas and Oklahoma to the East Coast. See what you get. *If*—and I'm telling you it's a mighty big 'if' — this is the work of a serial killer, he probably killed between 2008 in Mississippi and 2012 in Arkansas. Because you checked both of those states, you should look further afield."

"Okay," Nell said. "At least, we are sure now that there are two similar cases by an unknown assailant."

"Right," Ed said. "It is not reasonable that Dean March killed his grandparents. We can't *prove* that he is innocent, but both your mother and I believe it. And if he didn't kill them, someone else did." Ed smiled. "Now, the ball is in your court."

"It may take some time," Nell said. She thought of her responsibilities. This would be after-hours work.

"If you find something," Ed said, "you have my phone number and my email address."

"You can be sure I'll contact you if I find anything," Nell answered him.

"I'm sure you will," Ed said. "I'm sure you will."

Chapter 13

"Happy Mother's Day," Nell Jones greeted her mother at the door. "Thank you for coming to me today."

Nell ushered her mother into her home in northwest Little Rock, Arkansas. "I know I should have made the drive to your house. I know," Nell pushed her hands through her hair. "Come on in," she added. The two women hugged.

"Let's have coffee on the terrace," Nell said and led the way to the kitchen where one tray held a coffee pot and mugs and another held coffee cake from a nearby gourmet grocery store. Each woman took a tray and together they went onto the terrace to enjoy the May morning.

Although they had talked on the phone many times — almost daily — it had been over six weeks since they had seen one another.

"Myra sends her love," Joanna said after they were settled on the outdoor sofa.

Myra Ingram, Joanna's lawyer friend, had known Nell most of her life, had been an unofficial godmother to Nell. Although Myra came from old money and married old money, she had chosen to work, becoming a top attorney in Jackson. She also donated a good deal of her time to a program to help indigent people who were both innocent and imprisoned in Mississippi.

Joanna had lived in the guest house at the Ingram mansion while she and Myra worked on the petition to appeal for a new trial in Dean March's conviction.

As Joanna and Nell discussed the case, Joana sighed. "I started all this investigation and work because Dean asked me. Because I wanted to believe he didn't murder his grandparents. Then I really became convinced—based on everything we learned—that he is innocent."

Although Joanna had talked to Nell about the discoveries she and Ed had made, she repeated the main discrepancies in time and motive in the case.

She added, "The report from Ed's friend in the FBI confirmed our belief: the fire propellant was not gasoline. It was something slower, probably kerosene. Adding that report to the ones made by the fire inspector and the fire chief makes our case much stronger."

She took a drink of coffee and then looked at her daughter. "Myra thinks our case is strong enough for a new trial, but we have one big problem: we have no alternative suspect. No one profited by their deaths. What insurance they had paid for funerals and the rest went to that church they attended. The house, of course, was destroyed. Mr. March's brother paid to have the wreckage cleared and has been paying the taxes. I sincerely don't believe Dean killed the Marches, but damned if I know who did!"

Tears roughened her voice. "I am worn out," she said. "We must have prepared a thousand pages of material to present on his behalf. Myra's foundation will help with money, but everything has to be ready to present." She sounded both tired and discouraged. "It will be months before the petition is heard. Then, if Dean is granted a new trial, it will be months—maybe a year—before that happens. There are no guarantees of anything along the way."

Joanna looked at her daughter. "Ed said Dean is weak, whiney, and unlikable, and all of them are true."

"So why bother?" Nell asked.

"I can't imagine how awful it must be to be in prison. To know that you will be there for the rest of your life. But what if you know you are innocent? *Know* you didn't commit the crime. How horrible that must be! I feel a little better knowing that I am doing what I can to help Dean. It also helps my mind that Ed, looking at all the discrepancies, agrees with me. He may not find Dean a likeable person, but Ed believes Dean is innocent."

"One thing is true," Nell said, "if Dean is innocent, *someone* is guilty."

"And you think that someone is your serial killer," Joanna said. Nell nodded.

"How's your inquiry going?" Joanna asked.

"Oh, my God, Mother," Nell said. "What a mess I got myself into!"

"Really?"

"Really." Nell shifted on the sofa. "I sent a computer-friendly search to the M.E. offices in all the states that Ed suggested. Oklahoma and Texas on the western edge and the Atlantic Ocean on the East Coast. That's fifteen states."

At Joanna's nod of understanding, Nell continued, " I included the criteria as he suggested. Undetermined or unsolved arson/homicides. Older couples. How many could that be?"

She looked at her mother. "Let me tell you. To date, I have received over 135 possibles. Everyone—at least it looks like everyone—fed the info into their computers and cases were just spit into my email. In some cases, 15 years worth."

Nell shook her head. "It's like taking a drink out of a fire hose. Totally overwhelming."

Nell spread her arms in an encompassing gesture. Her eyes widened. "And, of course, this is on my own time."

She shook her head in a dismissive gesture. "No time to do any of this at work. With the cases we receive and the court appearances we have to make, our staff is busy all the time. In addition, I've been reorganizing the office to match my expectations. All of that means that I am tired when I get home. Then I face this."

"To repeat your question," Joanna said, "why bother?"

"I have wondered that," Nell said. "Often." She grinned. "Let me tell you. The first response I got was from Texas. Twenty-seven cases. *Twenty-seven.*" She rolled her eyes. "And how many of those are good possibilities?" She rolled her eyes again. "Not one. *Not one.*"

She shook her head. "They sent everything. They sent a case where two *children* had died in a house fire. One case was two older adults, but they died in separate apartments in a big building. Even the ones that more nearly fit my criteria were off for one reason or another." Nell held up her hands in a surrender pose. "I was ready, I mean ready, to give up."

"But?"

"But I was out of town testifying in a court case for three days. When I returned, there were results from several states. The first email I opened was from Louisiana and, Mom, the two cases there are so much like the two cases we have! Older couple. Fractured skulls. Arson after they were dead. And," Nell used her forefinger to emphasize her point, "those arsons were between your case and mine."

She sat back in her chair. "In fact," she continued, "those two cases in Louisiana are the strongest possibilities. One in 2009. The other in 2010."

Joanna's eyebrows rose. "That is interesting," she said. "And the other states?"

"After I discarded the cases that didn't fit the criteria for one reason or another, I have a total of fifteen strong possibilities. Well, actually sixteen, counting the Lodges case here in Little Rock. The case involving Dean March is also extra. Technically, that case is considered closed. Although we don't think it should be."

Joanna nodded. "That makes seventeen cases," she said.

"Yes," Nell said. "It covers fifteen years and eleven states."

"Wow," Joanna said. "I'm not sure which is more amazing: how many cases you found or how hard you have worked."

Nell looked pleased but said, "Right now, I have nothing but a lot of data. I'm hoping that Ed Flanders can make sense of it all."

She frowned. "I tried to call him Friday and again yesterday but just got his voice mail."

"He's gone fishing," Joanna said. "He should be home tonight. Or maybe tomorrow morning."

Nell looked sharply at her mother. "And you know this because?" she asked.

"We talk."

"You and Ed Flanders talk?"

"Yes," Joanna said, "on the phone and by email."

"About Dean March's case?"

"W-e-l-l," Joanna drew the word out, "about that sometimes. And just things in general."

"That reminds me," Nell said, looking suspiciously at her mother, "what about the trip the two of you made to New Orleans?"

"We had a lovely time."

"And?" Nell's eyebrows rose with her question.

"And," her mother answered, "that's all I have to say about that."

Chapter 14

When Ed Flanders entered his house in mid-morning on Monday, the first thing he did was to shower and shave.

He had spent from Thursday until late Sunday on an old friend's fishing boat. When Sam had long charters, Ed often acted as cook and crew. The two had docked late and spent the night on the boat, eating fresh fish and drinking cold beer.

Voice mail messages from both Joanna and Nell advised and warned Ed about the lengthy email waiting for him. He left them unanswered and the email unopened as he cleared other messages including one from his agent hoping a new book was in the offing.

After lunch and small household chores were accomplished, Ed sat down at the computer.

The message in Nell's email was brief. She was sending him a lengthy file containing data for 15 possible cases that seemed to her to resemble the two cases she had already given him.

"Fifteen!" Ed thought, *"Fifteen cases to examine?"* Ed sat for several minutes not actually seeing the email in front of him.

"Why am I even thinking about doing this?" Ed asked himself.

Even as he thought the words, the first answer came. "You promised," Ed said the words aloud. "You promised Nell Jones you would look at what she found."

Reluctantly, Ed admitted two other reasons. *"You are attracted to her mother,"* he thought.

He thought about Joanna Jones. Attractive, interesting, fun. He had enjoyed working with her on the arson case involving Drew March. He had also enjoyed their trip to New Orleans. Both of them had often been there although, of course, never together. Joanna showed Ed *her* New Orleans; Ed showed Joanna the places he enjoyed there.

Ed realized that if he wanted to have any kind of ongoing relationship with Joanna, he must honor his promise to Nell.

Finally, Ed needed a new book idea. He had several ideas churning around in his mind, but nothing was really urgent or even absorbing his interest. Having three rather successful books under his belt meant that his agent and his publisher wanted more.

Ed sighed. He downloaded the file Nell had sent.

Ed put on reading glasses and began to look at the cases Nell had chosen. Ed began to read case by case. He soon realized that all the cases were very similar, and that he could not remember details from one case to the next one.

He removed his glasses, rubbed his eyes, and checked the paper feed for his printer. Then he clicked on the button that would print the entire file. Every page he had gotten from Nell Jones.

As the printer spit out pages, Ed assembled and stapled the individual cases. All fifteen of them with an average of five pages per case. He added the preliminary versions of the two cases Nell had given him at their first meeting.

"The investigation begins," Ed thought with a grin. He turned his chair from the computer to face an empty work table. His first step was to put the cases in order by date. Because the reports differed in format and form, Ed used a marker to put the date — month, day, year — in the top margin of each report.

With the cases in chronological order and stacked with only the date showing, Ed was able to get an overview of the time involved. The earliest case was in January, 1996. The latest one: May, 2011.

Ed began to look for noticeable differences: gaps between cases or cases that were very close together.

Immediately, Ed noticed that the three earliest cases were in 1996 and 1997. Then there was a gap until 2001. In the years between 2001 and 2011, there were one or two cases per year with the exception of 2007 which had no reported cases that fit the criteria.

There were two sets of cases where the dates were in the same month, only days apart, two cases in May, 2003 and two in March, 2007.

Ed pulled the two from March, 2006 from the stack to examine them more closely. The first case, on Thursday, March 2 took place in Anadarko, Oklahoma. The second one took place the following day—Friday, March 3—near Huntington, West Virginia.

Ed turned his chair back to the computer and discovered that it is over 1000 miles from one place to the other. *"Possible,"* Ed thought. *Possible, but not likely. You kill a couple in western Oklahoma and drive a thousand miles to kill another couple in West Virginia the next day. Not likely."*

He added a blue star to the upper right corner of the two cases. They would bear a closer look, if only to eliminate one of them.

The two cases in May of 2003—one on Friday the 9th, the other on the following Monday—were also from different states. The first one was from Memphis, Tennessee; the second from just outside Greenville, North Carolina. *"Neighboring states,"* Ed thought.

Not recognizing the place in North Carolina, Ed turned again to the computer. *"Twelve hours plus driving time,"* Ed thought at he looked at the travel directions. *"Completely across Tennessee and most of North Carolina. Whew!"* Ed thought. He decided that, as in the other case, it was possible but unlikely that both cases were done by the same killer. He starred the two cases as he had the other ones.

Ed noted the gap between March, 2006 and January, 2008 but knew there were many factors that could have caused such a gap, even if there were an active serial killer.

First and foremost was the recurrent thought that law enforcement takes the path of least resistance. If a death occurred and no one asked questions, it would probably be written as accidental. Less paperwork. Less problems with the public. Homicide investigations are messy and expensive.

Ed also knew that state medical examiners were often not used by cities with their own staff of examiners. Cases that might have fit the criteria might never appear in the state files.

Finally, as Ed had stated several times, there might not be a serial killer. Ed had checked: each year in the United States there are several hundred thousand house fires. Several thousand people die in house fires each year. *"We may not want to believe in coincidence,"* Ed thought, *"but with over 2000 people per year killed by fire, we are going to have a lot of similarities."*

"Work with what you have," Ed said. He pulled a yellow tablet from a neat stack on a nearby shelf and began to list the cases. He numbered them chronologically. Beside each number, he put the day of the week, month, day, year, and place of occurrence.

Looking at the dates, Ed discovered that none of the deaths had occurred on Sunday. *"If there is an outsider – an active serial killer who moves from place to place – it makes sense that he or she or they would avoid Sunday,"* Ed thought. *"Too much variance in routine. Too many chances that the deed would be interrupted."*

In addition, he noted that there were no reported cases in February, April or December. He considered the month variation but came to no immediate conclusion.

"Now," Ed said, "time for a quick lunch and then we'll take a look at the *where* for each of the cases."

Back in his office, Ed turned to the internet for a printable map of the United States that showed only the outline of the states. With the help of the internet and using his extensive knowledge of places, Ed marked and numbered the seventeen cases on the map.

"I-40 corridor," Ed said as soon as he looked at the map. Interstate 40 is a restricted access, "super" highway that crosses the United States from east to west. Five of the cases were along that route. "I'll be damned," Ed said, "add I-75 and I-10 and you have almost every case." I-75 runs north and south through the center of Ed's involved area. I-10 is the southern route going east and west across the United States. "*If* there is a killer, he's most likely a bus driver, a trucker, a salesman, a moving van driver… Someone who does long distance driving."

Ed leaned back in his chair and considered his next step. He would have to do extensive traveling, contacting authorities in a wide range of places. It would be necessary to interview family members, neighbors, firemen, police officers. "*And I'm not sure there is* one *killer,*" Ed thought. "*Where do I start?*"

Ed sat in thought for several minutes. Then he took a highlighter and marked the two cases he knew most: the one in Hattiesburg, Mississippi and the one in Little Rock, Arkansas. The closest case to the two of them was case #7: Memphis, Tennessee.

He pulled the #7 report from the stack and began to read the coroner's report. Immediately, Ed was struck by the similarities to the other cases.

The couples in all three cases were nearly the same. Melinda and James Clifford were in their 80's — as were the Marches and the Lodges.

Their bodies had been found under the rubble of their home which had been engulfed in flames when a neighbor called 911.

Damage to the bodies had been extensive.

Mrs. Clifford had been dead before the fire started, killed by blunt force trauma to the back of the head.

"Very similar," Ed said.

Ed noted that Mr. Clifford's hands and ankles had been bound. He had died of smoke inhalation. *"That's different,"* Ed thought. He highlighted that information.

The coroner had ruled the deaths to be homicide and had turned the case over to the Memphis Police Department.

Ed leaned back in his chair and folded his hands across his stomach. He mentally examined the similarities in the three cases.

"I need more information," he concluded. For a moment, he thought about a trip to Memphis. He liked Memphis. Loved the bar-be-cue and the music. It had been, he reckoned, several years since he had been in Memphis.

Suddenly, he sat up in the chair and turned to the desk. He thumbed through the cards on the Rolodex until he found the one he wanted: Ron Webb, Memphis Police Department.

"You still chasing serial killers?" Ron Webb asked when Ed had identified himself.

"I'm trying," Ed said. "And I need your help again."

"Gonna put me in another book?" Webb asked. "I made sergeant on the last one. Bucking for lieutenant now." There was laughter in Webb's voice. Ed's solving of the chat room murders had cleared a murder Webb had been investigating. Without doubt, it was not the reason for Webb's promotion, but a murder solved and inclusion in a well-received non-fiction book that spoke very favorably of Webb and his staff certainly didn't hurt.

"You got it," Ed said, laughing.

"Tell me how I can help," Webb said, his voice becoming serious.

"I'm taking a fresh look at the homicide/arson case of an elderly couple from 2003," Ed said. "It's listed as unsolved."

"That's before my time as a detective," Webb said, "but give me the basic info and I'll see what we have."

After Ed gave Webb the information, Webb said, "I'll call you back in a few."

Less than fifteen minutes later, Ron Webb called Ed back.

"I'd say you were in luck," the big black guy teased, "if the investigator wasn't Ray Hanton." He laughed and then sighed heavily so that Ed could clearly hear him. "Lucky, because Hanton is still a detective and working today." Webb's laughter was held in. "Unlucky, because Ray Hanton is a Class A Asshole. Okay detective. Lousy person. I told him you would call. Told him to cooperate." Webb laughed again. "What can I say?" he said, "Memphis's finest." He gave Ed the extension number for Ray Hanton and said, "Give him a call."

"Yeah?" was the greeting when Ed called Ray Hanton's extension.

Ed introduced himself, stressing that he was working as a private investigator and crime writer.

"Yeah," Hanton said, "Webb told me."

"You were the primary on a case of arson/homicide in 2003," Ed said, "where an elderly couple was killed and their house burned."

"Yeah," Hanton said, "Cold case."

Ed waited. If Hanton wanted to be a hard ass, Ed could match him.

"Okay," Hanton said, "I looked it up. Old folks burned to a crisp." Hanton snorted, said, "Crispy Critters Case."

Ed closed his eyes. Gallows humor is common among fire fighters and law enforcement, but it's often the crudest of the crude. Ed figured Hanton hoped to get a negative reaction. Ed waited.

"Webb said you was a expert on serial killers." He made the statement sound like an accusation. "Well, Mr. Smart Ass FBI, this wasn't no serial killer. It was a shithead thug. Or a gang of them."

Hanton cleared his throat. "Here's what happened. 'Bout that time this gang of young black asses hitting on retards or cripples. You know. Like that. B & E. Taking jewelry, money, whatever. Knock the vic around. Take off."

"There had been other break-ins in the Clifford's neighborhood?" Ed asked, mentally translating "B & E" into "break and enter."

"Not on the same street," Hanton admitted, "but close. Hell, everything in Memphis is close."

"Do you know what was taken?" Ed asked. Then added, "If it was a robbery."

"Not sure what was taken," Hanton admitted. "Old lady kept jewelry in a big cabinet that fell through from the upstairs. Most of her stuff was damaged but recovered. Old man sometimes kept a couple hundreds in the big Bible but it burned up down to the cover." Hanton sniffed. "Nah, too much damage to be sure what was taken. " He sniffed again. "Normal B&E: the perps are in, take what's easy, and out."

Ed made a sound of agreement.

"Only this time, it all went to shit," Hanton said. "Hit the old lady too hard. She's dead. Then the old man gets home and catches him or them in the act. They panic. Tie up the old man. Set the house. It's all over but the crying."

"Did you check out any leads?"

"Fuck no," Hanton answered sarcastically. "What do you think?" Hanton snorted. "Of course, we checked out leads. We talked to the neighbors. Anybody home was inside with air conditioners running full blast. Woman down the street who called 911 didn't even know the old folks."

Hanton seemed to consult his notes. " Next. Who got the money? Their kids. Or should I say 'more old people'? They had two sons and a daughter. All in their 60's. All rich enough and busy enough not to kill the folks. Alibis checked out. Etcetera."

Hanton snorted. "What's left that fits the bill? Some asshole thug. We checked that. Ran the list of local bad actors. *Nada.* Pulled in gang members operating in that part of town. *Nada.* Checked with undercover for any street talk. Nothing. Nowhere."

He paused then added, "Twelve day turn around. Boss says, 'Where are you?' We got nothing. Case goes in the shit can." He spoke very distinctly, his voice dripping with sarcasm, "Wait a minute. I said that wrong. I should have said, 'The case went into an inactive file and then into the cold case department.'"

Before Ed could think of what to say, Ray Hanton finished saying, "Now, Hot Shot, you got it. That's all there is to that. "

Ed thanked Hanton for his assistance and hung up.

He called Ron Webb back and asked for a copy of the cold case file. Webb laughed. "One step ahead of you, my friend. I sent a newbie to get the file, copy and email it to you."

"That will get you in the next book for sure," Ed said. Both men chuckled.

"Was Hanton helpful?" Ron Webb finally asked.

"Ray Hanton is one of a kind, isn't he?" Ed said. "And that's a good thing." He sighed, added, "Yes, he was helpful. More by what he didn't say than what he did." Ed closed the conversation, promising to keep Webb in the loop if a loop developed.

Ed knew it would take some time for the Webb's new staff person to find the file, copy and email it. In fact, it took several hours.

Ed had finished the laundry and eaten dinner before the email arrived.

Ed immediately printed the entire file and sorted it into individual reports. He read through the entire file without taking notes, just trying to put himself into the investigation as it first appeared.

When he finished reading, he leaned back in the office chair which protested with a squeal. He folded his arms across his chest and sat for several minutes.

"Much as I dislike Detective Hanton and people like him," Ed decided, *"his conclusion – that it was a thug or thugs or a gang of thugs – is as reasonable as saying, 'We don't have a clue who killed these people and burned their house.'"*

His thinking went further: *"On their own, each of these cases reached a reasonable conclusion. It's easy to dismiss things that don't fit or don't make sense at the individual level."*

Ed concluded: *"Looking at these three cases together gives more significance to the unusual aspects."*

"Right," Ed said the words aloud. "Right. Unusual aspects common to all three cases."

All were elderly couples either killed or incapacitated before the fire. All lived in single family homes that were engulfed in flames before the 911 call was made by neighbors. In each case, the fire was assumed to have been to cover up the crime. *"Only, of course, it didn't,"* Ed thought. *"The fire didn't cover up the crime."* Ed had to consciously slow his sudden burst of thoughts. *"The fires weren't to cover the crime. The fires were part of the crime. Kill and burn. That's what he does. He kills them and burns them. It's a ritual."* Ed sat very still as he considered what he was thinking.

Then he began rechecking everything.

After he had re-read all three cases, he turned to his computer and typed an email to his agent.

It read, "I'm very confident that I have found an active serial killer. I am quite sure no one else is even aware of the connection between the crimes. I have several cases already joined together and several more to investigate. If we can get it all together, we can have the book ready as soon as we turn it all over to the FBI because it covers multiple states. I'll need an advance for travel, etc. Talk to the publisher and let me know. ASAP."

Before he left the office for the night, he made one more phone call.

"Nell," he said after she answered the phone and they exchanged greetings, "do me a favor. Check on the charring pattern from the fire in Little Rock. Particularly around the bodies but also near the doors both the kitchen and the front door."~

"Why?" Nell asked. "Are you on to something?"

"Just checking on a theory," Ed said. "Let me know what you find. "

He ended the call and left the office, turning off the light, but taking his cell phone. He took a glass of wine and went out onto the deck. Using quick dial, he called Joanna.

"I don't want to talk about murders," he warned her. "I'm mind weary."

They spent twenty minutes discussing favorite foods, good restaurants, places they'd like to visit.

After their conversation, Ed sat on the deck enjoying the night air. Finally, he went in and went to bed.

Chapter 15

"My favorite writer," Ed's agent said when Ed answered her call. "Definitely."

Ed waited.

"As we discussed earlier," the agent continued, "the advance will be wired to your account today. Ed Flander's fourth book is a go."

"Thanks," Ed said. "The contracts?"

"You should receive them by email today," the agent said. "Sign and return."

"Will do," Ed said.

"Now," she said, "get busy and make us some money." With a laugh, the agent ended the call.

It had taken less than two hours for the agent and publisher to agree to advance Ed money for the new book.

Ed sat again at the table, the three cases to his right, the remaining fourteen cases to his left. In the middle was the yellow pad with the chronological listing of all seventeen cases. Above it was the map with the cases by place.

The three cases Ed had studied extensively had all taken place during the month of May. In fact, two of the three had taken place on May 9th. Ed looked for other cases in the month of May. There was one. The second case listed chronologically was from May 8, 1996 in Everglades City, Florida.

Ed had been to Everglades City. He and his wife had vacationed there one winter. *"Must be fifteen years ago,"* Ed thought. On the Gulf of Mexico side of Florida, Everglades City is as far south as land goes. From there it is either swamp or Gulf. They had stayed in a condo, Ed remembered.

On a hunch, Ed looked up the number for the Everglades City Fire Department. The dispatcher didn't remember 1996 or the fire but gave Ed the number of a local man who had an air-boat business. "If Captain Vin don't remember the fire," she told Ed, "maybe he can tell you someone who can."

Captain Vin remembered immediately, even though years had passed. "Yeah, I remember it. Kind of a hippy couple. Maybe grew a little pot. Lived in an old trailer house. I don't think they ever knew for sure what happened. Both of them died in the fire. Her mama was sure someone set the fire to get rid of them. Neighbors didn't like them much, you understand. Her mama tried to get the sheriff to arrest the neighbors. But it didn't happen."

Ed thanked Captain Vin for the information and re-read the information included in the file. *"Doesn't fit,"* Ed thought. Couple in their 40's. Found in bed. Blood tested positive for both drugs and alcohol. Fire apparently started in the kitchen. Undetermined cause. Ed sighed.

"What am I doing?" Ed said. "Wasting time?"

Ed started over. He began to ruthlessly sort the cases by age. Only couples over 65 were considered. That eliminated three cases.

Then he looked for blunt force head trauma for one or both victims. That eliminated two more cases.

"What now?" Ed asked himself. He was saved from answering by his telephone.

"The fire inspector for Little Rock wants to know if you want a job," Nell Jones said. Without waiting for Ed's response, she continued, "Deep charring on the floor around both bodies. Not—let me repeat—not consistent with what we thought."

Ed waited.

"The fire department and the inspector both saw the damage from the fire on the stove and concluded that the fire centered there," Nell explained. "They are re-evaluating all the information including the sections from the floor, the videos, and the photos." She breathed deeply. "Well done, Ed. Well done!"

Ed thanked her and promised to explain all as soon as he had a little more information. "Right now," he explained, "I'm not sure enough of anything to share, but I'll know soon whether I'm right on track or have created a train wreck."

Ed was relieved that Nell didn't have time to talk.

"Accelerant!" Ed said. "He used a slow-burning accelerant." He sorted the remaining cases again looking for evidence of accelerants. The lack of it eliminated three more cases.

Ed had one more aspect to consider: how fully developed the fire was before 911 was called. *"Not enough information to determine that,"* Ed thought. *"For that, I need fire department or fire inspector records for each case."*

With that avenue of inquiry blocked at least momentarily, Ed considered two alternatives: focus on the serial killer or focus on the victims.

After staring at the yellow pad and then the computer screen for several minutes, Ed left his house and drove to Saint George Island. All the way at the end is the state park which is usually not crowded. Ed sat on a bench facing the Gulf of Mexico, watching the ripples and clearing his mind. He stopped for a late lunch at a small bar frequented by fishermen and returned home.

"Start with what you know," Ed said as he walked into the office.

Chapter 16

"What do I know about the serial killer?" Ed asked himself.

Although criminal profiling has been used for centuries, television shows and movies starting in the 1990's made the idea widely known and erroneously understood. Viewers are accustomed to a profiler saying, "White male between 25 and 40 who has had a difficult relationship with his mother and is a loner who doesn't keep a job." Then, within the allotted time, law enforcement officers magically find the one man that meets all the requirements and, *Voila!,* the case is solved, the criminal apprehended and tried before the final credits roll.

The truth of criminal investigative analysis is much more complicated. When enough cases warrant the suspicion of a serial killer, the profiler begins to list similarities in the crimes using a process similar to the *Who? What? When? Where? How?* and , of greatest importance, *Why?* formula used by investigators and journalists. It means sifting through information over and over. Statistics gathered over the years helps, but they must be carefully used. The serial killer may not fit all, or even most, of the statistics.

Ignoring the other cases, Ed focused on his three primary cases.

On the map, Ed used a pencil to connect the three cases: 140 miles between Memphis and Little Rock. 150 miles east from Little Rock to Memphis. 300 miles south from Memphis to Hattiesburg. 350 miles north west from Hattiesburg to Little Rock. *"He's a traveler,"* Ed thought. *"Probably a driver."*

Ed considered each portion of his statement. "He" meant that Ed thought the perp was a man. Statistically, most serial killers who have been caught have been men. That did not necessarily mean, as Ed knew all too well, that this was a man. However, statistics favored a man.

The designation "He" also indicated the singular. Once again, statistically, the serial killer works alone. There are, of course, examples of couples or groups that kill together. However, adding the length of time covered by the three cases made a joint effort even less probable. The three cases covered eight years. That meant a long long-term relationship between two or more perps.

There have been instances of couples who worked together that long, but they are extremely rare. Couples or groups who stage murders rarely stay together. Too much pressure. Too many secrets to keep.

Ed did not discard the idea that there might be more than one criminal involved in these cases, but he put it to the side, as he had the extra cases: something to be considered at a later date.

By the designation "A traveler," Ed meant that the perp was at ease with traveling and with being in a variety of different types of places. The Memphis Case was in a suburb; the Little Rock Case in a city; the Hattiesburg Case in the country. With limited bus service and no passenger train service available in these areas, the killer was restricted to driving a vehicle, riding freight trains, or catching rides with other travelers. Driving seemed the most likely, especially the distance that the Marches had lived from town or a major highway.

"He's comfortable moving around," Ed thought, *"and people are comfortable around him. They invite him into their homes."*

Ed considered that idea. *"Who do you invite into your home?"* Ed thought. *"Someone you know. Or someone you trust. A meter reader. A delivery person. A policeman."* Ed considered and then added, *"Are there still door-to-door salesmen?"* Finally, he thought, *"Someone who needs help. Someone in trouble."*

With those types of people in mind, Ed reached another conclusion: *"More than likely,"* Ed thought, *"he's white and of average height."* As much as Ed deplored racism, he admitted that fear—or at least mistrust—of black men continued, especially in the South, where all these cases were located.

Additionally, Ed knew that people are intimidated by someone who is tall.

Ed smiled ruefully. *"A lot of thinking to accomplish not very much,"* he thought. *"Still, you have to start somewhere."*

Ed moved on to the time of the incidents. He considered them by one item at a time.

Years by Date: 2003 in Memphis, 2008 in Hattiesburg, 2011 in Little Rock. *"He has been killing for at least eight years,"* Ed thought, *"probably with other killings between these three cases."*

Months by date: two of the three had taken place in May, the other the last day of April. Ed thought, *"Is this significant? Does he have a special memory or ritual related to the month of May? If so, why change?"*

Day by date: Two of the cases—the one in Memphis and the one in Hattiesburg were on the 9th of the month.. The third—the last one in Little Rock—was on the 30th. *"If there had been a reason for the 9th, why did he change dates?"*

Day of the week: Once again, the first two matched: both had taken place on Friday; one in the morning, one in the evening. The other one had taken place of Saturday morning. *"No discernible pattern,"* Ed decided.

Ed leaned back in his chair and looked at the yellow pad. "I know a few more things about him," Ed said. "He plans the murders. He must bring the blunt instrument and the accelerant with him. He kills old people and then burns them."

"How do I know these things?" Ed thought. *"By looking at the victims and the crimes."*

Chapter 17

Of his three primary cases, Ed knew the case of Leo and Peggy March most thoroughly. With this in mind, Ed read through the entire case file again. Then he began making notes.

Leo March was 84; his wife Peggy was 82 when they were murdered.

They lived in a single house with neighbors several hundred yards away.

They were religious, going to the Singing at a distant church every Friday night.

Leo March quoted the Bible to Dean March, warning him of "wrath and judgment of God" and calling him a "Son of Satan."

According to both the neighbor and to Dean March's mother, Leo March had become more conservative and more harsh in his religious beliefs and pronouncements following the problems with Dean's father and with Dean himself.

The Marches were not wealthy.

The Marches had no relatives living close to them.

Dean March mentioned the crutches or canes that his grandfather used, but the elder March drove his car often. He also used a riding lawn mower.

Peggy March was a good cook.

Leo March had been sitting in his recliner when he was murdered.

Peggy March had been near the door of the living room when she was murdered.

"Nothing," Ed thought. *"Nothing to tell me why they were murdered."*

He called Joanna.

"I am so happy you called," Joanna said as soon as she answered the phone. "I wanted to call you but knew better than to interrupt."

Ed sat back. He had not expected such an effusive greeting. Before he spoke, Joanna continued, "Nell called me after she talked to you. She says you are onto something."

"Oh," Ed said. "Yes." Ed hesitated. "I found another case. One that—taken with the other two—leads me to the conclusion that there is a serial killer. One who kills and burns elderly couples."

Ed outlined the case from Memphis, explaining how he had gotten the extra information from there. He concluded, saying, "Although eight years separate that case from the one in Little Rock, I am sure they are connected."

"Eight years," Joanna said. "That's a long time."

"Yes," Ed said, "and we have no idea how many of the other cases Nell found fit. And how many more cases were written off as accident or not reported to the state M.E."

They were both quiet as they considered the implication that there were, almost assuredly, other cases.

"Is there any way I can help you?" Joanna said. "I have finished all the paperwork for my friend Myra to petition the state of Mississippi for a new trial for Dean."

"Actually there is," Ed said. Truthfully, Ed had been reluctant to share what he knew until he had more information. He also wasn't sure whether Joanna had the time to help him. But she had volunteered. "I need to know more about Leo and Peggy March." The frustration in his voice deepened. "How did he choose them? Why did he choose that particular couple? Why did he kill them?"

"You are in luck," Joanna said. "The daughter of an old friend from Hattiesburg is getting married this weekend, and I've been invited to the wedding." She paused, continued, "I hadn't decided whether to go or not. I'll go. While I'm there, I'll revisit the people who knew the Marches."

"I'll pay your expenses," Ed said.

"You'll what?" Joanna asked.

"I'll pay your expenses," Ed repeated. "My agent and publisher are interested." He paused. "Interested enough to put some money into the investigation."

"Have you told Nell?" Joanna asked.

"I haven't had a chance," Ed said. "Haven't gotten the contract yet. Just got the call this morning."

"She will be delighted!" Joanna said.

"I hope so," Ed said. "I don't want her to think I stole her idea."

"She *gave* you the idea," Joanna assured him. "And she would never be able to do all the research this will take. She is so busy!"

"Okay," Ed said. "I had planned to call her this evening anyway."

"Does your phone have conference calling?" Joanna asked.

"Yes," Ed said, hesitantly. He didn't admit he didn't know how to use it.

"I'll call you back in an hour," Joanna said. "We can all talk."

Ed agreed.

An hour later, the three of them — Ed Flanders in Tallahassee, Nell Jones in Little Rock, and Joanna Jones in Greer's Ferry — were greeting one another in a conference call.

Joanna acted as a sort of moderator so that the conversation moved along. Under her direction, Ed related to Nell the facts about the case he had discovered in Memphis.

Although Nell was pleased to have her theory confirmed, all three of them were sobered to realize that a person was killing and burning people. They realized how difficult the task would be to catch a killer who had gone undetected for at least nine years.

"I believe," Ed said, "that we must find the common link between all these couples. That will answer the "Why?" question. Then we can look for the killer."

Joanna agreed. "Something sets these couples apart. We have to know them better to look for that link."

When Joanna explained her plans to return to Hattiesburg to learn more about the Marches, Nell apologized. "I would love to be able to do the background work for my case. For the Lodges," she said, "but I am just covered up." She paused. "What I can do," she decided, "is get the other reports on the Lodges. The one from the police department and the full report from the fire department and fire inspector."

"That would be very helpful," Ed said.

The trio spent several more minutes discussing the cases. Finally, Joanna said, "Okay, I'm going to Hattiesburg. Nell is going to get reports in Little Rock...."

"And I'm going to Memphis," Ed said.

Chapter 18

On Thursday afternoon, Ed checked into the Peabody Hotel in downtown Memphis. It seemed an unnecessary expense — there are plenty of cheaper hotels in Memphis — but Ed liked staying there. Liked being close to the food and the music of the area. Liked the ducks.

Ed had called Ron Webb on Wednesday. Ed would spend Thursday afternoon and Friday doing background work on the Cliffords. Friday night and Saturday, Ed and Ron would enjoy Memphis.

On Sunday, Ed would decide on his next steps in the investigation. "And recuperate," Ed said as he thought of his itinerary.

Ed quickly unpacked and set up his laptop. He reviewed the case of James and Melinda Clifford. Using the police report, Ed had prepared maps with street directions to reach the children of the Cliffords.

Ed added a small notebook and pen to his jacket pocket and took a digital voice recorder with him. Even if he did not record conversations, he could use the recorder in the car after each interview.

Just after four o'clock, Ed pulled into Larry's Best Autos, the used car lot owned by Lawrence Clifford, the Clifford's youngest.

A young salesman directed Ed to the office where Larry Clifford stood to greet Ed. Tall, slender, gray-haired, Larry Clifford had a ready grin and a quickly out-stretched hand.

"What can we do for you today?" Clifford said. "Can we sell you a car?"

"Can I have a little of your time?" Ed said.

"What are you selling?" Clifford asked.

"Not selling anything," Ed protested. "I just need some information." Although Larry Clifford frowned slightly, Ed continued, "My name's Ed Flanders. I'm an investigator and I'm taking a new look at the murder of your folks."

"It's about time," Larry Clifford said. "Guess all my bitching got you started." The two men sat down.

"Wait," Ed protested. "I'm not with the Memphis police."

"I should 'a known," Clifford said, disgust in his voice. "They never gave a shit. 'Nothing we can do,' was all they ever said." Clifford looked across at Ed. "If you're not with MPD, who are you?"

"I'm retired FBI," Ed said. Sometimes he immediately told people of the connection; other times, he didn't. He thought that the FBI connection might work with Larry Clifford. It did.

"The FBI?" Clifford repeated, "Now we're getting somewhere." He leaned forward. "How can I help you?"

"I have the files," Ed said, "but I need to know a little more about your parents. It would help if I understood them a bit."

"I don't see how that would help catch the thug that murdered them," Clifford said.

"I'm not sure it will," Ed admitted, "but if I knew more about them, I might be able to determine how and why they were the victims."

Larry Clifford considered this and nodded his agreement.

"Just tell me about them," Ed said.

"Well," Larry Clifford frowned then started, "they got married young. Mom was seventeen and Dad was 20. They had Junior and Susanna and then me. Dad started a used car business when Mom was pregnant with Junior. He was good at selling cars. Built up business 'til he had four lots. All of them called Jay's Best Autos."

Ed nodded his encouragement.

"We had it pretty good growing up," Clifford said. "I started working here, at this location, when I was a teenager." He looked around. "I had a one-room office and five cars, if you can believe that."

"Very impressive," Ed said. The showroom was large with three of the best cars showcased. Ed had seen several offices and the door to a garage on his way to Clifford's large office. There were twenty or so cars of varying models in the lot outside.

"Not that Dad was ever totally pleased with the way I run my business," Clifford said. "When the old man retired in '93, I bought this lot. Lock, stock, and barrel." He shook his head. "Not that he quit coming here and telling me what to do." He rubbed his hand across his lower face. "Ah-h-h-h, he wasn't bad, just thought the old ways was better."

"I tend to be that way," Ed said with a grin.

"My kids think that too," Clifford said. "Now *I'm* the old man!" He shook his head and grinned at the thought. "You got kids?" he asked.

"No," Ed said.

"Smart man," Larry Clifford said. "No kids? You got money. You got peace and quiet." He shook his head. "I got five. Two by wife number one. One by wife number two. Two by wife number three. My oldest is 38. My baby is 17."

Ed was unsure what to say so said nothing.

"Yep," Larry Clifford said, "I'd be a rich man today if I could have kept my pants zipped. Three marriages. Three divorces. Five kids."

"Did your parents enjoy being grandparents?" Ed asked, bringing the topic back to the elder Cliffords.

"Well, of course, they loved 'em," Larry Clifford said, "but Mom was—what do you call it? OCD?—about her house. Everything had to be spotless."

He looked at Ed. "Do you know what she said? She said, 'Leave your shoes outside.'" Larry Clifford looked his surprise. "Are you fucking kidding me? I wear hand-made Western boots. I'm not leaving $600 boots outside."

Ed looked properly impressed.

"Me and the kids just quit going there. I don't know. Five, six, seven years before they was killed. Stetson, that's my baby boy, was a toddler. It was just too much trouble to keep him out of all that stuff Mom had everywhere."

Ed nodded his understanding.

"Were your parents religious?"

"You heard about that, did you?" Larry Clifford shook his head. "My darling sister got them started to church with her. Not that I'm against religion. I'm not. But they went over the top. Always with the Bible. Always with the praying." He shook his head. He leaned closer. "You know what I call it when old people suddenly get religion? I call it 'fire insurance.'"

Both men grinned at the old joke.

"I guess in some ways, it was good for them. Kept Dad active. He worked out with a group of men about his age — you know my dad was nearly 90 — and organized that prayer breakfast. Which, let me add, I *never* attended. Mom and Susanna did woman programs or something. I don't know much about that," Larry Clifford shrugged his shoulders. "They bought Susanna that book store. All three of them spent time together I guess."

Ed nodded.

"Anyway," Larry Clifford confessed, "I just stayed away. Called 'em on the phone from time to time. If they started in on going to church or telling me how to live, I'd just say I had a customer or another call. Anything."

"Well," Ed said, "that about covers it." He thanked Larry Clifford and promised to report back if any progress in solving the crime was made.

"It's been nine years this month," Larry Clifford said. "Nine years." He looked sad. "That shouldn't have happened to them. They were good people."

Chapter 19

"Too late to catch either of the other Cliffords," Ed said as he sat in his rented car. He grinned. Nothing to do but go back to the hotel. *"Tomorrow is another day,"* he thought and grinned again.

Back at the Peabody, he checked email and phone messages. He answered an email from his favorite niece Ginny and one from Nell. He sent Joanna a text in answer to hers.

A quick shower and shave and Ed left the hotel, walking up the alley to line up for a rib dinner at Rendevous, an old favorite. Waiting in line, he met a young couple who invited them to share their table. After dinner, he invited them to stroll Beale Street with him. The trio bar-hopped and finally settled in a lesser known bar where an impromptu group was playing blues.

The young couple eventually left, but Ed stayed until the group quit playing as the bar was closing at half past one. The night air was warm as Ed walked back to the hotel.

At nine-thirty the next morning, Ed pulled into the shopping area where, among a variety of other stores, Susanna Clifford Hayward owned the Sanctified Life Book Store.

"Greetings and bless you for coming in today," came a voice from the back of the store as Ed entered.

The store was attractive. Books and magazines were displayed without crowding customers. There were also home decorations, all with a religious theme, on display. One area was devoted to Bibles of varying sizes and covers. In the center of the store was a reading area with comfortable chairs and small sofas.

Tall and slender like her brother, Susanna Hayward came to greet Ed with the same smile of welcome. She wore dark slacks and a green-checked shirt. A dark red apron with the word "Sanctified" stitched on it completed her outfit.

"How about a cup of apple cider with a hint of cinnamon?" she asked.

"Sounds great," Ed said.

She brought two mugs and poured from an urn that was shaped like a large tea pot.

While they both waited for the cider to cool, Ed introduced himself and told her his purpose for coming to the shop.

"So tragic," she said. "Just tragic." She sighed. "They are in a better place. I'll see them again."

"It would be helpful if you could tell me a little about them," Ed said.

"They were wonderful," Susanna said. "So supportive. Just wonderful Christians."

"They were religious?" Ed asked.

"Oh, yes," Susanna assured him. She sat down in a chair and signaled Ed to sit near her. "God came into our lives in such a marvelous way." She sipped her cider. "When my husband was taken from me at a much too young age, I—well—I lost my way. I just couldn't cope. Fell into depression and just couldn't find my way out." She looked sad then brightened. "Then, one day, I was waiting in line at the grocery store and the Lord just spoke to me."

Ed must have looked surprised because Susanna smiled. "Oh, I don't mean clouds and lightning and a deep voice," she said. "There, in front of me, was a poster that read, 'Are you depressed? Have you lost your way?'"

She looked at Ed. "Don't you see? That was me. Exactly." She smiled at the memory. "The poster was from Abundant Blessings Fellowship. I just thought: that's what I want. Abundant Blessings." She took another sip of the cider. "And I went to that church the very next day which was a Sunday."

She set the cup down. "Halleluiah! Praise the Lord!" she said. "I found Jesus. It turned my life around. Turned it around."

Ed took a drink of the apple juice with cinnamon. What she considered cider was not what Ed considered cider. No alcohol. Just apple juice with cinnamon.

"I knew my parents, God love 'em, were lost. Lost to Jesus. Not with God. So I witnessed to them. I showed them how God was working in me. I showed them the road to heaven and the road to hell."

She looked at Ed. Ed didn't speak.

"Praise the Lord and thank you, Jesus!" she said, clasping her hands together. "My daddy had a spell. Not a *real* heart attack but a little scare. He was in the hospital and a group of men from my church just went and laid hands on him and prayed. And the Holy Spirit just came down on him and he was saved right there. "

She paused for breath, tears in her eyes. Ed took a drink of the apple juice.

"And he and my Mama got baptized on the same day just one month later, and, oh, Ed, there was not a dry eye in the church."

Ed nodded and sighed inwardly.

"And Daddy's gift from the Holy Spirit was the gift of exhortation. He was led to urge—fervently urge—others to be saved. He was given a view of the days to come when God will judge all people. From that day on, Daddy spent his time exhorting people to repent before it was too late."

"And your mother?"

"Bless her heart," Susanna said, "my mother was a lovely person, but she was just impatient. Just impatient with people." She sighed deeply. "Let me give you an example: we both joined Mall Walkers for Jesus." Susanna noticed Ed's look of confusion. "Mall walkers are people who go to a mall before most of the stores open and get their exercise by walking from one end to the other or make a certain number of rounds. You understand?"

Ed understood the idea; he just couldn't imagine ever doing such a thing. When he went to the mall, it was get in, get out, as quickly as possible. And only go when absolutely necessary.

"Well, our church has mall walkers who go to all the big indoor malls in Memphis, and we carry little cards with our church name and a Bible verse and give them to other mall walkers or to workers we meet."

"Hm-m-m-m-m," Ed mumbled into the apple juice mug.

"Anyway, I was telling you about my mother," Susanna said. "She would get so impatient if people wanted to talk. You know, sometimes you give people that card, they have questions. Some of the people in our group just want to stop and visit. You know." She looked over the rim of her reading glasses at Ed. "Not Mama. When she was walking, she was walking. She would get just a little bit grouchy if she had to stop very much. Just a little grouchy."

A look of sadness and shame crossed Susanna's face. "Oh, my, I should not be speaking bad about my Mama. Not after what happened to her!"

Ed nodded appropriately.

"I know they are in a better place. That's what comforts me. They are in a better place. Waiting for me. Praise the Lord!" She looked at Ed and her mouth tightened. "And those awful men who killed them will be cast into the lake of fire."

Ed blinked.

"Cast into the lake of fire," she repeated. "Reserved for the devil and his angels." Her mouth tightened even more. "And that's what they deserve."

Ed nodded sagely.

"Enough of that sadness," Susanna said. "Now, Ed, tell me about you. Do you live here in Memphis? What church do you attend?"

"No," Ed said, "I don't live in Memphis. Just here for the investigation."

"Of course," Susanna said, "how silly of me! But will you be here on Sunday? I would love to take you to church with me."

"I'm leaving tomorrow," Ed said. "I'll have to take a rain check."

Susanna reached into the pocket of the apron she wore and took out a business card.

"Here," she said, giving Ed the card. "My cell phone number is there. Let's stay in touch."

Ed took the card and promised to let her know if he found any information about the deaths of her parents.

"Of course. Of course," Susanna said. "That's what I meant." She smiled at Ed. "But if your plans change and you are still here on Sunday, give me a call."

Ed set the mug down and stood.

"Could we just have a word of prayer together before you go?" Susanna said. She reached out with both hands and took Ed's hands.

"Sweet Jesus," she said, "be with this dear man. Aid him in his endeavors. Walk with him and help him find the sinners who killed my lovely parents. I ask this in Jesus's name and for his sake. Amen."

Susanna looked at him, tears shining in her eyes. Ed extracted his hands and turned, walking out the door of the shop and getting into his car without pause.

Chapter 20

As he drove the ten miles east to Arlington, Tennessee where the eldest Clifford was manager at a bank branch, Ed spoke into the voice recorder on the seat beside him, adding notes on the information from Susanna to the ones from her brother, Larry.

"Let's see what the other Clifford thinks about his parents," Ed thought. When he had called the previous afternoon, he had made an 11:30 appointment with Jim Clifford.

At exactly 11:30, a secretary came to where Ed was seated in the bank's waiting area. "Mr. Clifford will see you now," she said, leading the way to an inner-office.

"Mr. Flanders," Jim Clifford said, rising to shake Ed's hand, "how may I help you?" Clifford bore little resemblance to his siblings. Shorter than either of them, this Clifford was also darker with darker, thinning hair. His suit was of excellent quality but fit a little snugly.

Once more, Ed introduced himself and explained that he was taking a fresh look at the murders of Clifford's parents.

"A bad business," Clifford said. He folded his arms across his chest and said, "I hope you are not going to stir up all that again."

Ed looked surprised but said nothing.

"Look," Clifford said, "my parents were killed by a deranged person. No use bringing all that up again." He frowned. "Nasty business all the way around."

Although Ed expected a quick brush-off, he said, "Could you tell me a little bit about your family? It would really be helpful."

"My family?" Clifford asked. "My son is a dentist; my daughter is an elementary teacher. My wife does not work. She keeps a beautiful home."

"Excellent," Ed said. "And a bit about your parents? Your siblings?"

"Oh," Clifford said, "them." He thought a moment then said, "My father was demanding but always fair. He worked hard to provide an excellent upbringing for me and my sister and brother. My mother was a disciplinarian but loved us very much. She kept a beautiful house. They both wanted the best for us and expected good things from us."

"There were three children?" Ed asked.

"Yes," Clifford said. "I am the eldest. Named James for my father. Called "Junior" until I was in high school when I became "Jim." He smiled briefly.

"Second is my sister Susanna," he said. He closed his eyes and shook his head. "Always the problem child. Always." He carefully put both hands, palm down, on his desk. "What can I say?" He nervously licked his lips. "Better to say nothing," he concluded.

"Lawrence" he said, "also called Larry." He shook his head again. "His life's a mess; business is very successful."

"Were your parents religious?" Ed asked.

"Yes," Clifford said. "For several years before their deaths my parents were deeply involved in a church in Memphis."

"Do you attend that church?"

"Me?" Clifford asked, astonishment in his voice. "No," he added. "My wife and I are Methodists."

"I have been trying," Ed confided, "to figure out why your parents were killed. I just can't understand that. "

Jim Clifford leaned forward and motioned Ed forward.

"I am pretty sure I know who killed them. Or had them killed," he said, his voice low and confidential. "I told that detective." Clifford nodded his head.

Ed waited.

"Early on, when Dad was building up his used car business, he borrowed money from a man. A man with a shady reputation. Man named Sandy Lynch. Dad paid him back. Every nickel. Lynch always said he was supposed to be a partner. That Dad cheated him."

Ed nodded and taking the notebook and pen from his jacket pocket, wrote "Sandy Lynch" on the blank page.

"When Dad sold all four of the car lots — one to Lawrence, the others to different people, Lynch was furious. Demanded half of the money. Threw a fit at a restaurant. Threatened Dad. People heard him."

Jim Clifford threw his hands up into the air. "Do you think the police investigated that when my folks were killed? That Hanton snickered. Snickered!"

Clifford leaned forward again. "You think people don't hold a grudge? You think they won't wait *years* to get revenge?" His eyebrows rose again. Then his eyes narrowed. "You better believe they would." He looked at Ed. "You want something to investigate. Investigate Sandy Lynch."

"I'll do it," Ed said.

There was a discreet knock at the door. Jim Clifford sat back, straightened his tie and jacket, smoothed his hair, and said, "Come in."

"I'm so sorry to interrupt," the secretary said, leaning around the door, "but you will be late for lunch if you don't leave now." She retreated.

"Lunch with the other managers," Jim Clifford said, shrugging his shoulders.

Ed thanked him quickly. The two shook hands. The exited the building together.

Ed watched as Jim Clifford quickly drove away in a Lexus convertible.

"Whew," Ed thought, *"nice car. Nice car if you have $30,000 more or less to spend."*

Ed got into the rental car and returned to Memphis.

Chapter 21

Back at the Peabody, Ed reviewed the information he had gathered from the three Cliffords.

James Clifford appeared to have been demanding, judgmental, and interfering. He had also apparently been a good salesman and had worked to provide well for his family.

Melinda Clifford had been the impatient disciplinarian who kept a beautiful house by not allowing people to wear shoes. Ed grinned as he typed the description into his laptop.

They had been religious, attending a church that Ed discovered was massive. Nearly 2000 people were members. The web site showed the live orchestra, the choir of nearly 100. The programs listed in the church's outreach section were widely varied: a day care center, two dinners each week, the mall walker program. The church even owned a gym with trainers.

The Cliffords had been fairly wealthy. Not millionaire rich. But certainly very comfortable.

James Clifford worked out; Melinda Clifford was a mall walker. They must have been in reasonably good health, particularly for their ages.

Ed took the notebook from his jacket and called Roy Hanton.

"Oh, Jesus," Hanton said when Ed asked about Sandy Lynch, "Sandy Lynch. Where the hell did you dig up that name?"

"Jim Clifford seems sure that Lynch was behind the murders of his parents," Ed said.

"I should 'a known you wasn't gonna quit!" Hanton said. "I kept my notes handy, waiting for you." Hanton laughed. "I know exactly what you're thinking. You're thinking we *ignored* what could have been the big breakthrough."

Hanton waited, but Ed waited too.

"I'm gonna tell you about Sandy Lynch," Hanton said. "We had to go to a fucking nursing home to interview him. The man was older than dirt. Said he loaned Clifford the money. Said Clifford paid it back. Admitted he threw the fit in the restaurant. Said he was drunk. Said he called Clifford and apólogized. Clifford had filed a complaint against Lynch but dropped it." Hanton paused. "We checked on Lynch's associates — the few that was still alive — and his son who lives over in Arkansas. Nothing." Hanton sighed. "Of course, that didn't stop Clifford's son. As you well know."

Ed apologized for bothering Hanton and thanked him for the information.

"Well," Ed said, "that takes care of that."

Ed had planned to fly from Memphis to Little Rock on Sunday but discovered that there are no direct flights between the two cities. He would have to fly to one of the bigger hubs — Dallas or Atlanta, for instance — and then on to Little Rock.

"I'll just drive," Ed thought. *"It's cheaper and quicker."* He called the car rental agency and arranged to drop the car off when he finished with it in Little Rock.

Using Nell's address as a central point, Ed used a map search to find nearby hotels. He found a hotel on I-630. It was part of a chain of hotels he had used previously and was less than two miles from Nell's home. Unsure of when he would make the two-hour drive, Ed didn't make a reservation.

Ed was waiting outside the Peabody the next morning at 11 when Ron Webb arrived.

"Escaped the crowd," Ed said. "It's duck walk time." A Peabody tradition, twice a day the ducks ride the elevator down and walk the red carpet to the marble fountain in the lobby; then they go back to the elevator and to their home on the roof. It's a tradition and a tourist draw.

"Enjoyed the evening," Ed said as they drove away from the hotel. "Your wife is delightful."

The previous night Ron Webb and his wife Yolanda had taken Ed to dinner and to a variety of small clubs off the beaten track.

"She's the best thing ever happened to this ol' boy," Ron Webb cheerfully admitted.

The two men joined five more off-duty policemen at a boat dock south of Memphis and spent the next five hours fishing out of two boats on the Mississippi River, moving from the main channel to backwater sloughs and to several of the small lakes that edge the river.

Ed was totally lost when the two boats pulled up to a dock next to an old tin building with a big front porch. Ed could see cars and trucks parked to one side of the building.

"Get away cabin," Ron told Ed. "Cops only."

During the next hour, the men cleaned the fish and peeled potatoes. One man assembled the two huge pots on tripod bases that were butane-fueled cookers. He added oil from restaurant-sized jugs.

Other men unloaded coolers of beer and other drinks from a variety of vehicles.

A strange variety of chairs and stools were pulled out of storage.

A big campfire was started.

By five o'clock, the first of the food was being cooked. Pan fish, catfish, and several types Ed couldn't identify were fried in the hot oil of one cooker. Potatoes were fried in the other.

Some of the men left before midnight; others arrived.

The sky was beginning to lighten when Ed and Ron took the boat back toward Memphis.

Thoroughly chilled, Ed arrived back at the Peabody. He made his way cautiously to the front desk. "I will be staying until Monday," he carefully said the words to the night clerk. Then he crossed to the elevator and up to his room.

When he woke at four in the afternoon, he groaned and went back to sleep.

Chapter 22

"Choir practice?" Joann asked, laughing. "You went to an MPD choir practice?"

Nell looked confused.

"Choir practice," Ed explained to Nell while Joanna attempted to contain her amusement, "is the old term used when policemen get drunk together."

"I thought that was a joke," Nell said.

"Yesterday morning," Ed said, "my head thought it was anything but a joke." He grinned. "I was seriously over served."

The trio was in Nell's kitchen in Little Rock. Ed had made the two-hour drive from Memphis and had checked into the motel as he had planned. Joanna had also driven to Nell's that day, a six-hour trip from Hattiesburg.

They were assembling the ready-made meal that Nell had purchased at the nearby gourmet grocery.

As they ate, they chatted about inconsequential matters: the weather, the rapidly approaching summer, heat-resistant plants for Nell's terrace and garden.

When dinner was finished and coffee served, the talk turned more serious.

"I met with two people who knew the Marches well," Joanna said. "That woman preacher from Lucedale and Leo March's brother, Steven." She shrugged her shoulders. "Neither of them could shed light on who might have killed the Marches." She frowned then continued. "I did find out about Leo March and the canes."

Ed and Nell both paid close attention.

"Years ago," Nell said, "Leo was in an accident at the auto plant where he worked. Broke his left leg in two places. As he got older—especially in the last few years—it became more painful for him to walk. He used a wooden cane but then bought a pair of those canes that have handles and arm grips. According to Steven March, they gave Leo much more stability."

Ed nodded his understanding.

"Sister Murphy, the preacher, was quick to point out that the problems with his leg didn't interfere with Leo March's driving either his car with automatic transmission or the riding lawn mower either."

Joanna set her empty coffee cup on the table. "That's that," she said, "all I found. I am sorry."

"Don't be sorry," Ed said. "You tried. Hit the same brick wall I hit." He smiled at her. "I talked to the most likely people to kill someone: their closest relatives, the ones who stand to inherit their money. What did I find?" Ed shook his head. "Big nothing."

"Although Shirley Lodge and I didn't talk about the her mother- or father-in-law or their deaths," Nell said, "I spoke with Shirley on Saturday. She is a nurse at Arkansas Children's Hospital. Works 3-11." She looked at Ed. "I told her I would text her if you were unable to meet with her tomorrow at 11. I have her address."

"Great," Ed said. "I'll be there."

Nell handed Ed the address. "It's easy to find," she said. "An older house but beautiful."

The three of them talked a bit longer, but Ed was still feeling the after effects of the night on the Mississippi, and Joanna was tired from her weekend and drive home.

Ed excused himself and went back to his hotel.

Just before 11 o'clock the next morning, Ed turned off Cantrell Road at the address Nell had provided. He stopped outside the intricate wrought iron gates, looking for a call button.

A female voice came from an unseen speaker. "Could I help you?"

Ed identified himself.

"Of course," the voice said. The gate opened and Ed drove along a circular drive to park under the portico of a three-story house of red brick with white columns.

Before Ed reached the front door, it was opened by an attractive black woman dressed in slacks and a matching shirt. Of medium height and weight, she had short hair beginning to gray.

"Come in," she said, holding out her hand. "I'm Shirley Lodge. I'm so pleased to meet you."

She led Ed from an expansive entry, past a formal living room and a formal dining room and into a room that boasted a wall of books, a grand piano, and three areas of seating — one with a sofa and chairs, one with a wooden rocking chair, one with an overstuffed chaise lounge.

Ed paused to look at the wide range of framed photos that covered the piano top.

"My family," Shirley said. She smiled. She picked up one that showed her as a younger woman with longer hair in twist locks, a tall slender man beside her, and four children of varying sizes surrounding them. "My babies," she said.

Ed smiled at the photo, but his mind was racing. *"This is wrong,"* he thought. *"This is wrong."*

She reached toward the back of the piano top and brought a photo forward to show Ed. "My husband Paul and, of course, Bill Clinton." She smiled. "Of course, he was Governor Clinton then." The same slender black man but a much younger version smiled beside Clinton who went from governor of Arkansas to President of the United States.

Shirley Lodge returned the photo to its place. "Paul died four years ago," she said. "Cancer."

Ed looked properly solemn, but his mind continued to race. Finally, he spoke, "Do you have a photo of your father- and mother-in-law?" he asked.

"Oh, of course," Shirley Lodge said. She handed Ed a photo in a silver frame. The resemblance between Paul Lodge and his father was obvious: both tall and slender; both with a ready smile. Mrs. Lodge was much shorter and considerably less slender.

"They are black," Ed thought. *"Clyde and Zinna Lodge are black. Why didn't Nell mention this?"*

Shirley looked at Ed who appeared to be studying the photo.

"Such a tragic end to their lives," she said. "Such a waste."

Ed blinked hard to focus on what Shirley Lodge was saying.

"Do you take your coffee with anything?" she repeated. "Cream? Sugar?" She led Ed to a low table in front of the sofa.

"Neither," Ed said. "Thank you," he added. He sat down on the sofa.

"The Medical Examiner said you wanted to talk to me. . . ," Shirley encouraged Ed while their coffee cooled.

"Yes," Ed said. He mentally shook himself and began the interview. "I am taking a second look at the deaths of your in-laws," Ed said. "It would be helpful to me if I knew a little more about them."

Shirley Lodge looked confused.

"I am investigating similar fires, particularly among elderly people," Ed said, knowing that the deaths of the Lodges had not been ruled homicides. "I am hoping to draw some conclusions about the deaths by studying them in depth."

"Okay," Shirley Lodge said.

"I'm hoping that learning more about the people who died will allow me to understand what happened and why." Ed smiled. "I know this all sounds vague, but I really appreciate your time and indulgence."

Shirley Lodge thought for a minute, took a drink of coffee and then spoke, "I'm not sure what good it will do, but I am more than happy to share a bit about them with you."

Ed took a drink of coffee and waited.

"Paul's parents were both from Little Rock, grew up here, raised Paul and his two brothers here." She paused. "We called them Pappy C and Mommy Z—his name was Ezekiel Clyde but he went by Clyde; her name was Zinna."

Ed waited while Shirley Lodge sorted memories.

"Pappy C worked at a variety of jobs, mainly as a night watchman. Mommy Z worked in the kitchen in one of the fanciest hotels in Little Rock back in the day. They put all three boys through college. Paul became a lawyer; his brother Martin, a preacher; the baby, Robert, a university band director."

She indicated their house with a small motion of her hand. "When we got all of this," she said, "we bought that house for his parents."

Ed nodded.

"Pappy C was a man of few words," she said. "I always thought it was because he was ashamed of being poorly educated." She shrugged. "Whatever the reason, he often sounded abrupt when he spoke. More like making a pronouncement that simply speaking."

Shirley Lodge looked at Ed and grinned, "Of course, it may have been that he had so little chance to talk at home." She grinned again. "Mommy Z was a talker. And a whirlwind." She thought, explained, "If you walked into her house, Mommy Z would grab you by the arm and drag you into the kitchen. She would sit you down and feed you. Whether you were hungry or not."

"She was a good cook?" Ed encouraged.

"Excellent," Shirley said. "And cooked a wide variety of food. She learned a lot in her working days!" She sighed. "She was a good woman," Shirley said, "I wouldn't want you to think otherwise." She added, "but she was so insistent."

Ed waited.

"Our youngest son had a bit of a weight problem in junior high. He worked so hard to slim down. Then, we would go to Mommy Z's and she would attack him. Grab him. Drag him into the kitchen. Insist on feeding him pie or cake or cookies with hot chocolate or sweet tea." She sighed again. "Poor baby," she said, "we finally let him stay home." She shrugged again. "There was just no convincing her that he didn't want to eat."

"Did the Lodges attend church?" Ed asked.

"Of course," Shirley said. "They were charter members of the Baptist church in their neighborhood. Pappy C was a deacon. Mommy Z sang in the choir. They carried their religion home with them too. Studied the Bible together. Always held hands and prayed before eating. Even snacks."

"And their health?" Ed asked. "I know both were in their 80's. . . ." He allowed his comment to be unfinished.

"Considering how hard they had worked and their ages," Shirley Lodge said, "they were both in fairly good health. Pappy C had back trouble. Mommy Z had been on blood pressure medicine for years." She looked at Ed. "To tell you the truth, we were worried about Pappy C driving. He didn't drive much, but it worried me. His back trouble affected the way he walked and moved. I was afraid it affected his driving ability."

"Did you see them often?" Ed asked.

"I am ashamed to say that it wasn't so often after Paul's death." Shirley looked solemn. "Of course, I checked on them. Called them at least twice a week." She moved her hands in a small gesture of resignation. "What could I do?" she asked. "Martin is in Atlanta; Robert is in Ohio. They are busy. I am busy with work. I have this enormous house that I really should sell." She paused. "Those are all just excuses, I know."

"It's hard to balance everything," Ed said. "Even if we realize we are missing opportunities, we're busy with other parts of our lives."

"That is so true," Shirley Lodge said.

The two talked a bit longer, in general terms, and then Ed left.

Back at the hotel, Ed paced back and forth. *"Statistically so improbable as to border on the impossible,"* he thought for the hundredth time. *"Serial killers do not cross racial lines,"* he thought. *"In fact,"* his mind screamed, *"black people are very unlikely to be victims of a serial killer."* He amended his statement. *"There have been exceptions. Mainly prostitutes and homosexuals."* He said the next words aloud. "But still, no profiler would ever have predicted this."

On that thought, another thought jumped to his conscious mind. "Why didn't Nell tell me about that the Lodges were black?" he asked the mirror.

Two thoughts: first, she simply hadn't known or, Ed grimaced, she had known that given the two cases: one involving a black couple, the other involving a white couple, Ed would *never* have investigated them.

"And a serial killer would never have been suspected," Ed admitted. "And there *is* a serial killer," Ed said.

Later that evening, he repeated most of his thoughts to Joanna and Nell.

"I swear it was not deliberate," Nell said. "I knew that Dean March was white. I met him at Mom's years ago. I also knew that the Lodges were black." She paused. "I looked up information about serial killers on the internet. I knew most are white males, but several of the notorious cases involved both black and white victims."

Ed knew she was correct. Knew that his frustration was clouding his mind.

They sat on the L-shaped sofa in Nell's living room, Nell at one end, Ed at the other, Joanna in the middle.

"We seem to be back to square one," Ed said.

Each appeared to be lost in thought until Nell said, "What about the accelerant? Tell me why that is important."

"In each of the three cases," Ed explained, "a slow-burning accelerant was used. It served two purposes. It allowed the killer to ignite the fire safely and also to get away before anyone noticed him or the fire. I really think the other reason had to do with his ritual. That the fires are so intense and so engulfing — especially of the bodies — is a signal that the fire is important. Burning the bodies is significant."

"You're right," Nell said. "The fire inspector here was surprised at how completely the house was burned. "

"Maybe that's the key," Joanna said.

"Right," Ed said. "Nell," he continued, "can we look at the other cases and see if we can find one in our time frame where the house was engulfed in flames?"

Nell led the way into her office. As she opened her computer, Ed found the list he had sorted from Nell's longer list. The first two — one in Kentucky in 2001 and one in West Virginia in 2002 — did not seem to fit. The third one — West Virginia, March, 2006 — seemed right. The bodies of the couple had been severely damaged in the fire and when the floor beneath them gave way.

"Huntington, West Virginia," Ed said. "I hope they have an airport. And a connection to Little Rock. I don't want to drive."

"You're going to West Virginia?" Nell asked.

"Yep," Ed said. "It's our next good possibility. Our next good chance at finding that little something that ties all these cases together."

Chapter 23

By the time Ed reached Huntington, West Virginia, he had crisscrossed the eastern half of the United States. There were, he discovered, no direct flights from Little Rock to Huntington. He was routed through Charlotte, North Carolina and Chicago, Illinois.

Finally, at nearly 10 at night, he arrived in Huntington, the largest city in West Virginia although not the capitol.

The taxi driver took Ed to a hotel owned by a major chain. Ed checked in, went to his room, raided the mini-bar and went to sleep.

The next morning, Ed called the Huntington Fire Marshal's office. The administrative assistant told him that the fire marshal was in a meeting in the capitol and would be gone several days. When Ed explained that the information he wanted was for a fire some six years ago, the administrative assistant encouraged him to call a former employee, Billy Rayburn. "I reckon," she said, "he knows about every fire that ever happened."

When Ed told Billy Rayburn what the young woman had said, Rayburn laughed.

"That's Fred Fullham's youngest," he shook his head. "She looks to be about fourteen and thinks anyone over 25 is just sitting around, waiting to die."

Ed had called the number given him by "Fred Fullham's youngest" and had arranged to have lunch at a bar/restaurant called Fat Patty's. The food was good.

Ed introduced himself and said that he was a writer in search of a story. *"Big mistake,"* Ed thought, trying to steer the conversation away from the story of Billy Rayburn's life as a fire marshal and to the deaths of J. R. Kruk and his wife Angie. It was not easy.

The story, when it finally came, was a repeat of the other stories: elderly couple who lived alone, bludgeoned to death, their house set on fire, the fire fully involved when the fire department arrived.

Ed sighed inwardly.

"Damnedest thing," Billy Rayburn said, "I was at a meeting at the capitol maybe two months later, and don't it beat all? There was another fire marshal had almost the same fire where he lived."

"Really?" Ed asked. "Do you remember where that was?"

Rayburn tugged at his heavy lower lip as he thought. A florid man, Rayburn had his hair dyed an unnatural red and wore blue jeans, a blue denim shirt and suspenders. He had eaten with gusto and had drunk two beers to Ed's one.

"Greenbrier County," he finally pronounced. "Down by Lewisburg. Southeast part of the state." He scratched his chin and ordered another beer. "You know what that guy said — now what was his name?" Rayburn searched his memory. "Shit," he said, although he made the word into two long syllables, "I don't guess it matters."

The waiter brought Rayburn's beer. Ed ordered coffee.

"What he said was, 'That's three!" Rayburn nodded his head emphatically. "That's what he said. 'That's three!' I reckoned he meant three fires that was the same, don't you?"

"Could be," Ed said.

"Well," Rayburn said, "then the meetin' started and we didn't talk no more. That guy — I never did think of his name — wouldn't go to the bar with the rest of us that night. I never seen him at no more meetings."

Although Rayburn and Ed talked through two more beers, Rayburn had nothing else to offer.

Back at the hotel, Ed checked the list of cases he had sorted from Nell's longer list. Two in West Virginia: 2002, 2006. The 2006 case was the one from here in Huntington. The 2002 case had been as Billy Rayburn had said, in Greenbrier County.

According to the M.E.'s report, the couple had been struck with their own fireplace poker. The bodies had been burned but the burns were not as extensive or as destructive as those of the later fires had been.

"Wonder what happened there?" Ed asked himself. In all the later cases, no weapon had been found. *"Was our boy learning?"* Ed thought. *"When did he decide to bring his own weapon? His own accelerant?"*

Ed stopped his thoughts saying aloud "Whoa, Ed! You are jumping to wild conclusions here. Slow down and get it right."

He clicked on the file for the longer list — the one Nell had originally sent. No more from West Virginia.

"But the man said three," Ed thought.

He called Joanna and repeated the conversation. "I don't think," Ed said, "that Rayburn was just in his cups. I think the man said there had been three cases. I'm assuming he meant in West Virginia."

Both of them thought and reached the same conclusion at the same time, their words running over each other. "What if it's like Mississippi? What if someone was convicted of one of the crimes? What if there is another Dean March in prison in West Virginia?"

Both were silent for several moments, considering the implications. They had talked about the possibility that there were other cases that hadn't been reported or had been mistakenly reported. That there might be another innocent person serving time was sobering.

"Ed," Joanna said, "I'm in my car on the way home. Let's think about this. I'll call you tonight."

"Right," Ed said. "Sorry to have talked when you were driving. You should have said. Drive home safely."

They ended the call.

"If the third case was in West Virginia," Ed thought, *"I don't have it. But, if it was in a neighboring state — close enough to make the news — where might it have been?"*

Although Ed knew U. S. geography well, he pulled up a map of West Virginia on his laptop. "Crap!" Ed said, looking at the map. West Virginia is a small, roughly tear-drop shaped state that has borders with five more states and is less than an hour's drive from several more. *"No way to easily sort that down,"* Ed thought. *"Back to square one. One more time."*

Ed made a decision. For the moment, he would assume that the third case of arson/homicide occurred in West Virginia. He couldn't be sure how it had been reported. It could have been reported as accidental, or it had been reported as arson/homicide and resolved.

"Either way," Ed thought, *"how do I find it?"*

No immediate answer came to mind. However, Ed had learned in his years in law enforcement that patience truly was a virtue. Unless there was a demand for instant action, the best course was often to do something else and allow the unconscious mind a chance to work.

Hoping that was the case, Ed watched a reality show on television and then went to dinner at an upscale restaurant in walking distance of his hotel.

Superb crab cakes followed by crème brulee and coffee made Ed feel better about the world.

"I'll figure it out tomorrow," Ed thought as he watched more television and then slept.

Chapter 24

"Could I help you, Sir?" the young man—undoubtedly a Marshall University student—stood behind the main desk of Drinko Library on the Marshall campus.

It was Friday morning. Ed had walked the two blocks from his hotel to the Marshall University campus main library.

"Would it be possible to look at newspapers for West Virginia for the past dozen or so years?" Ed asked.

"Of course," the young man said. "We have digital copies of almost every newspaper for the entire state for over 50 years. Let me get a tech rep to assist you."

In less than ten minutes, Ed was seated at a computer with the young tech rep instructing him on how to use the advanced search feature, setting search words and also beginning and ending dates. Ed was also shown how to use his credit card to pay for copying stories.

Ed set the date range for 2000-the present. He used three words: *couples, dead,* and *fire* as his search terms. He got a long list of stories. Much longer than he had thought he would find.

As Ed quickly moved through the stories, he was able to eliminate most of them. Quite often, the story was about a *couple* whose child *died* in a *fire.* Or something to that effect.

He also found numerous stories that covered the 2002 and the 2006 fires. He scanned those stories hoping to find a reference to a third case, but none was mentioned.

When Ed had gone through all the stories and found nothing helpful, he leaned back in the chair, took off his reading glasses, and rubbed his eyes.

"Having trouble?" a voice asked. Ed looked around and up to meet the eyes of yet another young woman. This one grinned. "Hello," she said, "I'm Cathy Wilson, the research librarian." She smiled again. "You look a bit frustrated. Maybe I can help." She sat down beside Ed.

Ed told her what he hoped to accomplish. She looked at his search and said, "Let's expand your time frame and see what we get. Use 1990-1999. And ask for the results in reverse chronology. That way you see the results from 1999 first."

Once again, Ed got a number of results.

The librarian smiled again. "I'll be back by in a few minutes," she said and left Ed to begin reading again.

Once again, Ed was able to eliminate most of the results without looking at more than the headline. A few stories seemed promising but on closer inspection, didn't fit the pattern Ed sought.

Just as Ed sighed in frustration, he found a story that piqued his interest. The story was from 1991 in the Lewisburg newspaper. The headline read "Stoneville Couple Die in Fire, Grandson Being Held." The follow-on a month later was very brief and stated that the grandson of the couple had been committed to the state psychological hospital for an indeterminate time. Because the grandson was a juvenile, his name was not listed.

Ed ran copies of both stories.

"Found what you wanted?" the librarian asked, as Ed prepared to leave.

"Not really," Ed admitted. "I found a similar story, but I'm not sure how it fits." He showed her the story.

"Interesting," she said. "If I were you, I'd look for their obituaries as well. Should be in that day's paper or sometime over the next week."

"Good idea," Ed said. He changed search words using their names and time frame.

Sure enough, obituaries for both Oather and Esther Springfield were listed three days later. Both of them were 80 years old. No survivors were listed.

No other information about either of the Springfields was forthcoming.

Ed paused to thank the librarian for her assistance and complimented her on the kindness and cooperation he had received at the library.

On the way back to the hotel, Ed found a coffee shop where he could sit in the sunshine and read the newspaper report from 1991 in depth.

Oather and Esther Springfield had lived near an unincorporated village called Stoneville somewhere near Mt. Nebo.

They burned to death in the early hours of a Sunday morning in May, 1991. Their teenaged grandson was taken into custody at the scene. The fire marshal had determined that the fire was not accidental. The follow-up story offered little more information except that the teenager was only thirteen and had been committed to the psychiatric hospital.

Because of it's proximity to the 2002 case--located in the same region and reported in the same newspaper--, Ed felt that this was the third case that had been referenced to Billy Rayburn.

"But does it fit our cases?" Ed thought.

Ed finished his coffee and returned to the hotel. There he called a car rental company and secured a car to be delivered the next morning.

Next, he called Joanna. After greeting her, Ed said, "I'm driving down to Lewisburg tomorrow. It's only a two-hour trip and gives me the opportunity to find more about that case from 2002."

Joanna agreed.

"I found something else today," Ed said. "Remember that guy telling me about a third case?"

"Yes," Joanna said. "Did you find it?"

Without consulting his notes for names and exact details, Ed told Joanna about the case from 1991. "It's a long way out of our time frame," he concluded, "and may be completely unrelated."

"On the other hand," Joanna said, "what if that couple's grandson is like Dean March? Was he the best suspect or was he a victim of the justice system?"

"I don't know," Ed said, "but I'm going to try to find out."

Ed had dinner in the hotel restaurant and went back to his room. He was watching television when the phone rang at just past 11 o'clock.

"I think I found something," Joanna said. "Well, I found something, but I'm not sure what it means."

"Slow down," Ed said. "What did you find?"

"Walking canes," Joanna said. "Remember Dean March talked about his grandfather's walking canes?"

"Yes," Ed said. He waited.

"I found them in the photos from the fire. They were on the floor beside his chair. Beside his body," Joanna explained. She continued, "They were the ones Leo March's brother told me about. Aluminum frames, handles — of course, the rubber grips were destroyed in the fire — and the remains of the cuffs that fit on Leo March's arms just below the elbow."

"Yes," Ed said, "I remember your telling me about those."

"Well, guess what," she said, "James and Melinda Clifford's bodies were very close together, but beside them was another pair of that same type of walking canes."

"Are you sure?" Ed asked.

"Absolutely," Joanna said. "I checked the fire department list. The canes had been partially destroyed, but there they were. On the list."

"To quote a character in a favorite movie of mine," Ed said, "'That don't make no sense!'" He rubbed his face. "The Cliffords were in good health. He worked out. She was a mall walker."

"Well," Joanna said, "I don't understand it, but the walking canes were there."

"I'm not doubting you," Ed said, "It's just...."

"I know," Joanna said. "I was looking at the fire department photos, looking for body positioning and there they were."

"What about the couple in Arkansas?" Ed asked.

"No," Joanna said. "I checked very carefully and looked at the fire department report as well."

They both sat silently thinking.

Finally, Ed said, "Shirley Lodge said her father-in-law had a bad back. She had been worried about his driving. I thought it was because of his age. But maybe not. Maybe he used canes when he left the house."

"Could be," Joanna said. She hesitated, "I have an idea," she said, but she didn't continue.

"What's your idea?" Ed asked.

"It's—uh-h-h-h-h—it's treading on your territory," Joanna said.

"*My* territory?" Ed questioned. "First, I don't have a territory. Second, we need to find and stop this killer." He let out his breath in an aggravated puff. "What is you idea, Joanna Jones?"

"What if I called Shirley Lodge and the Clifford's daughter and said I was your secretary doing a follow-up?" Joanna said, all in one breath. "I could ask about problems with walking or getting around."

"Excellent," Ed said. "As I told you, I'm going to Lewisburg tomorrow. You call Susanna Hayward and Shirley Lodge. Tell them you are my *associate*. You found the clue. You get the credit."

Joanna laughed. "Thanks, Ed," she said. "I'll play it by ear."

They talked a couple minutes longer. Finally, Ed said, "It's nearly midnight here in the Eastern Time Zone, and I need my beauty rest."

Joanna laughed. "I had forgotten the time difference between Arkansas and West Virginia. It's nearly 11 here. But I'll say good night."

"Talk to you tomorrow," Ed said, "after *I* go to Lewisburg, and *you* talk to the ladies."

Ed spent several minutes after the call ended, puzzling over the canes found near the bodies of James and Melinda Clifford. He went to sleep without reaching a conclusion.

The next morning, Ed called Joanna at 9 just before he left for Lewisburg. He had waited until it was 8 in Arkansas.

"Mornin' Jo," he said.

She laughed. "I haven't been called that in years."

"When we worked together in K. C. all those years ago," Ed said, "I don't think I knew your name was Joanna."

"Probably not," Joanna admitted. "I was being macho woman in those days."

"What happened?" Ed asked. "Why did you leave the Bureau?"

"I got in a situation at work that was pretty bad," she said. "When it was over, I decided Nell needed a mother more than I needed the Bureau."

"I understand," Ed said. Joanna didn't need to tell him the details. She had gotten into a situation where she was in grave danger. It had happened to Ed a couple of times. *"In the heat of the moment,"* Ed thought, *"you don't think. Later, you think about your family. How your death would have been for them."*

"And I was getting no support. My husband and his family weren't happy with my career choice. I caved." She said the words simply then continued, "I chose marriage, school and motherhood." She paused, "But the marriage didn't survive."

Ed waited.

"Did you call to hear my true confessions this morning?" Joanna asked, her voice volumes lighter.

"No," Ed said, "actually, I called to ask you to ask those two women, Susanna and Shirley, if they knew of any connection between the two families."

"You think they knew each other?" Joanna asked. "That's a stretch."

"You are right—a big stretch. And, no," Ed said, "actually, I don't. But I'm trying to eliminate possibilities. Still working on the *why* but also on the *how*... how did he pick these people?"

This time, Joanna waited while Ed's thoughts coalesced.

"There *must* be a tie," Ed said. "Is it possible they knew one another? Or had friends or relatives in common?"

Joanna made a noncommittal sound.

"Is religion the tie? They didn't all attend the same church but all were religious. Apparently more openly religious than others around them."

"Right," Joanna said, "the Marches went to the Singing and also to a local church."

"The Cliffords were very active in a huge, super church in Memphis," Ed said. "And the Lodges were charter members of a church in Little Rock."

"But it wasn't the same religion," Joanna said then clarified, "they weren't all Baptists or Methodists or Catholics. That sort of thing."

"True," Ed said. "I don't know," he admitted. "I keep grasping at straws, hoping that we'll hit on that one commonality that will help fit all the pieces into some form."

"Me too," Joanna said.

"With that profound admission," Ed said, "I'm off to Lewisburg."

"Drive safely," Joanna said.

"Talk to you this evening or tomorrow," Ed said. "May we both have news to share!"

Chapter 25

It was nearly noon when Ed exited I-64 in Lewisburg, West Virginia. On this Saturday, the town of nearly 4000 was bustling. A farmer's market with a variety of stalls was busy. There was a crowd of cars at several of the local restaurants. Traffic was heavy enough and slow enough to allow Ed a good view of the town. *"Pleasant looking place,"* Ed thought.

He passed one fire station but knew that the fire department was further into town. When he found it, he parked in the place reserved for visitor's and went inside.

There was no one at the counter, but Ed could hear a voice in a nearby room. He waited at the counter for several minutes before an older woman dressed in orange slacks and a brightly flowered blouse came out, coffee cup in hand.

"Oh, land," she said when she saw Ed, "you startled me. Have you been waiting long? Good land. I am sorry." She set her cup on a desk and walked toward the counter. Ed guessed she was near his age, probably a bit older. She was of medium height and weight with nearly white hair worn short. "I was back there eating my lunch," she added. "I bet you heard me singing. Or talking to myself. You should 'a' hollered." She leaned on the counter. "Now," she said, "how kin I hep you?"

Ed introduced himself and explained that he was an investigator and wondered if it were possible to talk to someone about a fire that had happened in 2002.

"Well, you kin talk to me," she said. "I bin workin' here nigh onto twenty years." She held out her hand for Ed to shake. "Mary Jean Slater," she said. "Proud to meet ya."

Ed smiled as he shook her hand. "I'm interested in the deaths of a couple named Raymond and Edna Burdette."

"Burdette?" Mary Jean Slater scratched her chin as she thought. "Hm-m-m-m-m, now you got me. I'm a thinkin'" she added.

Ed waited. He had the file from the West Virginia Medical Examiner, but he didn't want to offer it. People enjoy remembering and telling things in their own way. He would let Mary Jean Slater think through past cases.

"White Sulphur Sprangs," she said. "The fire wasn't in Lewisburg, it were in White Sulphur Sprangs."

Ed nodded. The file he had listed the Burdette's location as White Sulphur Springs. Mary Jean's accent made it "Sprangs," but Ed understood.

"I 'member that," Mary Jean said. "They was a elderly couple. Lived right near the interstate. " She stopped. "Now, let me think...." She put a hand on each hip. "Don't that beat all. . . ."

Just as Ed reached for his briefcase, Mary Jean Slater spoke, "Oh, land!" she said. "I got it now." She looked at Ed. Her eyes narrowed as she spoke, "They wasn't burned up in a fire. They was murdered." She nodded her head as she remembered. "They was hit in the head with their own poker. From their wood stove. " She nodded again. "Here's what happened. Our fire department was headed out to the Greenbrier Forest to do a burn. You know, burn some old trees that had fallen over the winter. Practice makes perfect."

She drew a deep breath and thought. Then she said, "My late husband was part of that crew." She paused and lowered her eyes.

"They was driving down one of them country roads and durned if they wasn't a man flagging 'em down. Said that house down there has got smoke coming out. So they just turned that fire truck into the driveway and, sure 'nuff, that house was about to burst into flames. That man saw it when he was a lookin' for his huntin' dog."

Ed nodded his understanding of her story.

"So, they put out the fire, but them poor people was dead already. And flames all around their bodies." She looked sad and shook her head. "It was awful. That's what it was."

She sighed deeply. "How I 'member it, they was good God-fearing people." She looked at Ed. "I hadn't thought about that in ages. Dog's years."

"Do you know if either of them was handicapped?" Ed asked.

"Now that, I don't know," Mary Jean Slater said.

Ed asked several questions, but Mary Jean Slater had no more information. She also rejected Ed's attempts to look at the old case file saying she had no authority. "They let me watch the desk here on the weekends," she confided, "but they wouldn't like it if I messed with papers."

Finally, she told Ed that if he came back on Monday, the fire chief would be there.

Ed thanked her and asked about Stoneville. She didn't know where Stoneville was but when Ed mentioned Mt. Nebo, she gave him directions on how to get there.

Ed thanked her for the information and left the station.

The crowd at the local Chinese restaurant had thinned, so Ed found a parking place and went inside. Helpings were generous, service was good, food was also good.

An hour later, Ed was in Summersville, West Virginia with no idea how to get to Stoneville which seemed non-existent on maps and GPS.

Ed stopped at a service station, filled the rental with gas, and asked for directions to the county sheriff's office.

Once there, he asked the dispatcher for information on getting to Stoneville.

"Well, Sir," the young dispatcher said, "it's out on the state road west of here about three miles." He grinned. "You better watch the mileage, or you'll miss it completely."

"I hear you," Ed said. "I have a question." Ed scratched his chin. "Do you know anything about a fire in Stoneville in 1991? An older couple died?"

"1991?" the dispatcher repeated, making the number into a question. "Whew," he said, "I don't remember that far back. I was maybe three years old."

"Right," Ed said. "Think there's someone around who might remember?"

The dispatcher tried to remember if he knew anyone that old. Anyone who was in law enforcement in Nicholas County that long ago.

"No," he finally said, "the sheriff back then died in a flood years ago. His deputy retired and moved to Florida. I don't even think they had a dispatcher then."

"Okay," Ed said. He doubted the truth in the young man's word but wasn't sure it was worth questioning.

"Let me call home," the dispatcher said. "My mama lived here then." On his personal cell phone, he made a quick call. After asking a few questions, he handed the phone to Ed.

"I remember when that couple burned up," the woman's voice said. "If I was you, I'd talk to Reverend Wentworth up at the Pentecostal Jubilee Church right here in Summersville. They went to his church."

"Thank you, Ma'am," Ed said and handed the phone back to the young dispatcher.

"Could you direct me to either the Pentecostal Jubilee Church or to the Reverend Wentworth?" Ed asked.

The dispatcher gave Ed directions to the edge of town church adding that the pastor lived in the house next door.

Ed found the church which, on this Saturday afternoon, was deserted. He walked to the house next door and knocked.

The man who came to the door was about Ed's age. He wore his hair slightly long in back, curling along his neck line. In the front, the hair was thin and combed to one side. He was nearly equal in height and weight to Ed and wore slacks and an open-necked shirt. He looked at Ed over the tops of reading glasses.

Ed introduced himself as a non-fiction writer in search of a story.

"James Wentworth," the man said. The two men shook hands.

"I have very little time to spare," James Wentworth told Ed. "I am preparing for Sunday service."

"I'm sorry to bother you and won't take much of your time," Ed said. "I am taking a look at an incident from Stoneville from 1991." As soon as he spoke the words, the preacher's face tightened. "The Springfields?" Ed turned their name into a question.

"Why?" was the single word James Wentworth spoke.

"Well," Ed said, "I am investigating several cases in which older couples died in home fires. The case of the Springfields came into my possession. I am just investigating to see if it fits in any way with the others."

"No," Wentworth said, "I would say it does not."

"Were the Springfields members of your church?" Ed asked.

"Yes, they were," Wentworth said.

"Could you tell me a bit about them, if you remember them," Ed said. "As you say, it may be totally disconnected from the cases I am investigating, but I'd appreciate the information."

"Come in," Wentworth said. He led Ed into the living room which was comfortably, if simply, decorated. Wentworth indicated a chair and sat down opposite Ed.

"Oather and Esther Springfield lived a few miles from here, down the old highway." He stopped, apparently to compose his thoughts. "They came to church regularly for a number of years."

Wentworth stopped. He started again to explain to Ed. "We are Pentecostals. Do you understand that?"

Ed shook his head.

"We believe — firmly believe — in three baptisms. The first is Baptism into the Body of Christ. Some people call this 'getting saved.'"

Ed nodded.

Wentworth continued, "The second baptism is by water. We believe in immersion. Immersion of the body to wash away the old and become the new."

Ed nodded again.

"Now, all of this," Wentworth said, "is when a person has reached the age of accountability. We don't hold with baptism of babies. When a person realizes his sinful nature and asks Jesus into his heart, salvation happens. Then he or she can ask the church to accept and baptize them."

Wentworth looked sternly at Ed. "The final baptism is when the Holy Spirit descends on a person and gives them special power."

Ed contained his skepticism and nodded.

"It is a cornerstone of our belief that the Holy Spirit came to the apostles as it is recorded in Acts of the Apostles in the New Testament. That event is called Pentecost."

Ed waited.

"Pentecost is celebrated 40 days after Easter in accordance with the Scripture," Wentworth said.

"Okay," Ed said. He *wanted* to say, 'Get on with it. Where are we going?' but years as an FBI agent had taught him patience. He waited.

"Let me show you something," Wentworth said. He went to the desk and brought back a Bible. It was covered with softest leather. The cover was embossed with the words "Holy Bible, Book Divine." An intricate cross had been embossed underneath the words. Below that was Wentworth's name in small letters that looked handwritten.

"This is the work," Wentworth said, "of Oather Springfield." He rubbed the cover gently. "His craft was a gift from God."

Ed agreed. The cover fitted over the original exactly; the embossing work, beautiful.

Wentworth spoke in a deep voice, "We are, you must know, in the last days. The days of war against Satan and his angels. We are at a time of spiritual warfare."

He continued, "The scripture is clear. We must yield ourselves to the Will of Almighty God. It is our only recourse in this sinful world."

Ed looked properly solemn as he waited.

"I truly believe this," Wentworth said. "And so did Oather Springfield. He was a true believer."

Ed waited while Wentworth sorted his facts, and the way he wanted to present them.

"The Springfields' son was a sharp pain in their hearts. The fallen away. In anger and rebellion, their son left here. Even as the Prodigal Son did, going to a most sinful city. He only came back one time. To bring the boy."

Ed wanted to sigh but held it inside himself.

"I *knew,* may God in Heaven forgive me, I knew Oather was too harsh with the boy. Too unforgiving. Too quick to demand repentance."

Wentworth looked at Ed. He rubbed his hands together as if washing them.

"Things happen for a reason. God is in control of them and it is his Will that makes them happen. You believe that, don't you?"

Ed did not meet the preacher's eyes.

"I trust that what happened was the Will of God," the preacher said. He spoke quietly, "That Pentecostal morning, very early, Oather and Esther were in the sanctified room in their home where they held private communion with the Holy Spirit. The boy said Oather attacked him and that he, in turn, locked his grandparents in the room and burned the house with them inside."

Wentworth sat with his hands on his knees, his head bowed in defeat.

Ed, quite literally, had nothing to say.

Wentworth straightened and said, "But, Praise the Lord, the boy has found Jesus and has asked for forgiveness. He has prayed with me. God be praised!" Wentworth looked at Ed, hope lighting his face. "The Lord's purpose will prevail."

"The boy must be a man now," Ed said.

"Yes, yes, he is," Wentworth said. "And a wonderful, God-loving, repentant man."

"Can you tell me his name and where he is now?" Ed asked.

"No, no, no, no," Wentworth said quickly. "That would be betraying a confidence that I must keep. However, you can be assured that I have spent time with him, and he is right with God."

"I do have one question," Ed said. "Were the Springfields in good health? Were either of them handicapped in some way?"

Wentworth looked confused at the question but considered it. "No," he finally said, drawing the word out. "No, I think both of them were in good health. They were both near to 80, as I remember, but I'm relatively sure they were in good health."

"And the boy was committed to the state psychiatric hospital without a trial?"

"Yes," Wentworth said.

"Is he still there? Do you know?" Ed pressed.

"The boy was saved. That I know. He is right with God, and the Mighty Hand of God guides him," Wentworth said.

The two men talked for a few minutes longer, but the conversation was stilted.

Ed thanked Wentworth for his time and started back to Huntington. Thirty minutes later, Ed thought he had taken a wrong turn. When the narrow, paved road turned to gravel, Ed was sure he was going away from rather than toward the interstate highway. He drove nearly a mile before the road widened enough for him to cautiously turn the car around.

Nearly an hour later, Ed was back in Summersville where he wisely asked directions at a service station.

Streetlights were shining in Huntington when Ed drove into the hotel parking lot.

He stopped in the lobby to order dinner and two martinis from room service and went to his room.

A shower, a steak, and two martinis later, Ed was lying in bed, the television making low noises, as he drifted off to sleep.

Chapter 26

On Saturday afternoon, as Ed drove across West Virginia, Joanna Jones called Susanna Clifford Hayward at her book store in Memphis.

"Good afternoon," Joanna said when she had Susanna on the phone. "I'm Joanna. I'm Ed Flanders' secretary." Without waiting for a response, she continued, "Mr. Flanders asked me to call and repeat his thanks for all the information you shared with him."

"It was a pleasure," Susanna Hayward said, "Bless his heart, he is a kind and compassionate man." She paused and casually questioned, "Is Ed still in Memphis?"

"No," Joanna said, "he is on an investigative excursion elsewhere today."

"Oh," Susanna said, "I had hoped to invite him to church tomorrow."

"What church do you attend?" Joanna asked.

"Praise the Lord and thank You, Jesus," Susanna said, "I am a member of Abundant Blessing Fellowship. Right here in Memphis. I am proud to say that God has richly blessed us making our congregation the largest in Memphis. By the end of this year, God willing, we will be the biggest congregation in Tennessee." Susanna spent the next ten minutes describing to Joanna all the wonderful programs available at the church and the marvel of their worship services twice on Sunday, on Tuesday afternoons, and on Wednesday nights.

"Is your church affiliated with other churches?" Joanna asked. "One of the Baptist denominations, for instance or other independent congregations?"

"Oh, no, no, no," Susanna said. "Our pastor, Brother Vaughn, was moved to join hearts and lives together in the power given especially to him by the Holy Spirit. We are dependent upon God and his Word alone."

"Excellent," Joanna said.

Susanna began to enumerate again the wonders of the Abundant Blessings Fellowship.

When she paused for breath, Joanna said, "That sounds wonderful to me." Without allowing Susanna to continue, Joanna said, "Mr. Flanders did ask me to verify a bit of information that you shared with him. Just to be sure." She laughed lightly. "Sometimes he gets so interested in talking and listening that he forgets to take notes."

"Well, of course," Susanna said, "we did have a lovely time together. But, just to be sure...."

Joanna said, "Although your parents were in their 80's, they were both in good health?" She turned the statement into a question.

"Oh, yes," Susanna said. "They were both healthy and active."

"What about the walking canes?" Joanna wanted to ask. *"Why were there walking canes in their living room? Did the killer bring them, leave them there?"*

"Of course, my Mama, God rest her soul, hadn't been so active. I told her she would just have to be a Mall Walker in spirit."

"Oh?" Joanna questioned.

"Well, yes," Susanna said. "She had knee replacement surgery that spring." Susanna quickly added, "but her health was exceptional. That's what the orthopedic surgeon said. Exceptionally healthy."

"I'm afraid my mother is facing that surgery," Joanna lied, "and she is really worried. She loves her daily walk."

"Tell her to get it done," Susanna said. "My mama was doing so good. She was so ready to throw away those canes. Just hated the looks of them."

"She had canes?"

"Yes," Susanna said, "and you'd better believe she hated them. Wanted an elegant cane if she had to have anything. But her surgeon insisted. 'Last thing we need,' he told her, 'is to have you fall.'"

"So true," Joanna said.

"So Mama was stuck with that kind of walking cane that has the grips that fit your arms," Susanna explained. Then she remembered. "Poor Darlin'!" she said. "She and my Daddy are watching over me from Heaven. I can just feel them." She sighed. "Just a minute," she mumbled. Joanna could faintly hear Susanna blow her nose.

When Susanna was back on the phone, Joanna apologized saying that she didn't mean to upset Susanna. "I have one more question," she added. "Mr. Flanders wondered if your parents might have known a Leo and Peggy March, a couple from Hattiesburg, Mississippi. Might be relatives, or old friends, or business associates."

Susanna repeated the names. "March," she said. "March." She thought then said, "I don't remember that name at all." She questioned Joanna, "What was her name? Peggy?" She thought again. "No," she said, "I don't think so." She added, "Of course, Daddy might have known Mr. March. Daddy was in the used car business a long time." She thought a bit more. "I doubt that Daddy knew Mr. March. He didn't like Mississippi people much. Didn't trust them. Wouldn't hardly do business but cash only with them."

Joanna and Susanna talked a few more minutes. Joanna promised to pass on greetings to Ed and to remind him that he was more than welcome at Abundant Blessings Fellowship or at the bookstore Susanna owned.

Finally, Susanna wished Joanna a "most blessed day and weekend," and the call ended.

Joanna made notes on her talk with Susanna Clifford Hayward and smiled to herself. *"Ol' Ed better watch out,"* Joanna thought. *"I think Susanna is sweet on him."*

Fresh class of iced tea in hand, Joanna called Shirley Lodge, daughter-in-law of Clyde and Zinna Lodge. The call went immediately to Shirley's voice mail. Joanna left a message asking Shirley to return her call.

Joanna then called Arkansas Children's Hospital asking for Shirley and discovered that Shirley Lodge would not be on duty until Tuesday afternoon.

Joanna sat on the deck that looked out over Greer's Ferry Lake. The house was bigger than she had intended to buy, but she loved the piece of land that jutted out into the lake offering her views of the clear blue water from almost every room in the house.

Today, however, she didn't focus on the scenery. Mentally, Joanna Jones was in the classroom reviewing classes she had taught in criminal justice. In particular, she was looking for a certain type of criminal, a certain type of killer.

"Angel of mercy," she said, "Angel of death." She nodded. Over the years, a type of killer had been identified as focused on the act of killing and, in particular, on "playing God" by killing members of a particular group. The most infamous of this group are doctors or nurses who say that they kill to relieve the suffering of their patients.

"Is this the medical connection?" Joanna thought. *"Is this a nurse or otherwise medical person who sees killing these people as a mission?"*

She would save her theory to discuss with Ed.

Chapter 27

On Sunday afternoon, Ed called Joanna.

"I have a bit of a theory," Joanna said.

"So do I," Ed said. "Ladies first."

"First," Joanna said, "Melinda Clifford was using walking canes."

"She was *what?*" Ed's voice rose.

"She had had knee replacement surgery," Joanna explained.

"And her witless daughter didn't think that was a health problem?" Ed said. He smacked his forehead. "Susanna What's-her-name said her mother was a mall walker."

Joanna was having difficulty suppressing her amusement. "She was a mall walker. Just *in spirit*. And temporarily."

"Close your ears, Joanna," Ed said. He put his hand over the cell phone to muffle the sound of his profanity.

When he was silent, Joanna teased, "I guess this means you won't be attending the Abundant Blessings Fellowship with Susanna. Huh?"

"No, not at any time," Ed affirmed. His good humor prevailed, and he laughed. "Crazy woman!" he said.

"In her defense," Joanna said, "I understand what she meant. A couple years ago, I had a problem with my knee. I stepped wrong and developed what's called a Baker's cyst. Very painful. I had to take medicine and walk with a cane for two weeks or so, but I never thought of myself as unhealthy." Joanna paused, laughed. "I was in good health. I was just momentarily crippled. I was healthy *in spirit*." Both of them laughed.

"Now," Ed said, finally, "your theory?"

"I think the killer may be a nurse."

"A nurse?"

"A nurse or someone pretending to be a nurse," Joanna explained. "She—or maybe he—would easily be admitted to a house. The victims are elderly. The nurse may be one of the "Angel of Death" killers.

Ed considered the idea. "Does this fit the cases that we know?"

"Well," Joanna said, "Leo March and Melinda Clifford had medical problems of one sort or another."

"What about Clyde Lodge?" Ed asked.

"I haven't talked with Shirley Lodge," Joanna said. "I left a message, but she may be out of town. She's off work until Tuesday afternoon. She did say, though, that her father-in-law had back problems." Joanna continued, "Their ages, their medical problems, their isolation—none of them had relatives next door or even very close—all those together made me think of the "Angel of Mercy/Angel of Death" syndrome.

Ed said, "You know, I have a similar theory. Not "Angel of Death" but the idea of playing God. I'm looking at the religious angle. All of these people seem to be involved in heavy religious experiences."

Joanna waited while Ed sorted his thoughts.

"I don't necessarily mean weird religion," Ed said, "just stronger or more aggressive forms of religion." He continued, "Susanna said her father had been given the gift of—just a second—exhortation." Ed read from his notes. "He was given the power to urge people to repent."

"That sounds a lot like Leo March," Joanna said. "Remember the phrases that Dean repeated. Verses about repenting."

"I know," Ed said. "Once again, we're not sure how fierce Clyde Lodge was, but we know he and his wife were charter members of a church."

"What are you thinking?" Joanna asked.

"I'm thinking maybe it's an itinerant preacher," Ed said. "An old time evangelist traveling from place to place. I'm sure religion is tied into the killing in some way."

Joanna tried to control her snicker, but it escaped. "I've jumped to one conclusion; you've jumped to another."

"Right," Ed said. "We don't know anything more than we did but we now have not one but two killers."

The more Ed thought about their conclusions, the funnier they sounded.

"I know…I know!" Ed said, laughter deepening his voice, "we have a traveling evangelist and his wife…."

Joanna interrupted, adding, "who's a nurse and they roam the South…."

Ed added, "in search of religious nuts…"

"And zip them off to Heaven," Joanna finished.

Both of them laughed at the absurdity of their own thinking.

"Ah-h-h-h, Joanna," Ed said, "I'm enjoying working with you." His tone became more serious. "It's been a long time since I had someone to laugh with about work."

"Gallows humor isn't for everyone," Joanna said, thinking of the times she and others had seen the absurdity of life in the tragedy of it.

"True," Ed said. "Ellen never wanted to hear about my job. She was a lovely person but always fearful of what might happen. But never did."

"Will was that way too," Joanna said. "He's the same with Nell. Proud of his daughter but would have preferred her to become a plastic surgeon or a pediatrician. Something less, oh, gruesome."

The silence between them was comfortable.

After a couple of minutes, Ed said, "Here's my game plan: tomorrow I drive to Wheeling to the state psychiatric hospital. That is where the grandson was committed in 1991."

"Do you think he's still there?"

"I have no idea," Ed said. "In fact, I have very little hope that I will find out anything."

Joanna agreed. "Juvenile records and mental facility records are usually very difficult—if not, impossible—to access."

"It's worth trying," Ed said. "I found out more yesterday than I had hoped." He paused, added, "Then I'm driving to Columbus, Ohio to catch a flight home."

"Ohio?" Joanna asked.

"Yes," Ed said. "Believe me, I have looked at many, many ways to get from West Virginia to Tallahassee, and that's the easiest."

"Okay," Joanna said. "I'll call you on Tuesday after I talk to Shirley Lodge."

"Good," Ed said. "Talk to you then."

"Stay safe driving. And flying," Joanna said. "And good luck with the psychiatric hospital. I hope they don't decide to keep you."

They ended the call with laughter.

Chapter 28

"Good morning, Mr. Flanders" Roberta Sales looked up from the business card and greeted Ed as he entered her office. "How may I help you?"

Ed had driven to Wheeling and had been sitting in the outer office of Dr. Roberta Sales, resident psychiatrist, for the state psychiatric hospital for well over an hour. Although it was a Sunday, the psychiatrist was on duty.

"I'm a writer and am researching for a new book," Ed said, shaking her outstretched hand. "I am currently involved with a case from Mississippi in which a young man was accused of killing his grandparents and setting their house on fire. He was quickly convicted of the crime and is serving life sentences for their deaths. I believe that the young man is innocent of the crime." Ed continued, "During my research, I came across a case here in West Virginia that is almost a mirror image of that case in Mississippi. I am curious if the case here might not have been another rush to judgment as was the case in Mississippi."

Roberta Sales waited.

"The records show that the young man in question was admitted to your hospital in 1991. I wonder if you could give me some information on his case."

Roberta Sales took off her glasses and looked at Ed. "It's a matter of public record," she said, "that our patient confessed to the crime and was committed here for treatment."

This time, it was Ed who waited.

"However," Roberta Sales continued, "I can give you *no* information about the patient or his treatment."

"Is he still confined here?" Ed asked.

"I *told* you" Dr. Sales said, her voice angry, "I cannot release *any* information about my patients."

"Yes," Ed agreed. "I understand and appreciate your seeing me." Ed rose to leave. "You have my card with my phone number. If there is anything you can think of that might help me, please contact me."

"I can't imagine that happening," Dr. Sales said. She didn't offer Ed her hand to shake.

Ed left her office. *"Well,"* he told himself, *"that went about as well as I had expected."*

By ten o'clock on Monday night, Ed was home in Tallahassee, Florida.

On Tuesday morning, Ed did laundry, checked his email and regular mail and, in general, re-started the routine of living at home.

After a light lunch, Ed went to work in his office. Two work tables and an office desk made a U-shaped area.

When Ed had first begun writing, he had owned only one computer. He had bought it eight years ago when he moved to Florida, making it an antique in the rapidly changing world of computer technology. Ed had bought a flat-screen monitor but otherwise had kept the computer as it had been.

Although connected to the internet and to the printer, its chief use was as a word processor. When Ed faced it, he also faced the closed end of the "U."

To his left, at the back of the work table was the stack of twelve arson/homicide cases yet to be investigated. Closer to the front of the table, the five cases — Arkansas, Tennessee, Mississippi, and two from West Virginia — that were currently being investigated. Next to them was Ed's laptop with all the notes he had taken on his recent trip. The voice recorder was there as well.

To Ed's right, on the office desk proper, was the monitor and keyboard for Ed's newest computer. With several browsers and several sites available, this computer was for research.

For the next several hours, Ed worked: pounding out words, organizing notes, checking information. In addition to a bulleted list of information case by case, Ed began the task of correlating information common to all cases.

Ed's two goals were to begin to prepare the information for inclusion in the book he would eventually write, but, more importantly, Ed was reviewing everything, looking for what had, perhaps, been overlooked initially. A good investigator — even the best of investigators — often misses that all-important clue on the initial search. Getting an over-all picture would help him answer the two most important questions: How did the killer choose his victims? Why did he burn the bodies?

When he found the answer to those questions, Ed could begin to search for the identity of the killer.

"Then," Ed thought, *"then, I give the information to the local police or to the FBI and let them clean it up."*

It was nearly dark when Ed took off his reading glasses, rubbed his face, stretched and said, "Tomorrow, I start a storyboard." One wall of his office was covered in a fabric that allowed him to use push pins without leaving marks. He would put bits of information from each of the cases on paper and begin to look for commonalities and ties between the cases. With the information spread out in front of him, Ed hoped he would see the pattern which would lead him to the killer.

Leaving the office for the day, Ed cooked a simple meal and ate. He was sitting on the deck with an after-dinner brandy, when Joanna called.

After an initial conversation that was both friendly and general, Joanna said, "I spoke with Shirley Lodge this afternoon."

"Good," Ed said.

"Clyde Lodge had a degenerative back condition that had affected his mobility significantly. In spite of this, he continued to drive his car—a situation that Shirley saw as dangerous to himself and others. "

"Okay," Ed said. "That's about what she told me."

"However," Joanna said, "she also said that Martin Lodge, their son from Atlanta, had been in Arkansas less than a month before their deaths. And—" Joanna paused dramatically, "—had contracted with a local home health group to have a therapist and also a nurse work with both of them."

"Ah-h-h-h-h," Ed said. "So that means...."

"That means," Joanna said, "that the Lodges were accustomed to having a nurse-type person come to their house."

"Supporting your theory, of course," Ed conceded with a grin.

"Yes," Joanna said. "Martin had also bought his father a power lift chair. You know, push the button and it goes from seated position to vertical position."

"I've seen them advertised on television," Ed said.

"Shirley Lodge wasn't sure what medical group Martin used and wasn't sure if he bought the chair here in Arkansas or had it shipped to his dad. She promised to call him and ask both questions."

"Well, Miss Smarty," Ed teased, "did you find out anything else?"

"Yes," Joanna said, "she wasn't 100% sure, but Shirley was relative sure that her husband's parents had no connection with neither the March family from Mississippi nor the Clifford family from Tennessee."

"Superb work!" Ed admitted freely.

"What about your meeting with the psychiatrist?" Joanna asked.

"As we both suspected, she said she could give me no information."

"But?" Joanna could hear the hesitation in Ed's voice.

"When I mentioned the case in Mississippi and said that it mirrored the one in West Virginia, she showed absolutely no interest. If there was a chance, even a slight chance, that the two were related, I think she would have been curious."

"So, in her mind, there's no connection?"

"Right," Ed said.

"Sounds like she knows he *did* kill his grandparents ," she said.

"Yes," Ed said, "she said it was a matter of public record that he had confessed to killing them."

"Do you think he is still there?"

"Yes," Ed said, "I do. She called him 'my patient' as if he were still her patient. Looks to me like she is sure he was guilty of the one crime but could not possibly have done the second one."

They both thought for a minute or so.

"Oh, well," Ed finally said, "it was a long shot. One less case to scrutinize."

They talked randomly for several minutes and then said good night.

Chapter 29

On Wednesday morning, Ed slept late and was awakened by a phone call from his agent. Ed spent the rest of a groggy morning preparing a blurp to be used in advertising the new book — the one not yet begun.

"I'm stuck in research," Ed thought, *"and they want to know how the book is coming. How it begins. How it ends. How do I know?"*

After a trip to the grocery store and lunch at a nearby café, Ed was ready to begin putting information on the wall. Using tape, he divided thee wall into three sections, one for each of the cases he had investigated most thoroughly: the Marches from Mississippi, the Lodges from Arkansas, and the Cliffords from Tennessee. Using a marker, he began to prepare labels.

At half past three on Wednesday afternoon, Ed's phone rang. Ed growled under his breath. He was just beginning to put information on the board and resented the interruption.

"Conference call," Joanna said when Ed answered the phone. "Stand by," she added.

"We have a new case," Nell said without greeting Ed and her mother." She didn't wait for their words of surprise but continued, "I got the call less than an hour ago." Her voice sounded grim. "Jonesboro."

Neither Ed nor Joanna interrupted Nell's staccato recital.

"Just like the others. Couple in their late 70's. Reverend J. B. Abbott and his wife Hannah. She was bed-ridden. Visiting nurse called 911. Fire department arrived before the house began to fully burn."

When Nell Jones paused for breath, her mother said, "Oh, Nell, I hate to hear this."

"He killed them and then set them on fire," Nell said. "Just like the others."

Neither Ed nor Joanna corrected Nell's slight inaccuracy.

"We sent our wagon to collect the bodies," Nell said.

The trio was silent.

Finally, Ed said, "If this case matches the others, our killer is still active."

"Very active," Joanna said.

"We have to be careful," Ed said. "This is too important and too dangerous for us to go much further."

Neither woman spoke.

"If — if — this case is part of our pattern, we will put together what we know," Ed said, "and turn it over to the FBI and to Arkansas authorities."

"You're right, of course," Joanna said.

"Yes," Nell agreed. "I talked to the state fire inspector who is headed up there. They have a county inspector, but the state man will investigate too."

"Good idea," Ed said.

"Because the visiting nurse got there when she did, there was less fire damage," Nell said. "We may get some details that would have been destroyed otherwise." She sighed deeply. "I have to go," she said. "I have two case reviews this afternoon. I'm training new staff and have to check their work closely."

The three said goodbye and Nell ended her portion of the call.

"I need to talk to the inspector and to that nurse," Ed said. "I need to be sure that this case matches. That our boy is active."

"Yes," Joanna said, "with a fresh case, it's possible to look for similarities that were overlooked in earlier cases."

"Right," Ed said. "I'll call you back in five — maybe ten minutes."

The connection went dead.

Fifteen minutes later, Joanna's phone rang.

"Okay," Ed said, "I booked a flight to Little Rock today. Tomorrow I'll drive to Jonesboro and interview the people there."

"What time is your flight?" Joanna asked.

"In an hour and a half from here. Then a layover in Atlanta. I'll be in Little Rock about 9 tonight."

"I'll pick you up at the airport," Joanna said. "We can both stay at Nell's—she has three bedrooms---and drive to Jonesboro tomorrow."

"That's not necessary," Ed said.

"Are you leaving me out?" Joanna asked.

"Not if you want in," Ed said.

"See you at nine," Joanna said.

"I seem to have acquired a partner," Ed thought as he packed. The thought did not bother Ed at all.

Joanna greeted him at the Little Rock airport with a hug. Once again, Ed voiced his hesitation over staying at Nell's home.

"Don't be silly," was Joanna's response. That and Nell's affectionate hug upon his arrival reassured Ed. The guest bedroom and bath were his.

At 7:30 the next morning, Ed and Joanna were in Joanna's car on their way to Jonesboro, the largest city in northeast Arkansas. With close to 70,000 inhabitants, Jonesboro is home to the Arkansas State University, the second largest university in Arkansas.

As Joanna drove, Ed took notes and then made a list of questions that he would use with the fire inspector. They also made a list of questions for Joanna to use in questioning the visiting nurse who reported the fire.

As they approached Jonesboro, Ed's phone rang. Nell had set appointments for them. Ed was to meet Alan Greenway, the fire inspector, at the site of the fire. Joanna was to meet with Tiffany Ragsdale, the visiting nurse, at the clinic that was her home base.

Following the car's GPS instructions, Joanna left Ed at the house and went on her way.

Chapter 30

Alan Greenway, the state fire inspector, got out of his car before Joanna drove away. He had parked in the driveway that extended from the street, past the house, and to the detached garage. Greenway had been filling out forms as he waited.

Greenway held out a hand to Ed. As tall as Ed, Greenway was about Nell's age — mid-30's — and dressed in jeans, a golf shirt with a fire logo, and work boots.

"I owe you thanks for the tip on the fire at the house in Little Rock," Greenway said, shaking his head. "I missed the accelerant on that one. The fire from the cook stove caught my attention, and I just missed the other." He shook his head several more times again. "I could use the amount of destruction — the house was almost completely destroyed — as an excuse. But I should have caught it."

"You weren't thinking 'accelerant' and weren't looking for it," Ed said. "I was."

"No missing the fact that an accelerant was used on this one," Greenway said. "Let me show you." The two men walked from the driveway to the front of the house. From this angle, only a bit of the fire damage was visible. The large oval glass in the front door had been broken by the firemen and the area above the front door had smoke damage.

Greenway led the way onto the broad front porch and showed Ed the hallway. "Lots of scorching here," he said, "and damage to the floor."

Ed could see that the center of the hallway floor was charred. The walls and ceiling streaked by smoke.

"The most severe damage," Greenway said, "was confined to the back of the house, specifically to one room."

Ed nodded.

Greenway turned. "Let's look back there. We'll go around the house and in through the kitchen," he said. He led Ed around to the back of the house. Here the damage was noticeably severe. The roof had burned through on a portion of the house. A large hole indicated where a window had been. Smoke damage and charring were extensive.

The heavy, acrid smell that comes when wood and other burning materials are doused with water almost covered a heavier, nastier smell — the smell of burned human flesh.

"Very little fire damage here in the kitchen," Greenway said. The ceiling and walls were streaked with smoke but not charred. He led the way into the area where the hallway to the front door met the door to the kitchen and, next to it, the doorway to the room that was now a soggy, rancid mess.

"The hottest part of the fire was there," Greenway said. "Obviously," he added. The floor was burned through in several places.

Greenway showed Ed patches and outlines that had no fire damage and areas that had extensive damage. The steel frame of the hospital bed was tilted toward the open expanse that had once been windows.

"The unburned portion of the mattress," Greenway said, "is where her body covered it." From just outside the doorway, Ed could make out the roughest of rectangular whiteness in the charred mattress remains.

A similar pattern was on the floor beside the bed.

"The man's body was there," Greenway said.

The two men stood silent, studying the scene before them.

"I've taken photos," Greenway said, "and the county man did too." He added, "I'll send Nell copies along with the reports. We haven't finished processing the scene yet. I haven't done the floor cuts. Nell wanted you to see it before I did those."

"Thanks," Ed said.

The two men walked back through the kitchen and outside.

Greenway reached into his pocket and pulled out a packet of the lemony-scented hand wipes associated with restaurants. He handed one to Ed and used one himself. After Greenway wiped his hands, he held the hand wipe to his face and breathed deeply. Ed followed suit.

"I have some questions," Ed said.

Greenway grinned. "I thought so," he said. He led the way to the front steps and sat down.

Ed followed him.

"As Nell probably told you," Ed said, "I am an investigative writer looking into several similar cases of arson/homicide."

"Yes," Greenway answered. "Nell told me that she suckered you into looking at the case from Little Rock and another one."

"And *several* more," Ed said, his grin admitting how thoroughly Nell had gotten him involved. "I know a little bit about fires," Ed said. "Most law enforcement people have more experience with arson than they want. But I need to know more."

Greenway's nod showed his understanding.

"In your opinion and off the record, do you think this fire was set by a professional? Could someone with little knowledge of fires have set this?"

"If not a professional arsonist," Greenway said, "this person was at the very least knowledgeable in the way fires work."

"Expand on that, please," Ed said.

"The person who set this fire used a slow-burning fuel. The fire started, I believe further testing will confirm, at the front door and moved to the room where the bodies were located. The bodies and the immediate area around them had been doused with fuel."

Greenway looked at Ed and continued, "The fuel was slow-burning, but it was also hot-burning. There is one place in the hallway where a good-sized drop of the fuel evaporated rather than burned. I think it will test out as kerosene."

He looked at Ed. "In the United States," he said, "we don't do that much with kerosene, but worldwide, kerosene is used for lighting, cooking, powering motors, and heating homes. Very wide spread."

At Ed's look of interest, Greenway continued, "Kerosene doesn't flash like gasoline does so it's a safer fuel. It burns hotter and cleaner than many other petroleum-based fuels. The only other fuel that nears it for use throughout the world is lamp oil." Greenway grinned. "Except, of course, for gasoline and diesel for vehicles." He grinned again. "You get me started on fires, you may have trouble shutting me up."

"I'm listening and learning," Ed said.

"My unofficial guess is this: the arsonist had a container of accelerant and poured it on the bodies and furniture in the room where they were found. Then that person made a trail of the accelerant from the room to the front door."

"How much accelerant are you talking?" Ed asked.

"Not as much as you might think," Greenway said. "About the amount of liquid you'd get in a 2-liter Coke bottle. Maybe half that if the arsonist was careful."

Ed was surprised. *"So little accelerant,"* he thought, *"so much damage."*

"Then," Greenway said, "the arsonist lit the fire, made sure it was burning, and walked out of the house, closing the door behind him — or her."

"Why did the Lodges house in Little Rock burn more thoroughly than the one here in Jonesboro?" Ed asked.

"There are three reasons," Greenway said. "First, the 911 call came early. The fire wasn't fully developed. It had just begun to burn."

"How long do you estimate the fire had been burning?" Ed asked.

"Good question," Greenway said. "I'd say somewhere between 4 and 7 minutes."

"Really?" Ed asked. He looked surprised. The damage was extensive for that short period of time.

"The fire would have traveled very rapidly down the hallway. Given fuel and oxygen, the fire would have doubled in size each second. It would have reached the room where the bodies were located in as little as a minute. It would have spread immediately. Plenty of fuel; plenty of oxygen."

Ed waited while the inspector organized his thoughts mentally.

"The fire would have slowed soon. It was eating up the oxygen rapidly," Greenway continued. "Then the nurse arrived. Her call saved the house." Greenway added, "Well, her call and the fact that the fire station is less than two blocks away. That cut total response time down significantly. That's the second reason there was much less damage."

Ed nodded his understanding but didn't interrupt.

"Here's the process: someone calls 911 and reports the fire and location. The 911 dispatcher calls the appropriate fire station and gives location. Then the fire fighters suit up and roll. Then there is travel time. Then time when they assess the fire, get the gear ready. Then they begin to attack the fire."

Ed knew this but hearing it in step-by-step order reminded him of how much time lapses from start to finish.

"The standard turn-out time for a call during the day — from 911 call to fire trucks rolling — is 5 minutes. Travel time obviously differs." Greenway added, "Because of the early call and the closeness of the fire station, the fire department was on scene in under 4 minutes. The fire was ventilated and contained quickly." He paused. "The nurse who called 911 was still here and notified the captain of the crew that there were likely people inside the house." Greenway added, "That hurried them along as well."

"The third reason?" Ed asked.

"Older houses, as a rule, burn slower than newer ones," Greenway said.

At Ed's look of surprise, Greenway continued, "Newer houses have bigger rooms with higher ceilings. More oxygen to feed a fire."

With an interested listener, he continued, "Newer houses have thinner interior walls, often made of more flammable materials. New houses usually have lighter furniture covered and cushioned with synthetic materials which are, as a rule, more flammable. An older home, such as this one, may take up to 30 minutes to reach flash point. A new house with new furniture can take as little as five minutes."

Ed nodded his understanding.

"There is one more thing that is unusual," Greenway said. "The central heat and air conditioning unit was shut off." Greenway frowned. "I checked on the house from a year ago in Little Rock. It was turned off there as well but not so unusual. It was a cool day. It had rained," Greenway reported. "It was hot here yesterday. The house would have been very uncomfortable."

Ed waited.

"I think the arsonist turned off the AC to slow the fire down. Give it less oxygen. Get the fire going fully before it was noticeable from outside."

Ed's eyebrows rose. "Deliberately, then," he said.

"Yes," Greenway said. "That would account for the extensive burn in Little Rock. Over 50% of the time, a fire is contained in the room of origin. More often than not, the fire is limited to the object of origin. For instance, a careless cigarette sets the sofa on fire. Over 50% of the time, the fire is contained right there either with the sofa or the living room. There may be damage—basically smoke and water--in other places, but not to the extent we saw in Little Rock."

"Or the ones Memphis and Huntington," Ed thought, *"or Hattiesburg."*

"Had it not been for the 911 call," Greenway said, "this house would probably have been consumed as well. Whoever set this fire intended it to reach flashover before it was noticeable on the outside."

Ed nodded.

Greenway continued, "For flashover—also called roll over or burn over—to happen, the oxygen flow needs to be slowed while the unburned fuel forms a layer of gases at ceiling level. These gases are very hot but need oxygen to ignite. Usually, at this point, something in the structure fails—a window breaks from the heat, for instance—and a rush of oxygen causes the gases to ignite. If you made a thermal image of the structure at this point, it would indicate from 900 to 1100 degrees Fahrenheit."

Ed nodded again.

"One last thought," Greenway said, "if the nurse had opened the door, she would have probably been seriously burned. If she had arrived 10 minutes later and had opened the door, she would have died."

Both men looked sober at the thought.

"Your arsonist," Greenway said, "doesn't care if other people get hurt or die. The nurse. A fireman. Someone who just wanted to help."

Both men looked grim at the knowledge put into words.

Before they could lighten the mood, Joanna pulled into the driveway.

Ed thanked Greenway for his assistance. Greenway promised to get the reports to Nell. The two men shook hands.

"Lunch and reporting, in that order," Ed said as he got into the car.

Chapter 31

Earlier, Joanna left Ed with the fire inspector and drove to the clinic where Tiffany Ragsdale was employed.

The clinic was located in an older, yellow brick building, apparently built as a doctor's or dentist's office. *"Clean enough,"* Joanna thought as she entered the waiting room. *"Clean enough but a little shabby, a little worn."*

Tiffany Ragsdale had unnaturally blonde hair pulled into a low ponytail and wore a bit too much makeup. She wore a set of the bright scrubs that have become so popular with health care personnel. Lime green pants were topped with a brightly flowered shirt in tropical jungle print.

She greeted Joanna with a warm smile and a friendly handshake.

"We have a small conference room," Tiffany Ragsdale said. "We can talk there."

When the two women were seated, Ragsdale said, "Your daughter said that you are investigating other cases of arson?"

"Yes," Joanna said. "We are looking at similar cases."

"I hate to hear that there are similar cases," Ragsdale said. "That was horrible."

"I agree," Joanna said. "Could you tell me what your routine with the Abbotts consisted of?"

"I wasn't even supposed to be there on Wednesday," Ragsdale said. "I go — or went — on Tuesday, Thursday and Saturday. Give Mrs. Abbott a shower. Check her for bed sores or rubs. Change the bed linens. Refill her medicine box for the coming days. Take their blood pressure. Both of them. That's it."

"Why did you go by on Wednesday?" Joanna asked.

"He called on Tuesday. Said they had company and could I come on Wednesday. Okay by me." Ragsdale shrugged.

"Mrs. Abbot was bed ridden?" Joanna asked.

"Yes," Ragsdale said. "She had a stroke four years ago. With help, she could sit on a chair or use a bedside commode. For a few minutes but not much longer."

"How long had you been employed by the Abbotts?"

"Two years in January," Ragsdale said.

"Tell me about yesterday," Joanna encouraged.

"I got to the house at 1:58," Ragsdale said. "I try my best to always be on time."

"Me, too," Joanna admitted with a small smile.

"When I walked up onto the porch, I could smell something weird. Not really like smoke. Maybe oily. Then I saw the gray on the glass in the front door. They have this old-timey door with a big oval glass." Ragsdale used her hands to show an oval that was taller and wider than she. "About that time, I realized that the sound I was hearing might be the fire alarm in the kitchen. But I wasn't sure."

Ragsdale thought herself back into the situation, using subtle motions of her hands to aid her recollection. "I just stood there...I don't know...a couple seconds...kind of putting it all together. I had my cell phone in my hand and called 911."

Ragsdale looked down at her hand as if the cell phone were there. Then she rested her hands on the table. "I told the 911 operator I thought there was a fire and told her the address. She said for me to not open the door. She said that like four times. She said for me to move off the porch and away from the house. She said to not hang up."

Ragsdale stopped her recital and looked at Joanna. "You know," she said, "I've been a visiting nurse for over ten years. First time I ever had to call 911. It's weird. I couldn't think what to do. That woman was almost like a voice in my head telling me to be calm."

Joanna nodded understanding.

"Anyway," Ragsdale said, "it seemed like I stood there at the edge of the yard a long time. Then the fire truck got there. One man came to me and asked did I make the call and was there anybody in the house. And I said there was supposed to be. Mrs. Abbott was supposed to be in the bed in the back. He told me not to leave. The 911 woman told me not to leave too."

Ragsdale pulled her lips together and then let out a puff of air. "Then they broke in the front door and Whoosh, there was fire coming out the door."

Joanna waited while Ragsdale thought. "Then a policeman asked me my name and why I was there and where I worked. Things like that."

Joanna nodded.

"I'll tell you the weird thing," Ragsdale said, "When they said I could go ahead and leave, I turned around and there was police cars and more fire trucks, and I never heard none of them get there." She raised her eyebrows and added, "And when I got in my car and looked at the clock, it was 2:19." The surprise still registered on the nurse's face. "All that happened in barely 20 minutes."

The amazement in Ragsdale's face vanished. Her face became grim, "And they were dead. I knew when the ambulance came but didn't have the sirens on. I knew." Ragsdale looked at Joanna. "*That* I knew." She nodded. "Sirens and lights means someone's alive. No siren means 'No need to hurry.' Too late."

The two women sat quietly for a moment.

"Was there someone else who worked for the Abbots?" Joanna asked before the silence between them became too heavy.

"Oh, yeah," Tiffany Ragsdale said, "they had a woman come in and clean house and do laundry on Fridays." A deep frown creased Ragsdale's face. "Poor old thing," she said. "she can barely walk herself. Looks like she's about 150 years old. Had cleaned their house for years. Poor old thing!"

"Was there anyone else—maybe another nurse or something—who might have come there?"

"Not likely," Tiffany Ragsdale said, making a dismissive face. "They was damned lucky to have me." She looked at Joanna. "Who else would put up with them? Not to speak ill of the dead, but who else?"

She leaned back in her chair. "I'll tell you about the Abbotts. Years ago, maybe twenty-five years ago, J.B. Abbott was the pastor of one of the big Baptist churches here. Him and his wife Hannah was big stuff. "

Ragsdale leaned forward to confide in Joanna. "That was a time us teenagers called 'Pick a Sin.' Preachers would pick a sin and a Bible verse to match and preach away. Well, wouldn't you know, Brother J. B. was against almost everything." She waved her hand. "I could tell you some of his chosen sins, but the list gets too long."

Ragsdale leaned back again. "Fast forward twenty years. He's retired from the church, but he's still preaching against sin. Old Brother Abbott gets more and more stuck on this sin and that sin. Mrs. Abbott doesn't want to hear about anything new. Just wants the good ol' days back."

Ragsdale sighed. "Then Mrs. Abbott has that stroke and they need help." Ragsdale leaned forward again. "First, they tried the expensive home care people. Either the Abbotts fired them or they quit. Couldn't stand working for the hateful old people."

Ragsdale leaned back again. "Then they come to us. First off, they get Ron. He has a ring in his eyebrow." Ragsdale pinched the outer edge of her own eyebrow to equate Ron's. "They won't have him in their house." She rolled her eyes.

She began to enumerate, using her forefinger to count off the people. "Robert? Gay. Amber? Smells like cigarettes or maybe dope—whatever that smelled like to them. Crystal? Married to a black guy. Kristina? A Democrat." She looked at Joanna. "Get my drift?" she said, shaking her head slowly.

"Finally, it's my turn," she said. "They tried me. Kept asking me questions. What I thought about this. What I thought about that. My religion. My politics. My life story. I just played dumb."

Ragsdale looked intently at Joanna. "Here's how it goes. I have a daughter with special needs. It takes all the money Glen and me can make to keep going. I need the job."

Ragsdale nodded her head abruptly. "One day, Mrs. Abbot, she tells me to just leave. So I do. Don't go back for a week. Then Brother Abbot, he calls. Says will I come back. I say I have to have more money. He says okay. I say leave my life out of it. I don't want to hear about it. He says okay." She shrugged. "That's that."

Joanna nodded agreement. Then she asked, "Mrs. Abbott didn't use walking canes, did she?"

"No," Tiffany Ragsdale said, "she couldn't walk. In fact, we had to use a patient lift to get her to the shower." Ragsdale frowned. "You know, I forgot about that," she said. "They just bought a new lift. Oh, not long ago. Maybe a couple of weeks." She frowned. "They thought Brother Abbott could work it, but he couldn't."

"Do you know where they got the lift?" Joanna asked.

"From the pharmacy they used, I expect," Tiffany Ragsdale said. "Just a minute, I'll check on which one they used." She stood and left the room.

In less that five minutes, Tiffany Ragsdale came back with a slip of paper. Reid's Pharmacy and the address were written on the card. "Here's where they got prescriptions filled," she said.

"Thank you," Joanna said. "I have one more question, if you don't mind."

Tiffany Ragsdale looked at her watch. "So long as it's a quick one," she said. "I have to get back to work."

"Yesterday, did you see a vehicle or person near the Abbotts's house?"

Tiffany Ragsdale frowned in concentration. "You know, I saw a car going on down the street. Saw its brake lights when it turned back towards the highway. It was red with those big tail lights." She sniffed. "Hm-m-m-m-m," she said, "I forgot all about that."

Although Tiffany Ragsdale stood, replaying the day in her mind, she couldn't remember any other vehicle or person in the area of the Abbots house.

Joanna Jones thanked her for her time. The two women exchanged business cards and went separate ways — Tiffany Ragsdale to her next client, Joanna to the Abbott's house where Ed was finishing his interview with Alan Greenway.

"Lunch and reporting, in that order," Ed said as he got into the car.

Chapter 32

Ed and Joanna ate lunch at a small café they found near the Arkansas State University campus. While Ed ate a cheeseburger and fries, Joanna reported on her interview with Tiffany Ragsdale. While Joanna worked her way through a huge chef's salad, Ed reported on his time with Alan Greenway.

Having beaten the lunch crowd, Ed and Joanna were able to enjoy a second glass of iced tea in relative quiet.

"All of the similarities between the Abbotts and the other couples are here," Joanna said.

"Right," Ed agreed. "Especially the religious angle and the medical one." Ed sat in thought. "You know, Joanna, it's almost like a loop of film that keeps repeating."

"You're right," Joanna said. "Take away the names and the general location—Arkansas, Mississippi, whatever—and you have the same story over and over."

"That's the *why*," Ed said. "That's why he does it. He's killing the same people over and over." Ed grinned. "Well, maybe," he said. "That may be a giant leap."

"Could be," Joanna admitted, "But it's a good theory for now."

They sat quietly for several minutes, each reviewing the cases to test the theory.

"It's not exact," Ed finally said.

Just as Joanna would have agreed, her phone rang. She excused herself from the table and went outside to take the call. A short time later, she came back in and sat down.

"Well," she said, "that's interesting."

Ed looked his question.

"That was Shirley Lodge. Her brother-in-law bought the lift chair for Clyde Lodge at a pharmacy in Little Rock. She's going to text me the name and address. Martin had them deliver the chair to his parents' house."

Once again, there was silence while each of them thought over what the message meant.

"All the couples had all just recently — within the month or so before their deaths — gotten new medical equipment of some sort," Ed said.

"I have the name and address of the pharmacy where the Abbots got prescriptions filled," Joanna said. "It's a place to start."

Ed paid the bill, and they left the restaurant. In less that ten minutes, Ed and Joanna were entering Reid Pharmacy.

As is the case with many independently owned pharmacies, Reid Pharmacy offered a wide variety of products, some related to medical needs, some not.

Greeting card displays, an area dedicated to scented candles and oils, shelves of attractive photo frames and other gift items vied for the customer's attention. Memorabilia from local schools and Arkansas State University offered a variety of brightly clothed stuffed animals. Ed and Joanna passed all these with only brief glances.

The left portion of the store was reserved for over-the-counter medications and supplies. Behind that, on a raised platform was the dispensary portion of the pharmacy where prescriptions are filled. Near the back of the store, an overhead sign indicated an area for medical equipment.

At the counter in the medical equipment area was a young man who greeted them. "Hi," he said, "Can I help you?"

Dressed in jeans and a plaid short-sleeved shirt, the man reminded Joanna of a teddy bear Nell had been given as a child. Something about the way their eyebrows curved — both the man in front of her and the teddy bear her daughter had loved — gave each of them a look of perpetual sadness.

"Mike," Ed said, reading the name on the plastic name tag, "we have a couple questions about medical equipment."

"That's why I'm here," Mike said. "Ask away."

Ed looked back and forth at the small area devoted to equipment. "Well,...," he said, looking confused.

"Is your first question 'Where is the equipment?'" Mike asked, a huge grin changing his face. "Here's how we do it," he explained. "Small stuff like crutches, canes, etcetera, we keep back here." He indicated a door behind him. "Bigger stuff we order."

When neither Ed nor Joanna said anything, Mike continued, "We can get almost anything you need same day."

"Same day?" Ed asked.

"Oh, yeah," Mike said. "Look here." Mike showed them a series of catalogues. "Suppose you need a wheelchair. You can either buy or rent. We help you find the one that will best meet your needs here." He indicated several binders, choosing one and opening it to show them. "Okay," he said. "So now we have a manufacturer."

He looked at Ed and then Joanna. "You with me so far?" he asked, a smile taking the sting out of the words.

"With you," Ed said.

"Now we find an equipment company that distributes the wheelchair. He turned the computer monitor so that they could see what he was doing.

"I'm putting the make, model, and name of the manufacturer into the computer. Here you have it. Now, we check with them for delivery and costs. We are close enough to Memphis, Little Rock and St. Louis to get delivery in hours if needed. "

Mike leaned forward. "We help you fill out the insurance paperwork. Handle all that for you."

Mike straightened up. "Now," he said, "what's on your mind? What can I help you with?"

"To tell the truth," Ed said, "we are doing a follow-up investigation on a fire. The Abbotts whose house burned...?" Ed made the statement into a question.

"They were customers...," Mike began. Then he stopped. A look of distress covered his face. "You don't think our equipment caused the fire?"

"We are still investigating," Ed said.

"What equipment did they buy from you?" Joanna asked.

"We did not sell them equipment," Mike said, his voice defensive. "Any problems they might have had would have been reported to the equipment company and to the manufacturer."

"Of course," Ed said.

Curiosity got the better of Mike: he accessed the Abbotts account, moving the computer monitor so that neither Ed nor Joanna could see it.

"Oh," he said, suddenly understanding, "those Abbotts." Ed raised his eyebrows.

"Art, that's the owner, calls people like the Abbotts his 'legacy customers.' That means he inherited them from his father who used to run the store."

Ed nodded in understanding; Joanna lowered her head to hide her grin.

"I called them other things," Mike said. "Constant complainers." He shook his head as if clearing away the complaints. "I told them a million times. Call the equipment company. Look at the card. Call the number. It's in big print. Right by the line that says 'We service what we sell.'"

Mike looked at Ed. "Then after threatening to get me fired, Old Man Abbott would say, 'Have a blessed, God-filled day.'"

Mike shrugged away the thoughts.

"Could you give us the name of the medical equipment company?" Joanna asked, smiling politely. "It would really be helpful."

"I guess I could do that," Mike said. He looked at the computer. "Last thing they bought was a patient lift from Best Quality Home Care Medical Equipment Company."

"Thank you," Joanna said, writing the name on a notepad.

"I shouldn't have said those things about the Abbotts," Mike said, "what with them dead and all."

"It will stay just between us," Ed said.

"Thanks," Mike said.

Mike and Ed shook hands. Ed thanked him for his help and, with Joanna, left the store.

On the two-hour drive back to Little Rock, Ed and Joanna reviewed their findings in Jonesboro.

As they approached Little Rock, Joanna handed Ed her phone. "Check my text messages for one from Shirley Lodge. It should have the name and address of the pharmacy where Martin Lodge bought the lift chair."

"Bless her heart," Ed said, "Shirley not only put the name and address; she gave us a link mapping it out."

Because they were coming into Little Rock from the east, it was a simple matter to stop by the Freeman Drug Store in the center of Little Rock. An old Rexall sign, painted on the side of the building, had faded from bright orange and blue to shades that almost matched the red of the bricks. Although it must have been a larger store years ago, there was little more than a long counter with a raised dispensary behind it.

When Ed and Joanna entered, it was after six. Only one person, a young black woman in a white lab coat, was in the store.

The woman, who was the pharmacist on duty, was unwilling to discuss either customers or products with Ed and Joanna.

"I would not want to give that information to anyone without permission from the main pharmacist," she said. In addition, she told them that the main pharmacist would not be available until Tuesday of the next week.

As Ed and Joanna turned to leave, Joanna tried one last question. "Could you give me a list of the medical equipment supply companies that your pharmacy uses?"

The young woman considered Joanna's request.

"You would be giving us no information about patients or products," Joanna pressed. She kept her voice quiet, speaking in a reasonable tone.

Finally, the young woman decided. "I think I can do that," she said.

She turned to the computer and began to search. After a couple of minutes, Joanna heard the printer in the dispensary clicking as it printed. The pharmacist went into the dispensary and returned with a printed page, checking it against the records in the computer.

"Here you go," she said, folding the sheet of paper and handing it to Joanna.

Both Joanna and Ed thanked the woman and left the store. When Joanna was behind the wheel of her car, she handed the folded paper to Ed.

"Number two on the list," Ed said. "Best Quality Home Care Medical Equipment."

They both grinned.

"We may have found the *how*," Joanna said.

Chapter 33

"We may have found the *how*," Joanna told Nell. They had arrived at Nell's house as she was preparing dinner. Joanna set the table, Ed opened the bottle of wine, and Nell set a bowl of salad in easy reach. She also removed lasagna from the oven.

When they were seated, Joanna continued, "We have all wondered how the killer selects his victims. Today, we found what may be a link." She explained what they knew: the Abbotts had recently bought medical equipment through a specific supplier. She also explained about the possible link through the Little Rock pharmacy. "It's not much," she said, "but it's more than we had this morning."

Nell and Ed agreed.

"I did the post mortems on the Abbotts this morning," Nell said. Her face settled into grim lines. She set her fork on the plate. "Mr. Abbott had the same type of wound to the back of his head as Clyde Lodge had."

Both Ed and Joanna nodded.

"Abbott was dead before the fire started. Mrs. Abbott had carbon residue in her lungs." Nell looked from Ed to her mother. "She died of smoke inhalation. He hit her hard enough to break her nose and damage her frontal bone," Nell explained, her left hand making a line from above her right forehead and across her nose. "The injuries were severe, but not enough to kill her. She died in the fire."

The three were silent, eating, for several minutes. Finally, Nell continued, "Why didn't he kill her? I don't understand."

"But he did kill her, Honey," Joanna said. "He killed her in the most vicious way possible."

"But why?" Nell asked again.

"We don't know why," Ed said. "We may never know why. What we do know is that the burning is his ritual. He incapacitates his victims so they won't be able to get away from the fire." Ed spoke quietly but emphasized each word. "The fire is the important thing."

Nell looked from one to the other.

"That's right," her mother said. "That's why some are killed by the fire while others are killed by whatever tool he brings with him."

"Interestingly enough," Ed said, "in the 2002 case — the one in southern West Virginia, he used what was handy. A fireplace poker."

"But in both cases in Arkansas, the wounds he inflicts are almost exactly the same," Nell added.

"Right," Joanna said. "Somewhere along the line, he realized that it was easier if he brought some sort of tool with him instead of looking for 'something handy.'"

"Agreed," Ed said. "Serial killers — like the rest of us — learn by doing. He has honed his skill."

"Of course," Joanna added, "that's a general statement, but it seems to be true."

"Right," Ed confirmed. "He's studied fires. Probably has read fire fighting manuals. Lots of information on the internet too." Ed took a drink of wine. "He's also studied accelerants. He comes prepared to burn the house in a most destructive manner." As the two women finished eating, Ed repeated the information Alan Greenway had given him. "The arrival of the nurse at just the right time didn't save the Abbotts," Ed finished, "but it saved the house and preserved evidence."

Over coffee, Nell asked, "Ed, you say the fire is the ritual. Do you think he stays to watch the house burn?"

Joanna spoke first. "I doubt it," she said. "The Marches' house was isolated enough to make anyone lingering around very noticeable."

Ed agreed. "At least one other of the fires we know about was in a rather isolated place."

"Something else he had learned," Nell said.

"He didn't have much time," Ed reminded the two women. "Greenway said the fire in Jonesboro was discovered in four to seven minutes."

Joanna sat quietly for a minute then jumped up and went to find her notes.

"A red car," she said when she returned. "Tiffany Ragsdale, the nurse, saw a red car going down the street when she got to the Abbotts' house."

"Do you think that was the killer?" Nell asked.

"It's possible," Joanna said. "Lucky for her that she didn't arrive while he was setting the fire. I think he would have killed her."

"He would have had no choice but to kill her," Ed said.

As Joanna and Nell discussed that possibility, Ed sat in thought. When their conversation ceased, they turned to look at Ed.

"Red car," Ed said. "Red car," he repeated. "The most popular color of rental car in the United States is red."

Both women looked at him.

"What are you saying?" Joanna asked.

"Hell," Ed answered, "I don't know." He leaned back in his chair then forward to rest his elbows on the dining table. "Investigations are made up of little bits of information that seem to be unrelated. Then a pattern or a picture emerges." He sighed. "I don't know whether the red car/rental car has any meaning or not. But it's another little bit to add."

"It's too late to call tonight," Joanna said, changing the subject, "but tomorrow I'll call Mississippi. If we can find a third connection to that medical equipment supplier...," she paused.

"If we can find a third connection," Ed said, his voice firm, "we take it to the FBI." He looked at both women. "This person is a killer. Right now. We put our case together and take it to them. Understand?"

Both women hastily agreed.

"I'll get everything I can on the two Arkansas cases," Nell said. "Alan should have his report ready tomorrow."

"I'll get the Tennessee case and the two West Virginia cases prepared," Ed said.

"And I'll call Mississippi," Joanna finished. "By this time tomorrow, we should be able to construct a combined strong case."

On Friday morning, Ed called the Little Rock FBI office and made a 10:30 appointment with the agent-in-charge. He spent the next half hour assembling his notes and entering them into a small notebook that would easily pass security measures in the building. The full report, including Nell's information and Joanna's information, would be ready later.

When Nell left for work, Ed was in the office and her mother in the kitchen. Joanna was drinking the last of the coffee and checking her laptop map search for pharmacies near the place where the Marches had lived outside Hattiesburg, Mississippi.

"Drat," Joanna said, a few minutes later. Within a five-mile radius of the Marches' home there were no less than six pharmacies. As she clicked on each of them to see more information, she said, "Futile. This is absolutely futile."

She straighten her back, took a drink of coffee and thought. "Ah-hah," she said. She clicked through her cell phone history to the calls made to Lucedale, Mississippi and selected one.

"Steve March?" she asked when a man answered the phone.

"Yeah," the man's voice drew the syllable out.

Joanna quickly explained who she was, reminding him of their conversation.

"Sure, sure, sure," Steve March said, "I remember you. Writer lady."

"Yes," Joanna said. She shrugged off the inaccuracy of the description. "I have a question if you have a moment."

"Any way I can help," Steve March said, his voice drawing each word to twice its normal length.

"You said your brother had purchased new walking canes not long before his death," Joanna reminded. "Do you know where he purchased them?"

"Sure do, Ma'am," March said. "I took him to that drug store just down the road. They ordered them for him."

"Do you know the name of the store?"

"Now, let me think," March said. Joanna waited while March thought. Finally, he said, "I just can't remember the name, but I tell you this. They got a neon sign in the window. Ugly as sin. Like the red cross but green."

While Steve March rambled on about the sign and its ugliness, Joanna turned to the map on her laptop. There it was. A photo of the exterior of Quality Prescriptions. The cross glowing green.

"Do you think the name is Quality Prescriptions?" Joanna asked when Steve March paused for breath.

"That's it," March said. "That's it. Quality Prescriptions."

Joanna thanked March for the information.

"That there druggist can tell you all about them canes," March said. "But don't mention how ugly the cross is. He is right proud of it."

Joanna smiled to herself and ended the conversation.

"Yes, Ma'am," the voice said when Joanna called Quality Prescriptions, "we can provide you with quality medical equipment."

In answer to Joanna's questions, the male voice assured her that they worked with a fine company that would bring any medical equipment to her home and would make sure that it worked.

"We use a company that matches ours in the way we deal with people and even the name. We have a contract with Best Quality Home Care Medical Equipment Company," the man added. "You get quality from us and from them as well."

Joanna thanked him for the information and ended the call. Before she left the computer, she found the website for Best Quality Home Care Medical Equipment Company. Then she reported to Ed. "Their home office is in Louisville, Kentucky," she told Ed. "They service Kentucky, West Virginia, Tennessee, Mississippi, Arkansas, and Louisiana."

"Good work," Ed said. "I'm off to the FBI office," he added.

Joanna smiled. "I'm glad we're turning this over to them," she said. "I have to admit, I've enjoyed the search, but getting this murderer off the streets is so urgent. They have the resources to find him before he kills again."

Chapter 34

"Good morning, Mr. Flanders — Ed," Max Fuhrman rose a bit in his chair and offered a hand to Ed. As they firmly shook hands, Ed thought, *"Stereotypical FBI agent: short hair, short-sleeved shirt, ugly red tie."* Fuhrman waited until Ed was seated and said, "Ed, how can I help you?"

"Since I retired from the Bureau," Ed began, "I have been an investigative writer."

Fuhrman looked at Ed but didn't respond.

"Over the past several months," Ed continued, "I have been investigating a series of arson/murders — at least two of them in Arkansas — which were committed by a serial killer who is active now."

Fuhrman leaned back a bit in his chair and placed both hands, palm down, on his desk.

For the next fifteen minutes, Ed used his notes to present an overall view of a case that united all the individual cases that he, Joanna, and Nell had discovered.

When he finished, Fuhrman nodded his head one time. "Very interesting theory," he said.

"Theory?" Ed thought. *"Theory? I brought you cases, details, exact information, and you call it a theory?"* Ed held his temper, but barely.

"Tell you what," Fuhrman said. "Why don't you write all this up? Put it in regular form. Then bring it back."

"You asshole," Ed thought. *"You want me to write your report?"*

"We're up to our ears in drug investigations and anti-terrorism problems, but as soon as we catch a break, we'll take a look at your report," Fuhrman said. "Just give it to whoever is at the desk when you get it finished."

The anger that Ed had been holding boiled over.

"You prick," he said, his voice low and intense. "You couldn't be bothered to turn on the recorder or lift a pencil to take one note, but you expect me to write your report?"

Ed stood and opened the door. "You can kiss my ass!" he said. He closed the door carefully behind him.

On the way back to Nell's, Ed vented his anger, using all the words he very rarely allowed himself to think let alone say.

Still seething, Ed parked Joanna's car in Nell's driveway. Before he went inside, he quickly called his nephew, Benton Owens, an FBI agent. The call went directly to voice mail as did calls to Benton's home phone and to his wife Ginny's cell phone. Ed's concentration shifted from his anger at Fuhrman to concern for his nephew and family. *"Where are they?"* Ed thought. Then he checked the phone for the date. "June!" Ed said. "It's June. June first." Benton, Ginny and their three boys were in Costa Rica for ten days, a trip they had been planning for months. "Well," Ed said, "so much for getting Benton involved." He sighed. He did, however, send Benton an email giving the bare basics and asking for Benton's assistance. *"When Benton checks his email,"* Ed thought, *"he'll at least know why I'm trying to contact him."*

"I can not believe it," Joanna said when Ed told her his tale of woe. "I can not believe they aren't interested in catching an *active* serial killer."

"They are too busy with druggies and terrorists," Ed said, his voice rough with sarcasm.

"What now?" Joanna asked.

"Not much to do right now," Ed said, "except continue with the combined report." He sighed. "We just have to hope that whatever sets our killer off doesn't happen until we figure out another approach."

Neither of them was happy with this decision, but Ed went into Nell's office and began to type the report on his laptop.

Joanna worked on the Mississippi case at her laptop in the kitchen. When she began to add the information about the walking canes, she hesitated and then turned to her cell phone.

"Good afternoon," the male voice answering the phone said. "This is Best Quality Home Care Medical Equipment Company. How can I help you?"

"I'm checking out medical equipment firms for my parents," Joanna lied. "They were in a car wreck and will need a variety of equipment when they get out of the hospital."

"I'm sure we will be able to provide whatever they need," the voice responded.

"Oh, good," Joanna responded. "You will deliver whatever they need?"

"Of course."

"What about taking care of it or problems?"

"We don't anticipate problems with the equipment," the voice answered. "However," he continued, "we are always ready to assist with adjustments or extra fittings as needed." His voice was warm. "We really mean it when we say that we service what we sell."

"Wonderful," Joanna said. "A friend of mine from Little Rock recommended your company. Are you based in Arkansas?"

The man on the phone repeated the information that Joanna had found on the company's web site.

"Very impressive," Joanna said when he finished explaining the wide range of products offered and the various states where they were available.

"Thank you, Ma'am," the voice said. "I built the company myself. From scratch."

"Oh," Joanna's voice registered her surprise. "You're the owner?"

"Yes," the voice continued, "and on this Friday, I'm also the receptionist and secretary." Amusement filled his voice.

"Sometimes it happens that way," Joanna said. "I have a couple more questions if I could...."

"Of course," the voice said.

"My parents live out from the center of town," Joanna lied, "and insist on keeping money in the house." Joanna paused then said, "I worry about strangers taking advantage of them. You do background checks on your employees?"

"Yes," he said, "we do." He continued, "In addition, we insist that new salesmen work with one of our more experienced salespeople until we are sure they know what they are doing. In our business, we deal with people who are disabled either temporarily or permanently. Our business and our integrity depend on our customers being able to trust us."

Joanna wanted to protest, wanted to say that someone was killing their customers, but she didn't. In fact, she couldn't think of anything to say.

"Now," he said, "when your parents need whatever equipment is required, give our office a call. We can deliver almost anywhere the same day or at most the next day. Guaranteed. When you call, tell them Robert House—that's me—told you we would give you a good deal."

"I'll do that," Joanna lied. "Thank you for the information."

Joanna ended the call and walked down the hall to Nell's office. "Well, Ed," she said, "I don't know what I learned, but here's what I did."

Although Ed and Joanna discussed Joanna's phone call at length, they were unable to reach a conclusion about its importance to the combined case.

"Is there a chance," Joanna asked, "that two or more of his salesmen are in on these murders?"

"No," Ed said. "Serial killers are loners. They are successful because they keep a low profile. This killer's gratification is personal." Tapping his chest near his heart, Ed continued, "The satisfaction or pleasure he gets from his action is in here. Inside him. He has no need — or desire — to share it. He follows a definite pattern if we were able to put it all together."

By the time Nell came home, they had abandoned the speculation and had returned to preparing individual portions of what they now saw as one case.

Ed insisted on taking the two women out to dinner. "I have imposed on your hospitality long enough," he said. "Time I started being useful."

An hour later, they were enjoying sushi at Little Rock's best Japanese eatery.

Between rounds of tasty sushi and other Asian dishes, the three discussed the case.

Finally, Joanna said, "We think we know how the killer meets the victims, but we don't know why he chooses to kill that particular couple."

"True," Nell said. "A medical equipment salesman must meet lots of elderly people. Elderly couples." She paused then added, "He can't kill them all."

"It *must* be a combination of characteristics," Ed said. "There's a common thread through the whole thing. That's what we are looking for. We have to find the pivot point that everything revolves around." Ed thought again of spreading all the information out onto a wall. That would make it easier to understand, easier to see commonalities. He found it difficult to talk to these two women who were only on the edge of police work. *"I'll get home tomorrow,"* Ed thought, *"and put it in a form that makes sense to an investigator."*

Joanna drew a pen from her purse and said, "Give me words that describe the victims."

As Ed and Nell gave her words, she wrote them on her paper placemat.

"Couples."

"Old."

"Handicapped either temporarily or permanently."

"Isolated — as in living in a house by themselves."

"Isolated — as in no close relatives or friends in the next houses."

"Not poor."

"Right. With a fairly nice house."

"Religious."

"Super religious."

"Strictly religious."

"Evangelical religion," Nell said. Ed paused in his thinking and Joanna paused in writing. They both looked at Nell.

"Well," Nell said, "they all preached their religion to people." She gave a tiny shrug of her shoulders. "You know the kind of people who ask you about your religion as they are shaking their hands for the first time. 'Hi, my name is Sally. What church do you attend?'"

"There are lots of people who do that," Joanna said. "Lots of very nice people." She frowned. "But more than showing an interest in other people's religious beliefs, the Abbotts, for instance, were very judgmental of others."

"You're right," Ed said. "Judgmental and *insistent* in sharing their religious beliefs."

"Wait just a minute," Nell said, She held her hands up, palms toward the other two. "I'm confused."

They waited.

"How did he — or they — know the couple would be religious?" She continued her thought process. "How did he know they were old?"

"He didn't," Ed said. In a flash of understanding, Ed said, "He went back. He had been there originally to set up the equipment or adjust the walking canes or whatever. Then later, he went back to kill them."

Joanna nodded slowly. "Of course," she said. "The Abbotts called to complain."

"Even if no one called," Nell added, "a good salesman might just drop by to see that everything was okay."

The three sat for several minutes, each one evaluating this information mentally.

Finally, Ed said, "Scenario: a piece of medical equipment is ordered...."

"from a local pharmacy," Joanna continued.

"And a delivery company brings it and sets it up," Nell added.

"Normally," Ed took up the story line, "the delivery person assembles it, shows how to make it work, adjusts it, checks to be sure the customer understands it, and leaves."

"But," Joanna said, "if there is a complaint or question, the customer calls the company and they send a salesman/representative to handle that. And, occasionally, the customer begins to harangue the salesman about religion . . . ."

"And *that* sets their fate," Ed said. "That's the trigger. It's not their age. It's not their health. It's not even their religion." Ed looked from one to the other of the women. "It's the ferocity of their religion toward him."

The three of them suspended talk about the case until they were back at Nell's with coffee, carrot cake, and a brandy apiece.

They went over their recent conclusions point by point, looking for flaws in their thinking.

"What do we do now?" Nell asked.

"I think the only course open to us at the moment," Ed said, "is to wait for Benton to return from vacation. I sent him an email with a thumbnail sketch of our case."

Both women looked discouraged.

"We could set a trap," Nell began.

"No," Ed said, his voice stern, "we could not. We don't know for sure that the killer is a salesman. If he is, we don't know which salesman is the killer. We don't know how much time elapses between his initial contact with the victims and the crime." For emphasis, he repeated, *"No!"* To ease the harshness of his pronouncement, Ed added, "When we have Benton and the Bureau on our side, *they* may decide to set a trap." He shook his head, "but they will use their own people. No civilians allowed."

Joanna agreed. "They might want to use a house like mine, but with me safely away."

"Your house is isolated?" Ed asked, his voice reflecting his surprise.

"You haven't been to Mom's house, have you?" Nell asked. "It's isolated."

"I have neighbors," Joanna defended, " I just can barely see them." She grinned. "I had thought I would invite both of you there for the weekend."

"Actually," Ed said, "I planned to go home to Florida tomorrow. Haven't had a chance to call the airport though."

"Actually," Nell repeated Ed's opening, "I have a meeting with my weekend staff tomorrow but could be there about five."

While Joanna and Nell sipped coffee, Ed excused himself, going to the office to contact the airport. When he returned, he said, "I guess another two days of imposing myself on you two won't kill any of us. I can't get a flight until Monday."

Both women smiled.

"You can grill the steaks for dinner tomorrow," Joanna said.

"O-o-o-o-o-o-o-o," Nell said, "and go with us to the arts and crafts show at Fairfield Bay on Sunday."

"Grilling steaks? Check!" Ed said. "Arts and crafts show?" he shuddered. "Couldn't I just cook again?"

All three of them laughed.

Later, as Ed lay in his bed in the guest room at Nell Jones's house, he thought again, *"When I get home, I will put all these facts and thoughts on my wall. Then I should be able to make the connections. I'll just have to wait until Monday."*

Chapter 35

"Good morning—or should I say, Good Afternoon, Mom Bert," Jesse Springfield said when Dr. Roberta Sales answered the phone. "How are you?"

Berta Sales smiled. "Oh, Jesse," she said, "it is so good to hear from you." She tried to cover her concern with a bright tone. "I was beginning to be worried about you."

"I'm sorry I haven't called in a while," Jesse said. "I have been so busy. "

They talked for several minutes about Jesse's job and the move, made several years previously, to Little Rock.

When the conversation lagged, Jesse said, "So what are you doing this lovely Saturday morning? Well, morning at my house. An hour later where you are." Jesse rarely thought about Roberta Sales and was uninterested in her life, but he didn't want to discuss his own life with her. *"She'll ask if I am dating seriously,"* he thought. *"She will want to know what I am doing."* Jesse realized the importance of maintaining a relationship of sorts with the woman who could destroy his life, so he kept in touch from time to time.

"I'm at the office," Berta Sales admitted. "Catching up on some paperwork."

"You should be enjoying the sunshine," Jesse said.

"So should you," Berta said, "instead of spending your time on the phone with me."

"I'm going out this afternoon," Jesse said.

"Playing golf or tennis?" Berta asked.

"Tennis," Jesse lied. He planned to go to the shooting range. After his move to Little Rock, he had been introduced to target shooting by a neighbor in the apartment complex where he lived. The discipline and control of target shooting appealed to Jesse, and, over the four years in Arkansas, he had acquired two pistols and a rifle. He had never shared this information with Dr. Sales.

Searching for a subject to keep Jesse on the line, Berta said, "Oh, Jesse, I meant to tell you about a kind of strange thing that happened."

"Oh?" Jesse stifled a sigh. *What now?* he thought.

"A man came to my office the other day and asked about you," Berta said.

"A man asked about *me?*" Jesse repeated.

"Yes," Berta said, "he was interested your story."

"What did you tell him?" Jesse asked. He kept his voice light, but his mind was working rapidly.

"Nothing, Jesse," Berta said. "You know I can't discuss your case with anybody. It's against the law because you were a minor, and your papers are sealed. There is also doctor/patient privilege. Finally, you *know* I would never talk about you."

Jesse made his thoughts stop. *"I'm safe,"* he thought, *"Of course, I'm safe. She will keep me safe."*

Berta spoke to fill the conversation gap. "The man is an investigative writer. Doing a story about a boy in Mississippi. He thought the boy's case and yours were alike. Thought there might be a connection. "

"Mississippi?" The thought sent red lights flashing in Jesse's brain. "That's weird," he said.

"Yes," Berta said. "The man said the boy was sent to prison for deaths similar to those of your grandparents. The man thinks the boy was pushed into confessing or not judged fairly. Whatever happened. I told him it had no relation to you."

"Thank you," Jesse said. *"Who the hell is this man?"* Jesse thought. *"What does he know? Does he know about the Marches?"* Jesse thoughts were in a jumble. *"I have to find the son of a bitch and kill him,"* Jesse thought. "You know, Mom Bert," he said, "maybe I could help the writer. If there's a boy suffering like I did, I would want to help him."

"Oh, Jesse," Berta's voice was soft and warm, "are you sure you would want to bring all that back into your mind?"

"To help another sweet soul," Jesse said, "of course, I would." He kept his tone sincere. "I have learned to live with all that behind me, but I know other kids weren't as lucky as I was. They didn't have you." Jesse added a thought: *"Now tell me where I can find that fucking writer, you stupid cow."* Jesse spoke softly. "You made all the difference in my life."

Berta Sales made a sound of protest.

Before she could speak, Jesse added, "If I knew how to contact the writer, I would do it. Tell him my story. See if it would help this other kid." He added emphasis to his voice, "You know I would, Mom Bert."

"Oh," Berta Sales said, "He left his card. I still have it. Just a second."

While she looked through her card file and desk, Jesse's mind raced. *"I'll call him. Find out where he lives. Hunt the bastard down and get rid of him."*

After Berta gave Jesse the name and phone number from the card Ed had given her, Jesse cut the call short. "I'm going to call this Ed Flanders right away," he said. "I won't have time to talk to him today, but I want to let him know I'm interested." He continued the thought: *"Interested in blowing his ass away."* Jesse would not risk using the steel rod and burning the man's house. He would simply shoot the bastard and leave.

"You are such a delight!" Berta Sales said. "Always so considerate of others. I am always so proud of you!"

Jesse quickly ended the call and carefully set his expensive phone on the desk. Then he allowed the blind fury to take over. The harsh guttural sound that came from deep in his throat rose in volume and tenor to a high-pitched keening as if he were gravely wounded. The near scream burst into a torrent of profanity. Every profane word Jesse had ever heard, every profane thought he had ever formed poured out in a flood of anger, hatred, and pain.

Left in the wake of the tsunami that had engulfed him, Jesse sat, weak and trembling. "He will not send me back," Jesse said in a whisper. "He will not."

Having allowed himself that burst of fury, Jesse began to gather his mind together to form a plan of action against Ed Flanders.

"Who is Ed Flanders? What does he know about me?" Jesse formed the questions.

"Ed Flanders," he said the name aloud. Then repeated it. He turned to the computer and entered the name into his browser. Several book sites listed Ed Flanders and the titles of his three non-fiction books. Going to one of the sites, Jesse discovered a photo and biography for Ed.

Any remaining doubt that Ed was an enemy out to ruin Jesse's life evaporated as Jesse read the brief biography. *"Son of a bitch,"* Jesse thought. *"Retired FBI agent."*

"Lives outside Tallahassee, Florida. Spends his spare time fishing in the Gulf of Mexico," Jesse read from the biography. *"Ten hours drive,"* Jesse thought. *"I can drive there in one day. Kill the bastard. Drive back the next day. No one will ever know. Or fly. Fly in. Shoot to kill. Fly away."*

Jesse leaned back in his chair, envisioning killing Ed Flanders. *"Just like shooting paper,"* he thought. He imagined the paper targets at the range, the ones that were roughly human shaped with x-zones in black. *"Just like shooting paper,"* he repeated.

Although Jesse looked at the other sites offering books by Ed Flanders and searched other sources as well, he found nothing more about exactly where Ed lived or Ed's family.

Jesse looked once more at the photo of Ed from the back of his latest book. "Ed Flanders," Jesse said, "what do you know about me? How did you get from 'a boy in Mississippi' to me in West Virginia?"

Jesse's hands tightened into fists, his fingernails cutting into the scars left from other times when his temper had been held rigidly in control.

Jesse drew a deep breath, forcing himself to relax. "I need to be sure," he said.

In his bedroom, Jesse carefully removed the suit box from its secure place at the bottom of stacks of off-season clothes.

Inside the suit box were two scrapbooks. Normally, Jesse only updated the latest volume, but today Jesse chose the scrapbook marked Punishment Book 1.

Glued to the first pages were photocopied accounts of the fiery deaths of Oather and Esther Springfield. Next came photocopies of the accounts of the death of the itinerant preacher, Lloyd Davis. Jesse had found the accounts in newspaper files long after their deaths.

The first articles cut from newspapers recounted the deaths of Harlan and Virginia Wakefield.

Jesse did not need to read the newspaper article to remember clearly that day.

Having worked as a sales rep for over a year, Jesse was comfortable with the variety of challenges that came his way.

On a warm July day, he had answered a service call at the Wakefield home in eastern Kentucky.

The living room, painted white, had been simply decorated. A few framed Bible verses hung on one wall. On another wall, three wooden crosses, the largest over three feet tall, hung behind the sofa.

Both Virginia and Harlan Wakefield had begun conversations with Jesse by asking about his religious beliefs and church attendance.

"For all have sinned and come short of the glory of God," Virginia Wakefield had said, her voice stern as she had pointed to the framed verse.

Jesse had tried to ignore them as he discovered a loose cable on the intricate walker Harlan Wakefield had purchased. Taking a wrench from his brief case, he had quickly repaired the cable. Still squatting beside the walker, Jesse had encouraged Wakefield to try the repaired walker.

Although the walker now functioned normally, Wakefield had difficulty understanding how to use the hand brake. Jesse had patiently showed Wakefield again and again how to use the wheels and the brake, but Wakefield continued to have problems.

"If you can't fix this piece of trash," Wakefield had said, "get it out of my sight." He pushed the walker toward Jesse, knocking Jesse off balance.

A startled Jesse had looked up at the old man towering over him. Behind the man, Jesse could see the three crosses which hung on the Wakefield's wall.

"You are going to be sorry," the old man had thundered.

Jesse had surged up from the floor, wrench in hand. "No," Jesse said, "you are going to be sorry." He hit Harlan Wakefield several times with the wrench. Then he went to the kitchen where Virginia Wakefield was preparing coffee. Hitting her from behind, he knocked her to the floor and hit her several more times.

A large bottle of oil for cooking was on the kitchen counter. Jesse used it to douse the bodies and the floor between them. Then he had taken matches from a box by the cook stove and began to light fires: curtains, the stove itself, kitchen towels, and finally the oil-soaked bodies. He had left the house, closing the door behind him. A block away, he had pulled into an empty lot and waited.

Jesse shook his head as he looked at that page. *"So careless,"* he thought. *"They had to be punished. Yes. They had to be punished. But I wasn't prepared."*

Jesse looked through the pages of the two scrapbooks. Looked at the newspaper clippings from all of the punishments.

He nodded with satisfaction as he thumbed through page after page. *"Punishment deserved. Punishment given,"* he thought. *"Repentance and fire. Fire and smoke. Punishment deserved. Retribution."*

The newspaper reports of the deaths of Leo and Peggy March were on the first pages of Punishment Book 2. Jesse re-read the accounts thoroughly. He skimmed through the rest of the scrapbook, arriving at the reports, not yet carefully glued into place, of the Abbotts.

Jesse held his temper in check as he carefully returned the scrapbooks to their box and the box to its place in the closet. Then he allowed the fury to escape once more. Another bout of cursing poured from him.

When Jesse finally calmed down, he said, "Ed Flanders has to die. It's him or me. And it will not be me."

"First, I have to talk to him," Jesse thought. *"I have to find out what he knows. Then, I have to get him to trust me. I have to get him to want to meet me."*

Jesse nodded his head in agreement with his thoughts. In a gruff voice, he added, "Then I will kill the bastard."

Jesse seated himself at his desk and picked up his cell phone. Jesse carefully touched the numbers, the ones that comprised Ed's phone number. "Let the games begin," he said, as he pushed the call button.

Chapter 36

Joanna and Ed left Nell's home in western Little Rock at just past ten on Saturday morning.

At Ed's request, they returned to the pharmacy where the chair for Clyde Lodge was purchased. Joanna waited in the car while Ed went inside.

Ed wore a rather puzzled look when he returned to the car. As they started toward Joanna's home, a drive of nearly two hours, Ed said, "There are three salesmen who work for our medical supply company. " He read from his notebook, "Larry Fetterman. Tony Diggs. And Jesse Springfield."

Joana looked her question.

"Remember the couple in West Virginia," Ed asked, "the couple whose grandson was committed to the state hospital following their deaths?"

Joanna nodded.

"Their name was Springfield."

Joanna drove while Ed considered the impact of that information.

"Of course," Ed said, "Springfield is a common name." He paused, added, "And we have no idea if their grandson had their last name." He thought again. "The psychiatrist spoke of the boy — man, now — as her patient, using present tense rather than past tense, as if he were still there." Ed frowned. "Could be coincidence," he said. He turned to Joanna with a rueful smile, "But you know how we hate coincidences."

Ed sighed. *"I need to be home,"* Ed thought. *"I need to be where I can organize, can think clearly, can get all of this information in a useable form."* Ed breathed deeply. *"Make the best of the situation,"* he thought. *"There is nothing you can do until next week. Nothing is happening with the case this weekend. Relax and enjoy yourself."* Ed turned his attention to Joanna and the drive west from central Little Rock.

Ed and Joanna stopped at a grocery store in Conway where Ed bought a variety of foods for that day's meal and for Sunday as well.

They turned from I-40 and continued north along a well-traveled highway. Joanna drove quickly through residential areas and small towns. The farther north they went, the fewer houses they passed. Traffic remained fairly steady.

"People headed for the lake for the weekend," Joanna explained. "While a some people live around Greer's Ferry Lake year round, there are many, many weekend rentals and campgrounds. Very popular."

They discussed the lake's reputation as a prime fishing spot. "You should take some time," Joanna said, "enjoy the fishing. There are plenty of equipment rentals. I know several guys who would enjoy your company."

Before Ed could answer, a beep on Ed's phone announced an incoming text. The message was from Ed's vacationing nephew Benton, an active FBI agent. It read, "email rcvd. will call mon pm."

"Ah-h-h-h," Ed said. "Now, we're getting somewhere," he told Joanna, explaining that Benton would call on Monday night. "He can get things moving on the case."

Nearly an hour after leaving I-40, they crossed an arm of the lake and turned north onto a street lined with trees. Building lots here were large with trees and shrubs offering only a glimpse of houses — some large and ornate, others more simple.

To the left, Ed caught enticing glimpses of the lake.

Where the road curved to the right, Joanna made a left turn into a broad drive. The drive branched into three parts, each leading to one of three houses set on the triangle of land that jutted into the lake.

Joanna reached to press the garage opener on her car's sunshade. The double garage of the middle house opened.

"Bob and Joy, my neighbors over there," Joanna said, indicating the white house to the left, "are on the channel and have the boat dock for all three of us."

Trees, shrubs, and the house kept the boat dock from Ed's view.

"Travis and Kate have the beach," Joanna continued. Ed could barely see the dark brown brick house to his right. Through the trees, he could glimpse the water.

"I have the rocks," Joanna said. "You'll see."

Joanna's house of dark wood and native stone had an off-set garage that extended from the house, giving Joanna a deep front entrance. Climbing roses and other flowers decorated the left front of the house.

As Joanna drove into the garage, she said, "I know the house is too big for me, but I just fell in love with it."

The two gathered the sacks of groceries and went from the garage into the kitchen. Cabinets and appliances were to Ed's left. A window over the sink looked out onto the driveway. A work island with breakfast bar stood between the kitchen and the dining room.

"Go," Joanna said as she and Ed set the groceries on the work space. With a flip of her hand, she indicated the living room. The entire back wall of Joanna's living room was glass looking out onto the lake. The deck that extended across the entire back of the house included an area the size of a living room shaded by the house itself and ending in a point that extended over the rocks and nearly over the lake.

"Wow," Ed said. "I can see why you fell in love with this. It's almost like living on a houseboat."

Joanna smiled. "Without all the inconvenience," she said.

The June sun at nearly noon was hot and, although the view of the lake was alluring, Joanna and Ed turned back to the house. Back inside, Joanna indicated a door off the dining room/kitchen area. "Nell's home-away-from-home," she said. Along the opposite wall, a door led into a small hallway. "My bedroom and bath," she said, indicating an area to their right. "My office," she said as they entered a room to their left.

The office reminded Ed of his own office — a worktable held a computer and accessories, a regular office desk held a telephone and little else. Behind them were shelves of books and, to Ed's surprise, a large safe.

Ed grinned at Joanna. "Keeping your millions safe?" he asked.

"Right," Joanna said with a grin. "The original owner was a gun fanatic. Had it installed when the house was built."

She took a set of keys from the desk and, choosing one, opened the door of the safe..

In the racks designed to hold twenty or more rifles or shotguns, one shotgun was in place. On shelves designed to secure perhaps 12 pistols, there were two pistols. Beside each pistol were magazines or clips loaded with ammunition.

"I kept my .9 millimeter from the old days," Joanna said, "and a .22 target pistol. The shotgun was useful in Mississippi to scare off skunks and snakes."

There were several containers on the floor of the safe. "Important papers," Joanna said. "Sorry, Ed," she added, "no millions to keep safe."

She closed the door to the safe and locked it.

Back in the living room, she waited while Ed retrieved his travel bag from the car and then led him downstairs. Two bedrooms, a bathroom, and a storage room completed the lower floor of the house.

Ed set his bag on the bed in the bedroom Joanna indicated, and the two went back upstairs.

Joanna sent Ed back onto the deck to enjoy the view while she put away the groceries.

Accustomed to the warmth and sunshine of Florida, Ed stood at the point of the deck watching boaters and fishermen in the distance.

His phone rang.

Chapter 37

Ed saw the words "unknown caller" but pushed the button that would connect the call.

"Hello?" he said.

"Mr. Flanders?" The voice was masculine and rather hesitant. "Mr. Ed Flanders, the writer?"

"Yes," Ed said. "This is Ed Flanders. May I help you?"

There was a brief silence while Jesse made his final decision: whether to be the successful salesman who spoke to clients or the slightly immature young man who talked to Dr. Sales. He decided on the latter. "Um-m-m-m," he began, "I'm not so sure where to start."

"*A teenager,*" Ed thought. In the five years that he had been a published writer, several students had managed to find his phone number and had interviewed him as part of a school project. "Just start anywhere," he said, his voice encouraging, "and I'll try to catch on."

"Oh," Jesse said, "Okay." Jesse kept his voice soft and hesitant. "My name is Jesse Springfield." He waited.

In a warm conversational voice, Ed said, "Hi, Jesse, how did you get my phone number?"

Jesse let the sound of a sigh flow into the phone. Once again, Jesse made his voice soft and hesitant. "Um-m-m-m-m," he hesitated then spoke quickly as if he were confessing a secret. "My doctor said you were interested in me. In my story."

"Your doctor?" Ed questioned. "I'm not sure I understand."

"Dr. Sales," Jesse said quickly, "Dr. Roberta Sales." Then he added, "From West Virginia."

"Oh," Ed said, feigning sudden understanding, "I spoke with Dr. Sales, but, of course, she didn't give me your name."

"She gave *me* your number and said you were interested in me."

Because Ed knew so little about Jesse, he tried to draw him out. "Why are you calling me?"

Jesse held his anger in check. "Dr. Sales told me about the other boy, and I just wondered if I could help."

Ed thought then said, "Well, Jesse that case has been resolved."

"But, but, but," Jesse said, not wanting Ed to hang up. Speaking quickly, Jesse said, "You are a writer. I thought you could tell *my* story."

"Well," Ed said, "I'm really involved with this book. Maybe we could get together another time."

"This is really important to me," Jesse said almost interrupting Ed. "Couldn't we get together so you could hear my story?"

"I'm traveling right now," Ed said. "Let me check my schedule and see when I can come to the hospital to talk to you."

"Oh," Jesse said, "I'm not in the hospital anymore, but I keep in contact with my doctor."

"It's him," Ed thought, *"without doubt. It's him."* Ed said, "Then give me your phone number, and I'll call you back."

"I don't give out my number," Jesse said. "Let *me* call *you* back."

"I won't be able to give you an answer until tomorrow morning," Ed said. "I hope you don't think I'm putting you off. You may have an interesting story for others to read. Give me a call about 10 o'clock tomorrow morning."

Jesse sighed. "Okay," he reluctantly agreed and ended the call.

Ed looked thoughtful as he went to tell Joanna the news.

Chapter 38

After the conversation with his enemy, Jesse did as he had planned. He went to the shooting range. He took only one pistol, a Glock, the same pistol used by many police departments. With each carefully placed shot toward the paper target in the stylized shape of a man, Jesse thought, *"There, you son of a bitch! Try to ruin my life and I will kill you."* After he had killed Ed Flanders 100 times, Jesse left the range.

When Jesse arrived at his apartment, he cleaned the pistol, reloaded the magazines with .40SW shells.

Then Jesse took the box marked "Bandages and Compresses" from the special briefcase. Opening it, he removed the wallet that contained Josh Faraday's identity. "Hello, Josh," Jesse said. "Would you be interested in a trip to Florida?" He grinned. "I thought so," he said. "Just a short trip." He carefully returned the empty box to the briefcase and the briefcase to its place in the closet, leaving the wallet on the desk.

Jesse's plan was simple. First, he would discover where Ed Flanders home was located in Tallahassee. Then, as Josh Faraday, he would fly to Florida, rent a car, kill Ed Flanders and return to Little Rock. "And the trail ends there," Jesse said. "Dead ends," he added with a small laugh.

During the evening, Jesse worked on the details of his plan to kill Ed.

Finding Ed's exact location would be easy.

As GPS tracking equipment became available, Robert House, owner of the equipment company where Jesse worked, had purchased the best and made it available to each of his salesmen. Jesse had a very sophisticated system on his cell phone, his laptop, and his recently purchased tablet, the newest computer form that combined the convenience of a cell phone with the screen size of a small laptop.

"Don't tell customers—especially the elderly ones—that you can find them," House had cautioned the salesmen. "It freaks them out. They aren't familiar with the technology that makes finding their house so easy. Heck, most of them don't even know you can lock onto their phones. Additionally, most of them are suspicious of anyone who knows too much about their 'business.' Call to set up the appointment. Lock into their phone and get the GPS. Zoom out until you find roughly where you are. Then let *them* tell *you* how to get to their house. Match what they tell you to the screen. When you have it, hit save. It's that easy."

It was, as Robert House had predicted, that easy. Customers were surprised and pleased that Jesse found them easily.

"Old Man Flanders is going to be surprised too," Jesse said aloud, "but not pleased."

With a grin, Jesse imagined Ed's surprise when he opened the door and Jesse was standing there, gun in hand. "He won't know who I am or how I got there," Jesse allowed himself to say the words out loud.

Jesse imagined the shots and the surprised look on Ed Flanders' face as he fell.

Jesse replayed the fantasy in his head several times. He drifted off to sleep with a vision of Ed Flanders falling dead playing in his mind.

Chapter 39

"I am *not* — absolutely not — hunting Jesse Springfield," Ed Flanders told Joanna and Nell Jones as they sat on the deck of Joanna's house sipping after-dinner drinks. "I will be more than happy to turn all of this over to Benton and the FBI boys on Monday night."

Ed and Joanna had been discussing Jesse's call when Nell arrived. The three of them reviewed all that they knew in light of Ed's conviction that Jesse Springfield was the serial killer responsible for the deaths of at least eight people in addition to his admitted killing of his grandparents.

While Ed had grilled steaks and Joanna set the table, Nell had combined all their information onto an external hard drive. It would be easy to email the information to Benton or to have the portable hard drive delivered to the appropriate authority.

There was little joy in the finding of the identity of the killer; too many deaths had occurred.

There was, however, a great deal of relief in the thought that the FBI or another law enforcement agency would be able to take the case forward.

"Jesse Springfield should be in custody before he learns how close we are to him," Joanna said.

"True," Ed added. "If he calls me back, I'll have to stall him. Benton and crew will need enough time for to cross check the information. I'll try to put him off until next month. That should give them plenty of time. Jesse Springfield need never know I've been in Arkansas or about your involvement in the investigation."

"I'm really glad we are handling our information this way," Nell said. "The thought that that guy lives near me — in the same city, at least — is downright uncomfortable."

Ed and Joanna nodded their agreement.

"About tomorrow," Joanna said, moving the conversation away from Jesse Springfield, "Nell and I plan to go to the arts and crafts show. An old friend of Nell's plans to be there too."

Ed grimaced.

"If you want to," Joanna continued, "you could do a little fishing from the dock. Maybe catch us some lunch."

Ed looked interested. Joanna explained where Bob, the next door neighbor, kept fishing equipment. "You can use artificial bait or dig for worms," Joanna said. "All the flower bed areas have a good supply of earthworms."

The next morning as she and Nell prepared to leave, Joanna repeated her suggestion, emphasizing, "We all share the beach and the docks, and my big rocks protect us from erosion when the water levels are high. Feel free to fish!"

Just before ten o'clock, Joanna and Nell were off to the arts and crafts fair.

Ed took the last of the coffee out onto the deck, pausing to watch distant fishermen when the phone rang.

Chapter 40

Exactly at 10 o'clock, Jesse pressed the button to make the phone call to Ed. As he had planned, Jesse was using his tablet, a computer not much smaller than a sheet of typing paper and not nearly as thick as a pack of cigarettes.

When Ed answered, Jesse said, "Hi, Ed. This is Jesse Springfield." Then, more hesitantly, Jesse added, "We, um-m-m, spoke yesterday." The hesitancy made the statement into a question as if Jesse were seeking reassurance.

"Oh," Ed said, "yes, of course, Jesse—uh—Springfield." Without giving Jesse time to answer, Ed added, "I'm sorry. If I sound a bit out-of-it, I just got home from the airport."

"Oh," Jesse said. He touched the icon for GPS tracking. "where do you live?"

"I live just outside Tallahassee, Florida," Ed answered.

Jesse's GPS screen showed the location of Ed's call. Because it was a close-up location, only the street address showed. Jesse touched the "zoom out" feature.

"You know, Jesse," Ed continued, "I'm in a difficult spot here. I want to hear your story, really I do. However, the deadline for this book I'm finishing is July 1."

The names of the places on Jesse's GPS seemed oddly familiar. He hit the "zoom out" feature again.

"I don't want you to think I'm just putting you off," Ed said. "Believe me, as a writer, I'm always looking for stories...." Ed let his voice drift away. *"What's happening with Jesse?"* he thought.

"Son of a bitch! Lying son of a bitch," Jesse thought. The second zoom showed exactly where Ed was—in Arkansas. Jesse glanced at the side bar. Ed Flanders was less than an hour and a half from Jesse's home. It was all Jesse could do to hold his anger intact.

"Jesse?" Ed questioned, "you still there?"

Jesse struggled to regain his composure.

"I know you must be disappointed," Ed said, "but I just can't be free until next month."

Jesse made a sound, cleared his throat, said, "Oh, that's too bad. I really want to meet you."

"And I want to meet you," Ed said. "I just hate for you to drive all the way from West Virginia to Florida when I wouldn't have time to concentrate on your story."

Jesse saved the GPS coordinates and information. Then, just to be sure, he ran the GPS locator again.

"I would drive there," Jesse said. "You are very important to me."

The GPS locator indicated the same address, an address on Greer's Ferry Lake in Arkansas. *"Gotcha!"* Jesse thought. He forced his voice to sound resigned. "I guess I have to wait," he said, "because I really want you to hear my story." He sighed heavily. "Can I call you in July?"

"Of course," Ed said. "I'll be looking for your call. The first week in July. I really want to stay in touch."

"Me too," Jesse said. His voice broke as he spoke the words, and he ended the call.

"Stupid, stupid old man!" Jesse said the words out loud. The anger dissolved into amusement. "You think you are so smart, Ed Flanders," Jesse said, looking at the GPS information he had saved. "You think you are smarter than me. But you're not!"

Jesse's amusement dimmed as he realized the need for immediate action.

"Change of plans," he thought. *"No need for Josh to fly."* On the heels of that thought came the realization that he could use the normal "punishment" routine carefully prepared over the years.

"No special briefcase this time," Jesse thought. From the closet he removed the holster he had purchased. According to Jesse's neighbor, the holster was "just like detectives wear."

At home, Jesse had practiced wearing the Glock in the holster, liking the feel of it attached to his belt. He had considered applying for a "concealed weapon" permit — they were available in Arkansas but hadn't gotten one.

With the Glock loaded and secured in the holster, Jesse added a summer-weight sports coat to the slacks and open shirt. When he looked in the mirror, he couldn't see the Glock unless he spread the jacket open.

Getting into "punishment" mode, Jesse drove to one of the medium priced motels near the junction of I-430 and I-630 in the center of Little Rock. He checked in using Josh Faraday's driver's license and credit card. Although it was not yet eleven o'clock, he was able to get a room.

From the room, he called Enterprise, the rental company that will deliver cars, and rented a mid-sized car. Within the hour, Josh Faraday had been picked up, had gone to Enterprise, had paid the rental fee, and was on his way.

"I should be to this house," Jesse thought, looking at the GPS location, *"by 2:30. Ed Flanders will be dead by 3 o'clock. "*

Chapter 41

"That was easy," Ed told himself as the call from Jesse Springfield ended. "Benton will have the time he needs to crosscheck our information."

Ed continued to sit on Joanna's deck for several minutes replaying the conversation with Jesse in his mind. *"If Jesse had any idea that our investigation has gotten as far as it has,"* Ed decided, *"he would have been more insistent on meeting."*

With the question of Jesse Springfield settled in his mind, Ed sat for over an hour watching the activities on the lake. Finally bored with the inactivity, Ed decided to take Joanna's advice.

"Can't remember the last time I dug for worms," Ed thought as he dug into the soft rich edge of the flower bed. In no time, Ed had bait and dirt in a cardboard container and was cutting across from Joanna's yard to the neighbor's.

In a building at the edge of the dock, Ed found the fishing gear. Rejecting the fancy rods and reels, Ed settled on a basic rod and reel placed beside a small tackle box. "For someone's grandkids, I'll bet," Ed said with a grin. The tackle box was well equipped. "Good enough for a bit of sunfishing," Ed mumbled.

At the door of the building, Ed found a stack of folding chairs, the comfortable kind.

On the dock, Ed surveyed the area, deciding where to fish. Near the dock on one side, the water looked to be fairly deep with an old brush pile spreading into the water.

Soon Ed was sitting in a comfortable chair, rod in hand, watching a tiny bobber float near the brush pile.

Accustomed to fishing in the Gulf of Mexico for much bigger fish, Ed had almost forgotten how much fun catching sunfish could be.

The first nibbles were from fish much too tiny to eat. They were carefully unhooked and released back into the water. Adjusting his fishing depth, Ed soon began to get stronger bites. *"Crappie,"* Ed thought. *"Feels like crappie."*

Instead of simply passing the time, Ed began to be interested in what he was catching. "Ah-hah," he said when he caught a crappie big enough for keeping—about the size of Ed's hand from wrist to fingertips. "Here comes dinner!"

Engrossed in catching fish, Ed had no concept of time. When he had caught a good "mess" of fish, enough for the three of them to share, he was ready to quit. However, there was one fish—at least Ed was sure it was *one* fish—that continued to evade his hook. It was hungry enough to steal his bait but cautious, very cautious. *"Almost as if it knows,"* Ed thought, *"as if it is playing with me."*

Ed almost caught it, but as he twitched the pole to set the hook, the fish escaped. A shiny hook, bare of its bait, was all there was at the end of Ed's line.

Although Ed tried again, the fish was gone.

Warm and thirsty, Ed returned the borrowed equipment to the building and, carrying the stringer of crappie in one hand and the worm container in the other, Ed walked back to Joanna's.

He paused outside to return the lucky earthworms to the flower bed before entering the house.

Ed laid the fish in one side of Joanna's sink and washed his hands in the other side. Then he drank a beer.

Ed glanced at the digital clock on Joanna's microwave oven and was surprised to see that it was 2:14.

"Better get a move on, Ed," he said to himself. "Joanna and Nell—and maybe Nell's friend—should be here any time."

Ed quickly gathered the equipment he would need to scale and gut the fish: paper to cover the counter next to the sink, a sharp knife, a platter large enough to hold the cleaned fish, and, wonder of wonders, a fish scaler. Ed would remove the scales from all the fish then gut them, leaving the bodies intact for grilling.

As Ed scaled the fish, he thought about the fun of fishing and the ease with which he had caught all the fish — except one. He thought again, as fishermen have done for centuries, about the one that got away. *"He played with me. He let me feed him and then got away. Smart little dude,"* Ed thought. *"Smarter than me."* An adjacent thought flitted across Ed's mind, but he couldn't catch it. He focused on the fish in his hand.

When the fish were are free of their scales, Ed moved them to the cutting board and carefully gathered the scale-covered paper, putting it into the trash. Joanna's garbage disposal would take care of the fish guts.

Turning on both the cold water and the in-sink garbage disposal, Ed cleaned the first fish, carefully slicing through the underside of the fish, removing the internal organs, and washing the fish in the running water. Later, he planned to marinate the fish in olive oil, salt, and slices of lemon. Grilled, they would make a tasty dinner.

Having cleaned thousands of fish in his lifetime, Ed worked quickly, efficiently, and with half a mind. The other half was on the imminent return of Joanna and Nell. He subconsciously noticed every car that passed in the street beyond the driveway.

It was the hesitancy of the white car that caught Ed's attention. As the car turned into the drive, it slowed. Stopped briefly. *"Checking the address,"* Ed thought. *"Choosing which of the three houses is the right one."*

The driver had apparently made a decision. The car moved, this time without hesitation, toward Joanna's house.

Ed put the fish he had cleaned onto the platter but continued to watch the white car. *"White car — second most common rental car after red,"* Ed thought.

When the car stopped, Ed could see that there was only one occupant, the driver, a male.

"Nell's 'friend'?" Ed thought. *"Maybe."* A second thought: *"More likely to be a Jehovah's Witness — this is Sunday — or another evangelical type."*

When the young man opened the car door and stepped out, the tingle on the back of Ed's neck — the tingle he had been ignoring — turned into a full-blown thump. *"He's carrying."* Ed's brain said the words as clearly as if he had spoken them aloud. To most people, the subtle bulge at hip level under the young man's jacket would have gone unnoticed, but to law enforcement officers, flashing neon lights would not have been more telling.

Leaving the water and disposal running, Ed sprinted — as quickly as a man in his sixties can sprint — past the front door, down the hallway and into Joanna's office.

"The key," Ed thought, *"where's the key?"* Ed quickly pulled the desk drawer open and reached for the key ring. *"Three keys! Which one?"*

The ringing of the doorbell was followed by a sharp knocking on the front door.

"Could this be Nell's friend?" the thought edged itself into Ed's mind. *"Is her friend a cop?"* The thought continued, *"She's in law enforcement. Could be her friend is too. However...."*

Ed drew a breath to calm himself and chose the most likely key. As he fitted it into the lock, he heard a voice inside the house, "Mr. Flanders? Mr. Flanders?" Each time the voice spoke, it became stronger, clearer.

"Not Nell's friend," Ed thought, recognizing the voice. *"Jesse Springfield."*

Although Ed tried to open the safe quietly, each of the tumblers made a small clicking sound as it disengaged. The safe door opened.

Instinctively, Ed reached for Joanna's 9 mm. pistol. Picking it up, Ed knew it wasn't loaded. *"The clip! Where's the clip?"* Ed focused on the shelf. Found the clip. Grabbed it and inserted it into the butt of the pistol. Chambered the first round.

Ed felt Jesse's presence inside the door of the office. As Ed turned, he saw the Glock, pointed toward him, coming up fast in Jesse's hands.

Before Jesse could shoot, Ed Flanders shot Jesse Springfield twice in the chest. Jesse crumbled to the floor, dying before the sound of the gunshot had finished echoing in the room.

Ed set the safety on the 9 mm and laid it on the desk. He sat down heavily in the office chair. Picking up the house phone, he called 911.

When the operator answered, Ed said, "My name is Ed Flanders. I am a house guest of Joanna Jones. I have just shot and killed a home intruder. I am not sure of the address here."

"We will use GPS to locate you," the operator told Ed.

"GPS," Ed repeated. He nodded his head. "GPS, of course."

Ed sat very still in the office chair for the next ten minutes. Finally, he heard sirens approaching from a distance. Then blue and red flashes of light shone through the office window. The sirens died. Ed heard car doors and the sound of footsteps. Knowing the front door was open, Ed continued to wait. Slowly, carefully, Ed raised his hands to shoulder height indicating that he held no weapon.

A young man, the patch on his sleeve stating that he was a deputy sheriff, cautiously peered into the room. Pistol drawn, he stopped at the door. "Sheriff," he called over his shoulder. "In here." He took a step back, continuing to hold his pistol in both hands, pointed toward Ed. He was careful not to touch the body of the victim.

The sheriff of Cleburne County, a slender man in his early forties, wearing jeans and a uniform shirt stepped into the doorway without obscuring the deputy's view of Ed.

Hands still raised, Ed very calmly and distinctly, said, "My name is Ed Flanders. I am retired FBI. That man is Jesse Springfield. He came here to kill me."

Although looking at Ed, the sheriff spoke to the deputy, "Secure the weapons," he said. The deputy hesitated. "Put the Glock and the 9 mil on the table there," the sheriff said, indicating a small table. "Close the safe."

The deputy holstered his weapon and followed the sheriff's orders, skirting the body on the floor and trying not to step between the sheriff and the man seated at the desk. When the two pistols were on the table and the safe closed, the sheriff said, "Check the vic for id."

The deputy leaned over the dead body and retrieved a wallet from the inside pocket of the sports coat. He glanced at the driver's license and frowned. He handed the opened wallet to the sheriff.

The sheriff looked at the driver's license and then at Ed. "Who did you say this is?" he asked, pointing toward the body.

"His name is Jesse Springfield," Ed said.

"According to his driver's license," the sheriff said, "his name is Josh Faraday." The sheriff looked grim; Ed's face had gone white. The sheriff said, "You need to come with me."

Aftermath

October, 2013

" Here's to a tiny bit of justice for Clyde and Zinna Lodge!" Nell Jones said, lifting her champagne flute. The three of them — Nell, Joanna, and Ed — touched their glasses together with a musical clink.

"And a bit for Leo and Peggy March," Joanna added. "And for Dean March who has been freed from prison."

"And all the others," Ed said. Their glasses clinked, and they drank.

They were seated in one of the finest restaurants in Little Rock compliments of Ed's publisher.

Four months after the incident at Joanna's house, Ed had returned to Arkansas, this time to a local bookstore to autograph copies of his latest book, *A Fiery Retribution: the Jesse Springfield Story.*

Events had moved quickly in the intervening four months.

That Sunday, the sheriff and Ed had barely been seated in the interview room at the Cleburne County jail when Joanna and Nell arrived. The credentials of the three — Ed, a retired FBI agent; Joanna, a retired professor of Criminal Justice; and Nell, the state Medical Examiner — had added weight to the outline they gave him of their investigation into the serial killer named Jesse Springfield.

In the meantime, the true identity of Josh Faraday had quickly come to light. Jesse's wallet with several forms of identification and the keys to his car were found in the motel room taken by Josh Faraday. Jesse's computer tablet with GPS coordinates was found in the rental car.

Ed was released from custody that day, but it was a week before the shooting was declared "self defense."

During that week and the ones that followed, various areas of Jesse Springfield's life had been investigated by the FBI spurred by the attempted murder of one of their own and by Benton Owens, Ed's nephew.

All the evidence found supported the investigative work done by Ed, Joanna and Nell.

The crime team that processed Springfield's apartment, aided by the knowledge that the occupant was considered a suspect in serial killings, was able to find what they dubbed as his "kill kit." Later tests would reveal that the chrome rod was, in all likelihood, the murder weapon. The team also found the scrapbooks, removing any last doubt that Jesse Springfield was a serial killer.

Working separately, other investigators discovered that Josh Faraday's credit card history, limited exclusively to car rentals, matched exactly the dates of all the murders dating back to Jesse's time in Nashville. Faraday's true identity was discovered and his family notified.

In the initial look at Jesse's work history, investigators were able to match the murdered couples to their interaction with Jesse Springfield. A disability, either temporary or permanent, put them in Jesse's world. Later, all of his previous clients were investigated to be sure that no other deaths had been missed.

As the work of investigators continued, Ed began to write the new book, telling Jesse's story and the stories of several of the couples he had murdered.

Dr. Roberta Sales, her reputation ruined and her personal life shattered, had allowed Ed access to a number of documents related to Springfield.

A psychiatrist specializing in the study of serial killers had verified the conclusion reached by Ed, Joanna, and Nell: when all the elements were combined: when an elderly couple predicted eternal fire for Jesse and demanded his repentance, Jesse reverted mentally to that young boy abused by his grandparents. The elaborate plans he used in killing and burning showed his premeditation.

"One last toast," Ed said, "To you, Nell Jones." Ed pointed his glass toward Nell. "Had it not been for your tenacity, the cause of all this destruction would never have been questioned."

"Thank you," Nell said. The trio had discussed many times the unusual chain of events that had led them to each other and to the discovery of Jesse Springfield, the serial killer.

"I do hope," Ed added, "that the next time you find a drama unfolding, you will wait and just tell me the story. I'd much rather *write* about looking down the barrel of a Glock or about being arrested than actually *living* it."

All three smiled.

"Do you really think there will be a next time?" Nell asked.

"Knowing you and your curious nature," Ed said, "I'd say it's a certainty."

The three looked at one another and laughed.

XXX

Made in the USA
Monee, IL
10 January 2023

24629963R00144